Judy

May the Night protect you!

the Lesser Devil

A Novel of the
Keening Chronicles

ISBN-13: 978-0692499696 (Custom Universal)
ISBN-10: 0692499695

The Lesser Devil

Cover by Teresa Whitehead

Red Thorn Publishing
Huntsville, AL 35811

Acknowledgements

I'd like to offer my thanks to my heroes, my therapists, my enablers and my instigators, without whom this book wouldn't have happened.

First, my deepest gratitude to my partner-in-crime, Shadrone. You offered me love and support that I didn't even know was possible. You believed in me even when I didn't. You are my love and my best friend and yes, I'm fucking done!

Thank you to Katheren Holmes, my mom, for your unwavering interest and input in my rambling ideas and midnight freak outs. You taught me the courage to be myself and the strength to back it up. I love you, mom.

To Dee, my mema, thank you for instilling a love of art and creativity in all its forms and to my Aunt Debra, for being my bus stop buddy. Love you both!

To my son, my heart, for loving a weirdo like me. I love you without limit.

And big shout out to the rest of my family, all you crazy ass people who supported my insane obsession, even if you didn't understand it or necessarily approve. I love you all.

A tremendous thank you to my technical team, my friends that helped polish my dream into something readable: it was no small task.

Teresa Whitehead for using her own special brand of magick on the cover, formatting and editing. You are amazing.

Jason L. Evans and Beth Roberts for their eagle eyes and amazing dedication. Y'all are awesome.

And let me not forget the many friends who encouraged me, helped me and were there when I thought I had nothing left. In short, I am very lucky.

Thank you.

This book is dedicated to all those who have ever felt persecuted for being different.

You are not alone.

"Hell is empty and all the devils are here."
—Ariel, *The Tempest*

Chapter 1

I awoke sitting up, my mind and body on knife's edge. The moonlight broke through the blinds at harsh angles that made even the harmless and ordinary seem cruel and otherworldly.

I had the childlike dread that if my feet touched the floor the creature under the bed would pull me under to my grisly death and I would never be seen again.

My eyes darted around the room, focusing on the slightly ajar closet door, which blocked the moonlight from illuminating its interior. The small space seemed to have endless depths where anything might live or be waiting.

Both of my black cats simply looked at me, stretched, and went back to sleep. Their soft purrs reassured me that everything was okay. I laid my head down on my damp pillow, pulled my covers tight and enjoyed my bed companions' warm small bodies next to me.

Every time I would begin to drift off, I would jerk awake as new sense of alarm would wash over me. I would imagine someone in the night's shadows watching and taunting me.

I finally consoled myself with the thought that if there was anything in this room, my cats, Morti and Grace, would be the first to know. I started to relax and let myself begin to drift into desperate sleep.

Behind my eyelids I would see fearsome flashes of something reaching for me; pale, long arms slowly stretching up from the depths of the shadows, monsters wanting to drag me into their gaping jaws. I would heavily open my eyes to the room and try to shake off the feeling and memory of the vision.

I would instead think of all I had to do tomorrow. "I need to work on my book, pick up cat food and some groceries: milk, eggs, bread..." My thoughts became fuzzy as I began to give in to the Sandman's call.

Click.

My eyes jerked wide open. Neither of my cats had moved from my side.

Scritch, scritch.

My eyes once again darted across the bedroom. The space seemed darker than before. The light from outside seemed unable to dispel the inky night.

Scritch, scritch.

The sound was coming from my now closed closet. I began to lose my breath, and my mouth went dry. I was now fully awake, every sense I had on full alert, but I played still.

Scritch, scritch.

"The closet. Maybe it's my belts hanging on the back of the door and the air vent..."

Scritch, scritch.

I poked at the cats, wondering why they didn't hear it or seem to want to check it out.

Scritch, scritch.

"Okay, Lydia, get a grip." I steadied my nerves and grabbed a heavy flashlight that I always kept beside my bed just in case an Alabama thunderstorm knocked out the power.

Scritch, scritch. Scritch, scritch.

It was becoming louder and more impatient.

I lifted Morti and put him beside his sister. I was about to put my feet on the floor when a sharp jolt of panic ran through me I remembered that the Boogeyman was waiting, underneath. My limbs began to weaken.

I placed one foot down on the semi-shag carpet, keeping most of my weight on the bed so I could get away quickly, if I needed to.

Nothing.

Scritch, scritch. Scritch, scritch.

"Don't be silly. Nothing is going to grab me from under the bed. The Boogeyman is waiting for me in my closet." I glared at my cats, who did not care that my heart was in my throat. "Spoiled ass cats. This is probably a mouse, and it's your job to protect me from said mouse!" They did not budge.

Scritch, scritch. Scritch, scritch.

I gritted my teeth. "Damn it! I'm coming." I screwed up my courage and made my way to my closet.

Scritch, scritch. Scritch, scritch.

I clicked on my plastic flashlight. It gave a reluctant yellow glow that barely did anything but cast more twisted, demonic shapes across the walls.

The scratching sound had stopped. I thought about trying to go back to my bed and pretend this had never happened.

This time a long, drawn out *scriiiiitch* went across the back of my closet door. My entire body began to tremble. I held my flashlight firmly in my left hand and reached with my right. As I stretched for the doorknob, I could barely lift my arm for the weight of my dread bearing down on it.

I turned the old scuffed brass knob slowly. I heard the click of it releasing its hold on the door frame. I had to remind myself to breathe. I could hear my heart pounding in my ears.

"*Fuck it!*" I jerked open the door.

Four glowing eyes jumped at me, and I let out a scream. The dim light revealed them to be nothing more than Morti and Grace. I slid down the door as the adrenaline flushed from my body. I nervously chuckled with embarrassment.

"Wait...something's not right... No, you were in bed with me," I said, as if trying to convince them.

A cold prickle went across my flesh like icy cobwebs. The room grew cold and dark. And darker still. I stood up and turned around to face my bed where I thought my cats laid sleeping.

Two low growls and hisses came from my feline friends at my feet as we all stood in shock at what we saw before us.

A great black hole opened over my bed. The Nothing was all consuming. No light but a purple hue swirling into the void. Great claws reached for me and grabbed at my skin.

Both my furry friends were puffed up, arched, showing their claws and fangs while their backs were to the wall.

I tried to pull off the ravenous talons, but my hands slipped through frigid viscous air. Shadows danced all around me. I could hear voices calling out. Picture frames lurched from the walls as shade creatures scurried furiously behind them.

Raspy and alien voices broke through the night. "She's *dangerous.*"

"We must *kill* her."

"*Dangerous!*"

"Take her! *Take her!*"

I dropped to the floor with my knees up, my face down, and my hands over my ears. I tried to resist the pull of the dark portal that summoned me.

It was not my flesh that was being ripped away but my very soul. Only the silver cord between my spiritual and physical self kept me from being lost into the nothingness. Its threads began to fray and snap one by one. I tried to crawl to the bedroom door, but my astral arms and legs were no longer connected to my muscles. I had to focus to connect my will to my flesh and bone.

The devil's mad chorus grew stronger. "Come with us! We *know* you."

"*You can not hide!*"

"She is dangerous! *Take her!*"

"No! *No!* Let *go!*" I screamed. I continued to try to crawl away as my soul was falling into oblivion. "*Help!*" The talons of the abyss morphed into a great undulating toothed tentacle that began to crush me. With every exhale, the coil compressed and crushed my lungs inch by inch.

Suddenly a strange calm filled me. It was like the great eye of a hurricane, beautiful peace in the middle of catastrophic chaos. I knew that I could defeat this, the creatures from the Nothing.

The calm turned into a warm fire within me and it reflected from inside the void. A small golden glow began to emerge within the portal. The bright flame grew steady and ever larger.

The shades began to scatter. The giant squirming tentacle held firm. My spirit's silver cord was on its last thread. My soul would be lost forever but still calmness remained.

I just knew I was not defeated, and at that moment the torchlight exploded into the room. The tentacle that held me so tightly putrefied into a sticky slurry. My soul and body crashed together with such force I awoke sitting up in my bed feeling the stark sensation of *déjà vu*.

Once again, the moonlight broke through the blinds at harsh angles that made even the harmless and ordinary seem cruel and otherworldly. I was still afraid, but not helpless.

Chapter 2

I tried to shake off last night's dream, but it lingered in the back of my mind. The echoes of the shades were still in the corner of my eye. It was hard to find focus and motivation.

I sat there looking at that damn blinking cursor as it dared me to think of something clever to write. I thought writing my second book would be easier. I was wrong.

My first book, *Hodge Podge*, had a very humble following, and I was surprised that the publisher wanted a follow up. It had been a pain in the ass, but this one just wasn't coming. I didn't know if it was because of the steady stream of night terrors or this abstract sense that something was heading my way.

Of course, my little how-to book of spells and crafts wasn't what you would call a masterwork. It contained lots of bright pictures, simple chants and home projects - none of the really good stuff.

The exception was one spell that I was particularly proud of. It had come to me in a dream many years before. It brought me a great ward and protection spell, but the rest of the dream itself had become a fog over time.

My dreams had always been a source of inspiration and pain. Most of my nights were filled with nightmares, but last night, and for that matter the past couple of months, had been on a different level and steadily getting worse.

If I was lucky, my nightmares could give me insight and

sometimes a glimpse into my future. That's if I could piece the images together before the event actually happened, but usually my epiphany was as the moment unfolded, and I said, "Oh! That's what that meant."

I sat there static. My computer screen mocked my efforts and gave no sympathy. I gritted my teeth as I felt the temptation to throw my laptop across the room like a Frisbee. The idea did make me feel a little better.

I was at the point of no return. *Fuck this. I am so fucking done. I quit. Even if I did write anything, who would fucking read it?*

"This is so stupid. Why is this so fucking hard?" I whined. I watched Morti softly snore on top of my unfolded laundry as Grace sat in the window flitting her tail thinking of squirrel for lunch. My clean but cluttered living room and yesterdays dishes beckoned me. It briefly crossed my mind to clean up around the house, but I decided against it.

"I need some hot chocolate." I gave up for the day.

I grabbed my worn leather jacket with its duct tape patches and headed out the door.

I pressed send to the last person who had called me on my phone, it too was held together with duct tape. "Hey, you wanna meet me at Beans and Things?" I asked as I hopped into my beat up truck.

The rough growl of the motor bellowed as I turned the key. I was barely able to hear Joy give me her answer of "Cool" over the engine and the explosion of sound from my radio. I frantically fumbled the volume control down.

Got a quarter of a tank; I can make it there and back. I checked my jeans pocket to see if I had money for my hot chocolate therapy. *WOOT! Ten bucks!*

"See ya there in fifteen." I hung up my phone and turned up the music.

Exactly fifteen minutes later and ten churches passed, I pulled into the Beans and Things. I sat broken-hearted as I listened to the end of yet another news report of a mass shooting. *Fifth one in as many months. What the hell is going on?*

The DJ popped in after the news report. "On a lighter note, a new comet was discovered has been dubbed Saint Nick because it will be making a pass this Christmas!" I clicked off the radio as I noticed that Joy was pulling in. Christmas was a month away and I wasn't a big fan. I was more of a Yule girl, pagan that I was.

Joy got out of her VW Beetle and she looked cute as always. Her Maniac Panic hair was Kool-aid red today, and her make up done with her usual bohemian flare. Joy wore her signature outfit: a short plaid skirt, big boots and Anarchy tank. She was the model of mainstream punk. Every item was torn perfectly and mismatched purposefully.

I was wearing my usual too, sadly. My fifteen-year-old jacket, dirty torn blue jeans and my favorite old t-shirt. *Is this a chocolate stain?* I looked at myself in the rear view mirror, depressed even further at noticing that my frizzy copper hair was falling out of its sloppy bun. *What is that... fuzz?* I plucked the mystery white fluff from my hair and redid a quick ponytail.

Joy was on her phone, as usual, going into the small mom and pop coffee shop.

I was no longer in my twenties, and my body was not a size 2 like Joy's. *But I am smart and creative. Oh wait... I can't even write two fucking sentences!* My own voice crashed in my mind. My frustration with my many recent failed attempts to write my book burned through me. *Time for my hot chocolate.*

Chapter 3

Beans and Things was a simple kitschy coffee shop in the middle of nothing and nowhere about five minutes outside the city of Huntsville, Alabama. It seemed a lot further because it was over the mountain. If it wasn't in Huntsville city proper it was "too far away" for most people. The converted speck of a house, now coffee hangout had a mini storage to its right and failed mini-mall to its left. They did, however, have the best coffee at the cheapest prices.

My presence was heralded by the permanent Christmas bells on the back of the glass door. The smell of fresh brewed coffee gave me the sense of being wrapped in a favorite blanket.

Joy's shiny purple lips smiled happily up at me. "You look like you need a break, Liddy."

I answered her with a yawn. I hated her calling me Liddy but had given up the fight years ago.

The barista handed over our chocolate caffeine addictions with barely a smile. He took our money and put his earbuds back in.

Joy walked over and sat at our usual table with my coveted cup of hot cocoa waiting.

"You look exhausted."

"I am." I took a tentative sip of my hot chocolate goodness. *Still too hot, but mmmm, heaven.*

I was happy to have a friend like Joy, but I envied her

youth and energy. I was in pretty good shape for my thirties, but I was no twenty something. My bones popped, and the lines had started to show around my eyes. I worked out when I could, when I had the energy, but I hadn't had any since October. That's when I had started having sleeping issues.

I took another sip of my drink and smiled as I listened to Joy ramble on about her latest troubles. I looked around the shop, seeing the same old country art and quirky signs. The cozy cafe had a spattering of fake fall leaves and week overdue Thanksgiving decorations.

The only other customers were a frazzled mom and two young kids. There was a buzz of chaos and some sadness around them, but I was just too out of it to focus. The little blonde girl looked up and I glanced away.

The teenage barista was back to working on his homework and rocking out to some music. His ear buds buzzed so loudly it gave me the disturbing image of a cicada digging in his ear.

Shaking off that horrible thought, I went back to looking across at my young friend. I didn't mind that Joy's favorite subject was Joy. It got my mind off my own failures and sometimes got me to remember the "Good Ole Days."

Joy sipped her mocha frappe, gleefully going on about the latest boy falling over himself for her. "I'm really not interested in Lee. He's way too young but he just won't take the hint."

"Isn't he your age?" I relished my hot mug warming my hands.

"Yes, but he is so dumb. He is all about how everything's stupid and people are stupid and this is stupid."

"Yep, that sounds about right." I could definitely relate to Lee.

"He never wants to have a good time. He's so fucking emo. I just want to have fun. You know?" Joy pouted.

"Sing it Cindi." I offered as I lazily raised my hands like I was in church.

"Who?"

"Cindi Lauper?"

"Who's that?" With that Joy succeeded in making me feel even older. I blinked hard to shake off that punch to my ego.

"You know the re-mix they play at the club. 'Girls Just Wanna Have Fun? '" I tried.

"You mean that's not the original? Oh yeah! Wow, that came out way before I was born." Joy giggled. I wasn't entirely sure if she was fucking with me or not. I was too tired to do the math.

I twitched, and thoughts of friendly homicide danced through my head. My lips tightened as I tried to hide my evil smile.

"Did you hear about the comet?" Joy noticed the sinister grin which encouraged her to change the subject.

"Saint Nick? Just heard about it on the radio. I'm more concerned with the fucking psychos. Another shooting."

"Don't forget another mom killed her kids. A woman up in Ohio and her five daughters. She wanted to 'save their souls.' How fucked up is that? Maybe it's the comet and full moon fucking with peoples heads."

"I know I'm not getting a lot of sleep." I yawned yet again. I didn't tell her that I was feeling a bit distorted myself.

"Yeah, I see you post that online a lot. You're apparently not the only one though. A lot of people have been complaining about bad dreams and freak outs."

"The holidays are enough to make people snap."

"Speaking of, how was your Thanksgiving?" She looked up from her phone briefly knowing that the holidays were always rough for me.

"I sat at home and shared fast food chicken with Grace and Morti." I knew what she was really asking is if I heard from my eleven year old daughter. "And I didn't get to talk to Ember. She wasn't feeling well. I haven't been able to touch base with her since just before Halloween. She said she wasn't feeling well then either. Her dad told me her tonsils were giving her issues."

I smiled, but it hurt. I was getting frustrated with the phone tag between me and her dad, but I didn't have the power to do anything about it. Her father moved out of state and started a new family. His and my relationship was destructive at best. The custody battle was brutal on me. He came from money and knew how to work the system. I had a court appointed attorney named Billy Bob. I should have known I was screwed then, but once it came out that I was pagan, bisexual and poor the case was over. I was not fit to be a mother in Alabama anymore.

Over time I sucked up the pain and found projects to lose myself in. That's how my first book got written.

He didn't keep Ember from me, but I didn't have the money to travel and pay for a hotel room to see her.

I was sure to always write her letters and call, but talks hurt. It was the emotion in her voice, her not understanding why I couldn't come to see her and the voice of the man who took my heart away that made it too hard. He and I played nice, and I respected and trusted his new wife with my daughter. It just hurt. All the time.

Joy noticed I was going down the spiral. "Hey, are you having classes this Saturday?"

I barely heard her. "Yes, at 3, The Chalice. We'll be talking about energy working. Got a few new people, so I will have to go over the basics." I had been supporting my habit of writing by teaching magick basics for beginners, doing readings and any other witchy work I could find. It was the only thing I was good at.

Besides the fact that trying to get a job in Alabama without being a part of a local church was next to impossible, most people knew I was different. They just didn't have the why and how. I was always described as the "weird red-head."

God fearing people didn't want that around, and the local witch or new age shops didn't need extra help. The owners were like me and had to create a means to make money. One of them did, however, let me rent her back room to teach

Chapter 4

Most people never noticed my little dirt road as they sped past it on Highway 72. Most were looking forward to their trips to the bigger more exciting cities of Chattanooga or Atlanta. My tires began to spin as they made the sharp turn onto Mays Road. They caught and lurched me forward down the uneven back street. My small house peeked from around the naked trees as I passed my neighbors' pasture. Their horses and mules went on about their business, eating and warming themselves in the sun.

My home was the original farmhouse on the land until my neighbor decided he wanted to sell it and build himself a bigger home on the other side of the acreage. I was more than happy to take it off his hands when I published *Hodge Podge*. I had gotten just enough for a very small down payment and continued to rent to own.

Rick Mays was a "get your hands dirty" kinda guy. His face was aged with hard work, but his mind was still sharp as ever. His wife, Camille, was also aged by a life in the sun, but still held a soft beauty. She was always ready to lend a hand with a smile. I was about the same age as their many kids. After their children had left the nest, Rick and Camille decided to keep me under their wing.

They went to church every Sunday and Wednesday. They were what I would call Christopagan. Christians with a very strong pagan influence. They knew what I was, but they didn't getting the hint I was no longer amusing to Joy, so I gathered up my jacket and keys.

"Oh yeah, how is your book coming?" Joy looking up from her distraction.

"I'm having a hard time coming up with ideas. I need some inspiration."

"What is it you always tell me? Be careful what you ask for, the gods are always listening."

I hope they are. I thought to myself.

Her phone buzzed. "Oh, it's him. Oh my God!"

"What?"

"He's coming into town this weekend!"

"Who?"

"The hottie vamp!!"

"Oh gods. Be careful. Please. I'll see you at class?"

"Yes." She smiled and she looked at me really for the first time that day. "'Chance lined up.' Isn't that what you tell your students magick is? When it comes to being real, it doesn't matter what others think. It's what you know. You have a gift, Lydia, that I would kill for. I can't see a damn aura to save my life. Now give me a hug, bitch!"

I gave her a hug, and the sweet smell of her perfume reminded me of cherry lollipops. *Ug, I hope she doesn't smell me.*

right?" I couldn't help but chuckle.

"No," she leaned in close and whispered, "He is a 400 year old vampire, and he says he is part of a 'House' in... somewhere around Nashville." Her face turned redder. She was obviously thinking about some of their cyber dates.

"OK. So he is a 14 year old boy." I laughed harder.

"You're a freakin' goth witch, how can you not believe in vampires?" Joy's face tensed.

"I believe in real vampires. I believe in psychic vampires because it's just the manipulation of auric energy, and I believe in blood drinking humans who like the taste of blood and get some marginal benefits from it. I don't, however, believe in immortals cursed to walk the earth. Just humans with some gifts and/or disillusions." I was trying so hard not to let Joy become a fantastical. "Look around this is it. This is all the magick there really is. There are no Krakens, only giant squids."

"We will see." Joy started typing on her bedazzled phone. "And how can you believe that? You've seen so much. Aren't you cleansing a house for Ethan tomorrow?"

"I have seen a lot but... sometimes I wonder if it's all in my head. Maybe I'm a fantastical too? What have I seen? Ghosts? Auras? And maybe my spells don't work, and it's just by chance things lined up." I wanted to believe, but doubt crept in.

She was right. I had memories of amazing things, but so much of it could be explained away. Most everything I've seen has been in the corner of my eye, in my minds eye, or something I "felt". Over time, the details that convince me of the reality of the experience wash away. I'm left with stories that sound like a bad movie, and my logical mind goes to war with my senses.

Joy looked at me blankly, not really wanting to deal with anything deep today. I shrugged it off. *I'm too tired to fight.* I sipped the last of my cocoa.

"Real or not, I had better get back to the grind." I was

classes.

Many of the students were what I called "fantasticals," people who tended to be way outside the box and lived in a fantasy world. I kept hope that at least some of my students where reasonable and logical witches and not thinking they missed the train to Hogwarts.

They were also the mundanes, the normal people, that would attend. It wasn't about the art of magick, it was them trying to feel special. They found it easier to light a candle instead of seeking real therapy.

Of course these were also the folks who had money to spend on classes. They could hold down real jobs. I'm not saying all real practitioners can't hold a standard job. I'm just saying very few of us have a knack for blending, no matter how hard we try, and the South is unforgiving.

"Yeah, it's getting frustrating that no one seems to remember to bring any money with them." I was trying to hint at Joy about not paying for any of the classes herself. Subtlety was never my gift.

"Damn, I hate cheap people." Joy clearly did not get it or refused to acknowledge it. "Oh yeah! I might be bringing a friend this time. Is that okay? He is a big fan of your first book."

"If he brings ten dollars." Smiling, I sipped down my annoyance with chocolate goodness.

"It's a friend of a guy I'm talking to online." Joy perked. "He is sooo hot." She leaned in close and purred, "He and I sexted all night last night."

She showed me a picture of a tall blond man with a strong jaw, perfect abs and piercing eyes. *Why would a man that hot be looking for a date online? Must be a stolen picture.*

"The guy you're bringing?" I was a little curious to meet this Don Juan.

"No, his friend, not the hottie. I don't have a picture of him."

"You know the 'hottie' is probably an 80 year old man

care. They had their own folk beliefs and traditions.

Both of them would venture down for my circle's grill-outs and discuss friendly about politics and religion, and on rare occasions, get into heated debates about Southern college football.

Both Camille and I collected wind chimes and had them proudly displayed on our front porches. The beautiful chorus of bells was always a great way to be welcomed home. Rick's dogs barked in happy greetings as they raced to the fence line.

You wouldn't think much of my old yellow house. It looked normal in most ways, but if you looked closely you could see the telltale signs that a witch lived there: chalk markings on the steps, a herbal broom or two and a odd stone here and there.

My ward around my home invited me in with its usual rhythmic hum. The ward, a type of invisible barrier, was there to keep me and mine safe from any harm, be it human or other. My "cinnamon" brooms still in their place showed that no one had trespassed. I had made my spell so that if anyone uninvited crossed my yard, my brooms would fall. Beyond that simple sign, there were a few more surprises, most not that passive.

Happy to be home I opened my front door to see Morti waiting for me impatiently. Morti, a very muscular black tomcat, was sitting high and proud on the top of his cat tree. He was a bit annoyed that I had left without waking him from his nap.

"Hey, Morti, I wasn't gone that long." His green eyes squinted in disapproval.

I threw my keys down on the coffee table and my precariously stacked collection of research books wavered threateningly. Once again, I felt the pang of chores that needed to be done. An inch of dust covered my cheap china cabinet that was bursting at the seams with crystals, stones and trinkets all reflecting my spell craft. The only piece of technology in the room was my computer. Its screen saver danced quietly awaiting my return.

I was pleasantly surprised that it had not been knocked off the futon by Grace. Unlike her brother, she was not the picture of noble quiet strength, but a ball of ferocity waiting to unleash her cruel vengeance on toes and any other appendage that happened near her.

"Grace?" I tried to listen for her bell. "Grace?" I walked towards the kitchen and Morti got down from his perch and followed me. This was the game we always played. Grace's hide and seek and Morti's mocking of me. "Morti, where's your sister?" He jumped on top of the kitchen table and stared at me. "Food right?" I went to the closet to get some more food.

Thwat, thwat, thwat! Grace's thousand paws of fury attacked my hand, then she went tearing through the house. "Oh." I looked at Morti, who seemed to be laughing to himself.

"Pay back for leaving earlier?" I smiled as I poured some food in their dish. He showed his forgiveness with a purr. I gave Morti a scratch, "Love you too."

What's that smell? The smell of sickeningly sweet dead flowers and rot was followed by a cold chill that raced up my spine, making my hair stand on end. I stood up slowly as the distinct feeling that I was not alone crawled within me.

Morti's hackles raised across his back, and his ears fell flat. He was looking behind me.

Clack! My brooms hit the floor. Morti took off running, following his sister. I turned, not knowing what I was about to see, but there was no one.

I tried to see with my third eye, but I was greeted with the feeling of a pickaxe to the brain. The air in the room began to grow heavy and hot. *How are you getting past my wards?* The breath of the devil bore down on me.

I nervously fumbled for a box of sea salt and a spice jar of rosemary and sage. I hurriedly mixed them in my hand. I focused my will as the room began to vibrate with a malicious presence. I thrust the salt mix in front of me. "You are not welcome here. Get out!"

Snap! The kitchen window cracked. Immediately the room became lighter and returned its natural state. I caught my breath as I held the left over mix in my sweaty hands.

"What the *fuck* was *that?*"

I spent the better part of Wednesday night and the beginning of Thursday cleansing and reinforcing my protection barriers. The best thing I could do after the intrusion and persistent nightmares was to find some quiet time for me to hold a sacred circle and center myself.

I gathered up my homemade candles, my favorite tools and took them out side to my altar. It was hidden behind the house where I had seclusion and privacy. It was made of an old oak tree that had its heart stopped by a bolt of lightning a couple of years ago. Rainbow waxen rivers were frozen in time as mushrooms and moss bloomed from the short blackened stump.

I had lined my sacred space with dandelions and cypress sprigs. I sprinkled my fresh picked herbs into my fire cauldron. The night was cool but not cold. The sky was clear and the moon was waning.

The incense sat heavy in the air as I placed a single black candle in the center of the altar. This was my patron's candle. I had made it with special care for my Goddess Hekate. *I hope you hear me tonight.*

Hekate was the goddess of the crossroads, keeper of the key and light. She was the one who went into underworld to bring back Persephone. She was the goddess of witches. I was fearful of her reputation when I was younger, but she called me. Much like the Catholic priests and nuns say "I was called."

She had always been fair and pragmatic to frustration. She was the goddess I most respected and feared, much like a young child to her mother.

I sat still and let the incense wash over me. The strong smell of sage and sweetgrass tickled my nose. I began to center myself.

Deep breath in, Deep breath out.
Calming my mind.
Deep breath in, Deep breath out.
Calming my body.
Deep breath in, Deep breath out.
Calming my spirit.

I began to feel the movement in the night. My yard was locked down with the refreshed ward of protection but this ritual would make it even stronger.

I unsheathed my athame, a dagger used only in spell work, and was ready to begin. I pointed my blade out in front of me. "I cast this circle of protection and power. None shall enter with out my permission."

I turned clockwise in place, creating a motion of a circle surrounding me. "From back to front," I envisioned a barrier of energy glowing on the borders of my land. "To my right and to my left. As above and so below." I extended my arm to the heavens and then stabbed my athame into the ground. My third eye saw clearly a shockwave from my dagger that bellowed out to form of a bubble solid energy encompassing my home. It reacted like a bug zapper where little random energies would test it.

I picked up my shell with my burning sage and smudged a smaller five-foot circle that was marked by river stones on the ground. I took in a deep breath and filled my body with a white light and then pushed it out with a grand exhale, filling the minor space.

"Negativity, you are not welcome here. All malign forces, you are not welcome here. All mischief-makers of pain and discord, you are not welcome here. Get out! I command you."

I became more grounded and centered. My inner power grew. The real me was being released. I didn't have to pretend here. I didn't have to worry about what others thought or their schemes. I was powerful. I was calm. I had no apologies.

I knelt back down on my knees in front of my waxen altar. I dropped my black velvet cloak and exposed my skin to the cool air.

I called the four corners and lit the coordinating colored candles with one flame to the next.

"Air, give me clarity and carry the seeds of communication Fire, light my way and give me strength of will.

Water, give me peace and inner wisdom.

Earth, give me strength and stability."

I settled myself, focusing my thoughts and energies to call my goddess.

"Goddess Hekate, I call upon you as your daughter to join me this night. I welcome you." I lit my black candle.

I closed my eyes and let the night surround me, enveloped my body with its cool embrace. Goose bumps marched down my flesh. Rick's dogs began to bark as heralds for their patron.

The white noise of the night fell silent. The breeze seemed to be nothing more than a phantom to the trees around me as they were eerily still. I opened my eyes, and the depth of the night was like the deepest ocean. Before me a figure of a veiled woman stood behind my altar. Her formed danced like a heat mirage.

Hekate had never been such a physical presence before. She was somewhere between my first sight and second sight. Not tangible, but real enough that I had forgotten to breathe. In all the times I had prayed and called, she was no more than a whisper or minds eye shadow but not this time. She was here.

A tickle began, deep inside my right ear, a symptom of hearing those who were not from this world. She stood silently, staring down at me impersonally. The tickle turned into the harmony of three female voices, a child's, a mother's, and the leading voice of a crone.

"I am here," she announced with no emotion. She formed a right hand from her body of mist and veil and held a floating ball of blue torch light.

"Thank you for honoring me with your presence," I humbly told her.

"You are welcome, Lydia." Her mirage form began to walk slowly around the inside of my minor circle. Heavy rusted keys clinked with every step.

"I can't sleep anymore. I'm having nightmares every night. No matter what I do, I can't get rid of them. And now something came into home." I felt like a newbie practitioner.

"Yes." Hekate was not one to give information freely. The correct questions must be asked. Her responses were earned. She did not suffer fools or stupidity.

"I was able to banish the being who came into my home, but the dreams I can't seem to stop." I was feeling even more humiliated that I had summoned her for "bad dreams."

The Dark Moon Goddess continued to walk around the circle. Frosted fog swirled behind her. Her all-powerful presence made me aware of my frailty.

"I know," again she answered matter-of-factly.

"How did something get into my home? What can I do to stop the dreams?" I dared not turn around as the goddess circled behind me.

"You welcomed it into your home. The dreams will not stop." She finished her walk back to center behind my altar.

"I welcomed it?" I was confused.

She looked down at me as if I should know the answer. She was not about to give it to me.

"The coffee shop." I answered my own question.

"Choose your words and will carefully. Someone is always listening and waiting." The Crone gave the advice I had earned. Hekate's answer shamed me, because it was something a dabbler needs to be reminded of, not a seasoned practitioner and teacher.

"What should I do about the nightmares?" I didn't want to strain her patience.

"Use them. They are gifts."

"Gifts?" I was beginning to shiver from exposure.

"Yes," her tone of voice said "of course, silly girl."

"From who?"

She did not answer. She stood over me, infinitely tolerant.

"What do these things mean?" I repeated.

"It is time, and you have been found."

"Time? And by who?" At that moment, my bubble ward began to pop and crackle fiercely.

"Not all things that need to be feared should or can be avoided."

The waking sun blushed the early morning sky. Time had been swept away by the conversation.

"What do..." I didn't finish my question because Hekate was no longer there. I was alone, kneeling among the dewdrops on cold earth.

Chapter 6

Friday night
16 days until Solstice

It was Ethan who met me as I pulled in, greeting me with a
perfect smile. He was good friend of mine and was the one
who called me in for this particular gig.

"Hey sweetie! Thank you so much for coming." He gave me
warm hug. "I know you don't like doing this, but your skills
will be much appreciated." He volunteered his time with local
ghost botherers group, or as it was better known, The Rocket
City Ghost Hunters. They had called him, and he then called
me. "You look rough. Are you okay?"

"I'm fine; just tired. So why am I here?" I asked already
exhausted from the night before. I'd rather be at home
working on my book, preparing for tomorrow's class or taking
a nice nap. I took a quick moment and assessed the average
house on the average street. On the surface everything looked
as it should, right down to the American flag marking the
threshold. I relaxed my eyes and let the auric fields begin to
reveal themselves. Instead of the warm glow of a home, I saw
a sickly shadow creating a kind of wound in the energy field
on the top floor. *Okay, let's do this.* I grabbed my bag from my
passenger seat.

"They've been having disturbances lately. She had their
local pastor in and tried to cleanse the house, but it seemed
to only make things worse. They won't even go in anymore."
Even when delivering dark news, Ethan always had a light
about him. "I wanted to warn you before you went to the

porch. The mom isn't happy you're here. She doesn't like 'your kind' going into her house."

"I am not going to force my help on someone." Annoyance hardened my jaw, and I threw my things back in the truck and pulled out my keys. Ethan grabbed my truck door and gave me a pleading look.

"It's not for her. She has a six year old and a twelve year old. The grandmother, who's here, is the one who wanted us to come in." He knew my weakness.

"Fine," I grumbled. I couldn't resist Ethan's charms.

Everyone was stationed on the porch nervously being polite to one another. Paul stood up pleased to see me. He was a little plumper and shorter than Ethan, and was definitely the butch.

Ethan and Paul both pretended to just be friends in front of the clients, but their auras danced around each other timidly touching and caressing, each aura always seeking the other. It was nice to watch something positive with my "gifts" for a change.

In contrast, a very tense woman sat impatiently on an porch swing. Her aura had the sick yellow of unease and frantic scarlet of annoyed anger. She was a very plain and unremarkable looking woman to me, but would have surely been the prom queen back in high school. Thin features and her twitchy movements reminded me of a frazzled terrier.

"Ms. Gill, this is my friend Ms. Keening." Ethan gently pushed me up the steps. *Why am I here?*

"Ms. Keening." Ms. Gill forced a polite smile, but her eyes didn't hide her distaste for me.

"And I'm her mother, you can call me May and her Jackie." May was just as average as her daughter, but her friendly nature made her all the more attractive.

"Hi. Nice to meet you, and I hope I can help." I shook both their hands.

Jackie fiddled with her cross ring as she watched me suspiciously. I was used to it. *Let's just get this over with.* I believe we both felt the same way. I kept my soft smile and remained neutral and cordial.

Ethan and Paul took turns on generally filling me in to give me a starting point without giving me a bias. They had done sweeps of the house and observed some activity such as doors slamming and objects falling.

I raised my hands to stop their geek-gasms and focused on Jackie. "Tell me in your own words. What are some of the things you have witnessed first hand?" I watched every flutter and color change of her personal energy. She uncomfortably squirmed in her seat. She didn't like me, but she was desperate.

"At first it was nothing much." Her aristocratic southern drawl ran deep. "Shadows. Voices." She pulled on her ring so hard her knuckle began to swell. "We didn't think much of it. Then our pups started to act up. Biting and barking at nothing. Chasing nothing."

She dropped her hands with tears bulging. "And then Missy our youngest Pomeranian died." Two tears slid down her fake tanned cheek leaving faint streaks of mascara. "Then it started in on my kids...and my mom...and me."

"How did Missy die?" I asked as something walked past the window, listening in.

"The vet said her little heart just gave out."

"How has it been affecting y'all?" I went on, giving no sign of the distraction.

"My six year old, Hunter, started talking to thin air. My twelve year old Brittany was having night-terrors. We all heard our names being called in the dark and have been getting scratches that burn like fire and bruises that won't heal." She lifted her sleeve and revealed an ugly bruise in the shape of finger prints on her right arm. "I got this when I was packing our bags to stay at my brothers. It tried to throw me down the stairs."

"Anything new or stressful going on in the house? Divorce... Abuse?" I watched her aura and body language, and there was nothing to indicate she was lying or delusional. *This entity is dangerous.*

"Their dad passed away right before Hunter was born." She took a deep breath. "Hunter is doing great in school and Brit just made cheer squad last month." She beamed. "Other than the... 'troubles'... everything has been going very well." She was telling the truth. *No emotional trauma triggers. So most likely no one is subconsciously making it happen.*

"You've lived in the house...?"

"Ten years," she answered. *Something new in the house then.*

"So when did you say this started?" My personal feelings aside I had to help her and her family get their home back.

"About three months ago, and it has gone from bad to worse. I just want everything back to normal." How I envied the idea of normal.

"I'm going to take a look around and see what we're dealing with."

"What are you gonna do?" Another pass in front of the window.

"I'm going to feel the house and its energies."

"Are y'all going to do the witchcraft?" Her brows bent hard in worry.

"Let's first see what we're dealing with. I want you to stay outside." I sternly warned them.

I stopped as I reached for the doorknob. "Jackie, you don't think your little girl might have been messing with a Ouija board or anything like that?"

"No, we're good Christians." She answered pridefully.

I ignored the implication and took her answer as a simple "no." "Okay, let's do this. You guys ready?"

Both Ethan and Paul grabbed their gear as I stilled myself and opened the door.

Chapter 7

Friday night
16 days until Solstice

Thick, stale air stuck to my skin as we stepped into the cookie cutter home. I knew whatever it was, it was upstairs. Waiting.

Every item here could be traced to a department store or catalog. The scene was predictable, average, and dull except for the very real cold and unnatural breath of the house. Its decorative crosses and professional family photos were recklessly thrown around. Neutral tones were accented with more neutral tones pock marked by a spattering of mystery stains and fluids.

We followed the evidence of the temper tantrum into the kitchen. Something creaked overhead as we tiptoed through broken clutter. I had done this many times, but I still had to fight my nerves. I don't think any one gets used to the unnatural collision of home and haunt.

I reached out with my mind's eye and confirmed the eerie absence of ambient energy in the home. It had been drained of any sense of family. "Paul, this should be a good place for you to set up." I pointed him to the kitchen.

Ethan gave Paul a quick kiss and then followed behind me. He readied his EMF, electromagnetic fields, meter and I began to try find the unwanted guest.

I nearly tripped over the tumbled bag at the foot of the stairs where Jackie had abandoned it from her close encounter. Steps could be heard above. Static brushed my arm as Ethan's EMF meter blinked.

A shadow flitted into a bedroom. It was more than a wisp; it was a woman. Cold gust curled up the back of my neck. A breathless whisper brushed against my ear.

This spirit was strong. Anger was all I could feel. It was so pervasive that I could barely hold a thought without it being corrupted with seething rage.

I must keep calm and centered. Breathe in, breathe out.

"There is so much anger. It's unnaturally strong." I said. Ethan nodded his head in agreement. His EMF lights came to life briefly. Most of the house bulbs had been turned off or broken except for the nightlights. This didn't bother me in the least, it was much easier for me to see auras in the dark.

Thud! Crack! Something fell to the floor. My auric feelers gently searched out every room till I was sure she was alone in the master bedroom.

It was hard to breathe in the stale thick air of the room. Within the four walls, a cold void bent the atmosphere around itself. There was definitely something here, something trying to take shape. I gestured for Ethan to hang back.

A neighbor's car headlights lit the room, and I could only make out the faint silhouettes of furniture. There was the predictable over priced comforter, piles of pillows, and on the floor, a silver framed picture of Jackie's family.

A presence loomed in the corner where it could hide from the light outside. It took the form of a hunched old woman's silhouette. I didn't turn to look directly at her because I didn't want her to disappear again. Better to know where she was than not.

I motioned quietly to Ethan with my hand. He picked up on the cue, moved his attention to the corner and pointed his digital recorder.

"Who are you? Why are you here?" I steeled myself as I looked directly at the shade.

The unformed thing trembled and evaporated into the shadows. Lights began to warp the room as the neighbor finally pulled away. I lost track of the phantom only to have my skin crawl as the spirit brushed against me.

I squelched my natural unease, and I relaxed my body as I sat on the Jackie's bed. *Calm and centered. Breathe in, breathe out.* I focused on the soft smell of potpourri that rested on a beautiful antique vanity.

The temperature began to drop and another flock of goose bumps flew across my skin. She was trying to manifest. "What's your name?" The temperature fell further. The tickle in my inner right ear began to grow.

"My name is Lydia." I made my voice and my thoughts clear and focused. I was struggling against my fatigue.

"Abby." The name was more felt than heard. The tickle in my ear became more intense as pins and needles went up my spine.

"Get out, Lydia," the words hissed.

I glanced up into the large round vanity mirror and saw an old lady in white standing ominously behind me. Her rage disfigured her face. She was still gathering power.

"Abby, why are you angry?" Again putting my will behind my words and fighting my very human instincts to run.

"Stolen."

"What was..."

"*STOLEN!*" Her form mutated into a hallowed face with pitch orbs for eyes. She flew through me and into the mirror. Static cold, slice and burn went through my belly flesh.

I had fucked up. I had gotten sloppy. I lifted my shirt and showed Ethan, who had turned pale, the three fierce scratch marks across my white stomach.

An energy glow caught my attention; its origin was within and around the vanity mirror. *Damn, I am getting slow.*

Chapter 8

I went to the porch with Ethan and Paul in tow and gathered the ladies. "Where did you get the vanity?"

"From an estate sale. A woman in our church had passed. Why?" Jackie's sweet tea drawl was giving me a toothache.

"And when was this?" I already knew the answer but had to lead her to it.

"About three months..." I watched as the realization dawned on her. She was the one who brought the ghost into her house. Abby had most likely died in front of that mirror and was pissed about her vanity being "stolen" from her home.

"The reason the preacher's cleansing didn't work is that the woman's spirit is linked to an object that you invited in. Well, actually, you kinda kidnapped her." I touched the scratches on my stomach as they stung from salty sweat.

"Wha..." Jackie was baffled and horrified.

"Mirrors are powerful objects; they can hold and manipulate energy. As a general rule, cleanse them before you bring them into your home. Holy water would be fine. I prefer an herb and salt water mix." I pulled out my bag with my supplies. I placed a sage smudge, my favorite sacred agate bowl, herb mix, and salt water on her expensive coffee table.

"If you want me to cleanse it, I will need your help." I told her pointedly. I didn't have any patience with freak outs, but I could see one coming as her face lost color and her aura began to get frantic.

"Me? I don't know anything about this devil stuff! Ethan said you're a pagan!" She impudently implied it meant that I was a devil worshiper. She wanted a fight because she didn't want to deal with the reality of a ghost hiding in her mirror, a natural reaction. Jackie grew more agitated and more scared which fed the spirit more energy.

"I am a *Pagan* witch not a *Satanic* witch." I was trying to remain diplomatic and sympathetic, but my tongue was beginning to bleed from biting it so often.

Ethan was about to step in, but I put my hand up, "I am pagan but there is no 'Satan' in my beliefs. We have positive, negative and neutral energy, but not all Pagans are witches. Not all witches are Pagan. I am a Pagan witch. You can be Christian and still be a witch. Witches are people who have the ability to connect to the universe by more direct means. I am neutral. I don't pick sides. I just try help where I can." As I said the words the bondage of my "gifts" began to tighten. *I do this because I can do nothing else.*

I took in a deep breath and picked up the smudge bundle. "This is sage. It helps to cleanse an area. It's good to lighten up energy. Negativity is heavy and thick. Sage acts like paint thinner. If it's just normal negativity, you burn this," I held up the bundle, "and it breaks it up. Then it's easier to clean it out. It can be done either with the natural flow of the space, or you can use your will to push it out." I paused and read the doubt on her face.

"The Native Americans used sage. Do you understand?" My burning green eyes met her tearful brown ones. I didn't understand why mundanes were freaked out by the term pagan, but if you said "Native American" they were fine. Gotta love white guilt. It won't let them carry the same prejudice towards the Native Americans as Old World or Eastern paganism. *"Us white folks should know better."*

I poured the water into the bowl and stirred in the oils and herbs with a clockwise motion. I pulled white light energy to my center and focused it into the agate dish as I said my blessing softly.

Jackie and May sat quietly. Jackie nervously tinkered with her ring yet again. She watched me carefully to see if she approved of my efforts, not that she had a clue what I was doing or what every small action meant.

Jackie and I carefully climbed the stairs as the sage burned steadily. I gently set the thick smoke free with my raven feathered fan. "This house belongs to Jackie and her family," I announced at the top of the staircase. I nodded to Jackie to begin. The house began to growl and moan.

Her voice, soft and unsure, repeated what I had told her verbatim. "You are no longer welcome here. No one or no thing shall enter my house without my permission."

"No one or no thing shall enter Jackie's house without her permission." I said in a loud clear voice trying to show her how it needed to be done. "You are no longer welcome here." I looked towards her. "You must put your will behind your words or they are just sounds."

She nodded in compliance, and she repeated the words over and over, each time getting stronger and more confident that no one was going to laugh at her.

I opened the door to her bedroom. She grabbed my hand hard as I looked up to see the white form standing the same corner as before across from the mirror.

"Stay strong and focused. This is your house, your space. You set the rules." I steadied her hands, which held the bowl of water.

I made my presence known to the ghost as I walked into the blackness. "We wish you no harm, but I will not allow harm to come to Jackie and her family. Do you think you could live here in peace?"

Jackie looked shocked at the idea. Most benign ghosts just wanted to be recognized and acknowledged. They could be very helpful and protective if given half a chance. Others are so caught up in their problems they become crazed and dangerous. Ghosts are people boiled down to their essence and their emotions. Raw powerful emotion.

I had the feeling this ghost didn't want to play nice, but to be fair I had to ask. The room grew cold, and both Jackie and I experienced an invisible weight crushing in on us. The spirit was gathering strength to lash out again. I directed the sage smoke into the room to break up the heavy energy so Abby couldn't manifest. I pushed with my will, and the smoke began to swirl. I watched as the black energy began to separate like oil in water.

Abby charged from the darkness, and a burning slash found my cheek. Jackie screamed, and I quickly grabbed the water bowl before she dropped it. She instinctively curled herself in a tight ball on the floor.

I had guessed the ghost would take refuge in the mirror, and she did. My fingers made quick work as they anointed the mirror with the sacred water and sprinkled some throughout the room. I ordered Jackie to continue reclaiming her house. She stood up warily and began to chant again. The vanity began to vibrate, and the mirror rippled.

I pulled a little bottle out of my pocket that contained my homemade binding oil. With haste my fingers once again marked the mirror and vanity.

Immediately the room began to lessen its grasp, and fresh air began to flow. I pulled a bed sheet out of a laundry basket and began to toss it over the mirror as I watched the spirit of Abby retreat deeper within. She was locked behind the reflection, but she was not alone.

The familiar smell of dead flowers and rot began to taint the air. It was the same scent from my home. The bedroom's atmosphere began to pop and sizzle. *Demon.*

I quickly tied the sheet across the vanity and turned to survey the room. "What's that smell?" Jackie's nose crinkled in distaste. Ethan ran up the stairs "Lydia!" His meter was going off the charts. "Ethan, take Jackie and get out of the house now!"

As soon as Jackie cleared the bedroom door it slammed closed, cracking the frame.

Knock, knock. I heard slow knocking on glass from behind the sheeted mirror. *Knock, knock.*

I brought my hands up, took in a deep breath, and focused. I envisioned a ball of white light energy surrounding the vanity. "Be gone! And no more! You are not welcome here!" The foul smell and ill presence faded immediately, too easily, leaving only the presence of poor Abby behind.

It followed me. I was certain it didn't care about Abby, Jackie, or her children. This was getting serious, but I played it off to everyone as nothing out of the ordinary; one last tantrum from Abby. Ethan and Paul knew better but didn't push it.

Outside I explained to them that Abby was trapped inside the mirror. "If you want to truly cleanse and get rid of Abby, set the mirror out in the full moon light and wash it down with this." I held up another bottle of my own mixture. "This is a release and cleanse potion called Morning Star. It will set her free and guide her to move on...but don't break the mirror." I warned.

Ethan and Paul could handle all of that. I was done for the night. I just wanted to go home and try to get some sleep before tomorrow found me for class.

"Are you okay, Lydia?" Paul pointed to the two small scratches across my face.

"Oh," I touched the marks with some pain. "Yeah, I'll be fine."

"Blessed be, my friend." Paul hugged me. He didn't try to hide his worry. Ethan stole a hug from me as well.

"Blessed be." I picked up my roughly packed bags.

Jackie suddenly rushed over and gave me a hug. I could sense her relief and her aura was clear, but I knew that if we ever crossed each other in the street, she would pretend to not know me. I was okay with that.

"Magick is anything but easy. It requires the ability to look at yourself and the cosmos without hesitation. You must earn your way, and there is no forgiveness. You must take your stripes across your back and move on." I paused to watch the faces of my students. Some took the warning and others thought they knew better. *They will learn.*

"I think that is a good place to leave today's class. Are there any questions?" I gathered my notes. "Okay, I'll see y'all next time. Please work on your dream journals, meditation and grounding. Next class will be spell crafting."

I got a spattering of "thank yous" and tough talk from my students. I didn't care. I was too worn out from the house cleansing, and I desperately needed a nap before I went out later on that night.

Everyone poured out of the cramped back room of The Chalice, the local witch shop. It was nestled inside a back street strip mall that had been long forgotten by the upstanding citizens of Huntsville. It was the only witch shop within two hours of the Huntsville area.

It stood out from the strip because Wicked Wendy had great pride in her store. She had some seasoned graffiti artists decorate the outside of her store with a mural of a wild garden with pagan influences. "Always out but never seen" was the slogan of the local witches, but picketing still happened from time to time around the holidays or when a new pastor needed to make a name for himself.

The Chalice acted as a sanctuary to those who had nowhere else to go. Some of the witches were still in the broom closet, so to speak. Their families, friends or anyone who wasn't amongst the Chalice group had no idea of their path because the undercover practitioners or witches feared the punishments the greater society would inflict on them. I couldn't blame them. My cost was my daughter.

The local non-practitioners in the area steered clear of The Chalice and her patrons. As with most poor sides of towns, people kept to themselves. "You don't bother me and I don't bother you" was the understanding. We all had bigger worries, the struggle to find our next meals and money to pay the bills.

I grabbed my bag and headed out the back room after I thought everyone had left. Unfortunately, people were still hanging around the store scanning the new books and supplies.

"Lydia, I loved your class. Would you mind?" Willow, a tall lanky girl with limp dirty blonde hair, handed me a copy of my only published book with a puppy eyed look.

"Sure," I signed my name with barely contained glee. Willow skipped off happily back towards Joy, who stood beside the counter with a strange look on her face. Others began to notice me, and I knew I needed to disappear.

I quickly ducked into the bathroom to avoid the forced conversation I would have to have with everyone about their personal witch issues. I wasn't in the mood.

I leaned over to the dirty mirror in the dark little bathroom. My eyes focused on the tiny scratches across my right cheek, and my hand fell over my stomach. A reminder of my close encounter. No one had noticed them, most wouldn't guess.

My hair was down today, my curls almost reaching the top of my ass. Other than my tired eyes and a barely noticeable mark, I felt that today was a good day for mirrors. *I can't hide in here forever.* I found my smile and prepared myself for the long conversations as I made my way back to the front.

"Lydia, how are ya?" Wendy called from behind her glass counter top as she was putting up some herb jars. To my pleasant surprise, everyone else had left. "Joy said she would call you later."

"Cool. Is everyone gone?"

"Yes, if you want to join them they're going to lunch at the barbecue across the street."

"I'll think I'll pass." I picked up some citrine stones and tossed them between my hands.

The store had a simple layout. Lots of natural light shone through the front windows despite the bars. Wendy didn't tolerate the cluttered look that most little shops had. Pristine glass shelves lined the walls, making the small space look more open. You could get almost everything you needed here and if you needed something really special, Wendy, with a nod and wink could get that for you too.

All the stuff in front was what any dabbler or casual practitioner, the new age section educated, would need off the street. Of course most of us start there. For some who have been doing this for a while, the hardcore components were kept in back and shared on a need to know basis.

"I guess I'm good, how 'bout you?" I watched as Wendy steadily climbed down a short ladder in her layered long dress to place back the last jar. She was a little taller and thinner than me. Wendy's dark espresso skin looked younger than her sixty five years. Only her more salt than pepper dreads gave a hint of her real age.

"Honey, you look like shit. Are you sure you're okay?" She walked from behind the counter. As she reached out for one of my hands her many bracelets chimed together. Her own hands, wrapped in scars from a past she didn't share, held an unequaled balance of strength and softness. I could feel the stress of the past couple of weeks welling up in my eyes. "I'll getcha some tea."

The light smell of sweetgrass and sage soothed my frayed nerves as Wicked Wendy prepared our tea. "You wan' it in here or outside?" She placed the tea set on a serving tray.

"Outside, it's beautiful today." I went ahead of Wendy and opened the front door with the usual bell chime.

She placed the tea service on one of the small tables next to one of the two large cement gargoyles. I had dubbed them Burt and Ernie, and the names stuck. They had been both decorated with beads and cloth and blessed by the patrons of The Chalice. Their permanent mischievous smiles and unblinking eyes watched over the locals' sanctuary.

Wicked Wendy had purpose with every movement she made as she set the loose tea herbs into tea cups. Even as she poured the hot water, her energy was focused. I watched as her aura shifted from bright purple to a fresh green as she infused her brew with healing energy. If she had been anyone else I would've been worried about what energies had been put in my drink.

I didn't wish to interrupt, so I lost myself in the very blue skies and gusty breeze of fall. The government housing across the street was hosting a cook out with all their community neighbors. Kids ran around and played tag. The elderly matriarchs watched over everyone and set up the picnic tables. It was someone's birthday. Rough looking gang bangers played hide and seek with their kids, their tough exterior faded into silliness. *An urban Norman Rockwell.*

"So what's going on? You aura is all kinds of fucked up, my dear." Wendy was reading me and the pressure of her thoughts asked to be let in, so I let her. I hoped she could help me with whatever this was I was going through.

I pulled my attention from the laughing kids and looked into Wendy's aged eyes. "I haven't been sleeping well. I can't think or focus. My book isn't working at all. I feel this dread of... I don't know what." As I spoke the confusion and frustration smothered me.

"Well, your book will come. You felt this way about your

first one. I want to know about your dreams, but before that tell me about..." she motioned with her pointer finger to the scratches across the face.

I was hoping she hadn't noticed. "I got it at the house cleansing."

Wendy gave me a disapproving look. I knew I couldn't lie to her. "I wasn't careful."

"How about the ones on your stomach?" Her dark eyebrow arched pointedly.

"How..."

"You're scratching your stomach along with your face."

Defeated, I told her "I forgot to put my auric shields up." She wasn't amused.

"Lydia, I know you. Your shields are always up. Naturally."

"You think I did it on purpose?"

"Maybe subconsciously?"

"Maybe I 'm just getting tired and sloppy."

"Maybe you need to be reminded."

I knew what she meant when the words left her full lips. I struggled with faith- faith in myself. Sometimes I worried that I was like so many of the fantasticals I'd met. Their lives were so out of control that they had to believe in something, and the church just didn't fit their values.

Am I like them? Do I only think I see what I see? Know what I know? Did I lose my daughter for a faith that isn't anything more than escapism? Of course, you could say all faiths are a symptom of loss of control but that doesn't mean they are any less real.

"Lydia? Lost again." Wicked Wendy big brown eyes smiled and revealed the lines of wisdom and life lived.

"Sorry." I shook my head to stop my inner debate. "I think you're right. I didn't put my guard up because I wanted proof that..."

"You're not crazy believing in all this." She raised her arm like Vanna White towards her store.

"Yes." I was ashamed.

"I understand, but even with all that you have done and seen, you lack faith. Most would kill to have the proof you've had."

Her words reminded me of what Joy had told me only a few days ago. "I'm not ungrateful. I'm thankful to the gods for what I have experienced, it's just..."

"You don't want to be played for a fool. You have a logical and grounded mind, so you struggle. I believe that is why the Goddess Hekate chose you." She was right that my heart and mind were at war.

"No faith is worth having if you don't have to fight for it or question it. Faith is making the choice to believe today." Wendy understood me better than anyone. "But be careful. Those of us who have to fight for so much tend to make battles where there is no need for one. Save your energy for the real battles to come." A knowing passed across her face like a soft shadow of a cloud passing by, it worried me. "Now tell me about these dreams of yours."

I decided to let her knowing go because she wanted to move on.

I took a big drink, sat still and reflected on the idea. "Maybe it was just a dream."

"Maybe, but maybe not." She smiled and watched the families across the way. Two kids waved at us as they played with balloons. We waved back happily. A matriarch quickly stopped and scolded them. We both frowned a bit and moved on with our conversation.

"You need to explore this. They seem to be having a real effect on you."

"I feel a bit lost lately." The hot tea of honey and herbs soothed me.

"No such thing as being lost, child, just traveling to a place without a name." She sipped her tea softly. "Those are the best places. I love surprises."

The crackling bass broke through the club like a torrent. I had been there close to two hours, but already my cheap corset bit into my sides and my legs burned. I stomped my heavy boots to the harsh vocals of remixed Manson and drank my aches and pains away.

The Alt was the only club in Huntsville brave enough to take a freak's money. The bar staff were more or less the typical frat and sorority types. They didn't understand us but enjoyed witnessing the strange pageantry that was the southern goth scene. The men enjoyed the ample corset cleavage, and the women blushed at the noble goths and their Old World charms.

The goth chicks wore their vinyl and men their kilts, and we gave away our hugs and smiles to our adopted family. Everyone knew everyone else. Being a freak in such a small city leaves no room for strangers.

The night club shared its building with another dance club which catered to the "normals." Normals were the people who lived safe little lives, didn't know or care what an aura was, and strived to emulate the latest fashions and trends.

The normals or mundanes would visit The Alt to watch the freaks. The tourists were easy to spot when the look of shock, disgust, and/or intrigue would wash over their faces as they passed from the safety of their world into the uncertainty of ours.

Another song began to merge and fight for dominance over the dance floor, and I lost myself to its primal rhythm. Everyone held their own part of the dance floor. All the freaks be we goths, rivet heads, gravers, steam-punkers or anything else under the dark moon, vibrated in unison. We danced together but never touched; there was just a silent exchange of acceptance. We were here to remind ourselves that we weren't alone. This is where being a freak was badge of honor, not a scarlet letter.

My body moved like water following the pulsating current of the dark wave music. I was lost at sea. *Just me and the music. Nothing can touch me here. This is mine. I am me.*

Everything fell away. I gave myself away completely. I let go of the stress of the book that wouldn't come, the nightmares that wouldn't cease and the feeling of impending doom. I set myself free adrift the light scent of cloves and dark beauty of The Alt.

My body grew thirsty for my rum and Coke, so I slid off the dance floor between beats. I took a sip and realized my corset had shifted. I leaned in to Joy. "I'll be right back. Watch my drink."

She nodded as she barely took her eyes off her phone in expectation of her vampire.

I saw that my friend Shadow was at the bar getting a couple of shots. I came up behind him and groped his chest playfully.

He turned with a wide smile and chuckled, "Hey sexy!" He picked me up and swung me around. "See you on the dance floor later?" Physically he was not very attractive. He was a very tall overly thin guy with long, thinning, greasy black hair, but he was the guy you could always count on to make you smile. He also smelled absolutely amazing.

"Of course, but first I gotta fix this damn corset!"

"Looking that hot is never easy." He smirked as he waved his hand, gesturing to himself in understanding.

I found my way down the back hall to the bathrooms. I

stepped into the restroom to find two girls and a guy taking pictures up against a mural painted on the wall. I nodded to them and made my way to the mirror. The group turned bright red and rushed out the door with hysterical laughter.

I struggled with my top and re-clasped some of the hooks. My makeup had started to smear under my eyes, and my lips had lost all color. I retouched my face, tightened my pig tails and briefly appraised my Lolita outfit with approval. I kissed my locket and headed out the door.

My favorite song began to play, and I rushed out to the dance floor with the rest of my friends. I closed my eyes, and the energy of the space swept me away once again.

I peered through the curtain of red curls that had fallen loose as I moved my body to the rhythm. The lights pierced the dance floor from the upstairs balcony where the DJ booth over looked the club. The booth was affectionately known as The Pit because of the permanent B.O. smell that lived there.

Right below The Pit was a boxed in table booth. The right side was a mirrored wall that paralleled the dance floor, and the other wall was shared with the second rarely used bar top.

A group of people had come in while I was in the ladies room and had taken over that corner booth. Their faces were hard to make out between the blinding strobes and the dark recess.

Joy skipped over to a tall blonde who had walked out from the shadowy alcove. With my curiosity peaked, I had stopped dancing, and he took notice of me. He smiled flirtatiously.

I decided I would wait to see if Joy wanted to introduce me to her friend. I went back to dancing and tried to forget they were there. I wasn't the only one who had noticed the strangers. Most of the girls were getting flustered and doing their sexiest moves to impress the mysterious newcomers. The guys were feeling the sting of being replaced and ignored.

After the song ended, I went over to Shadow's table and asked "Do you know them?"

"Nope." Shadow took a drink. He remained his usual

cheerful self with no concern or jealousy.

"Lydia, you should go over their and say 'Hi'." His thick eyebrows jumped up and down like Groucho Marx. "Looks like Joy is already making friends." The strobes had stopped their epileptic spasms, and it was now easier to see into the cave. Joy was leaning over the table playing up how "drunk" she was and fondling the blond's short goatee clumsily.

Raven had made her way over to Shadow's table. "Hey, who are they?" She looked like the 1950's pin-up model Betty Page though much taller and skinnier. "The one with the dark hair is fucking hot."

"We don't know," I said, "but we should find out." *Why be shy?* Raven took my arm and we did our sexy walk across the club. I felt awkward and silly for even trying for sexy next to Raven.

"Hey, Joy." Raven greeted with her steamy voice. Joy smiled at me but showed some disappointment at Raven's company. All the new faces looked up at us. I was taken aback by the intensity of their collective gaze.

"This is Raven and Liddy, I mean Lydia," she corrected herself. "I was just about to come get you. These are my friends. August, David, Delphine and Bjorn." She blushed holding Bjorn's hand.

Bjorn was a very tall and very muscular. His platinum hair and his blue green contacts gave him a unnatural look. It was perfect for the goth club. His smile broadened; a hint of fake fangs could be seen, "Like your moves."

"Yeah, I showed Lydia some of my belly dancing." Joy plopped down in his lap making sure I knew he was hers.

"Thank you." I smiled graciously and my face warmed.

August sat very still and silently dominated the space. He was the picture perfect goth with his ghostly pale chiseled face in sharp contrast to his harsh black hair. His eyes, like Bjorn's, had cosmetic contacts but were golden.

On August's left sat David. David's spiked flaming hair challenged my own red locks. His skin was speckled like mine with freckles, and his crystal blue eyes were almost hauntingly white. *Are those contacts?* His thin red lips curled up at me in a Cheshire Cat grin.

Delphine was the only woman in the new crew. She had a beautiful androgyny about her. She wore intense jade colored contacts which stood out against the background of her perfect onyx skin. Delphine's hair was almost completely shorn, only the thinnest layer of black curls grew. She reminded me very much of a panther waiting patiently for something to catch her interest.

"Would you like a drink, ladies?" Delphine gave a quick smile and it went just as fast. They all had a sense of wild quiet nobility.

Raven was quicker than me and sat down next to August as she answered an elated "Yes, a vodka and cranberry please!"

Everyone waited for my answer but something told me to keep my distance, although I felt an irresistible urge to talk to them. "That's okay, I already have my drink on a friend's table."

"Bring it over, Liddy, we'll watch it for you." Joy insisted. I couldn't think of a good excuse to get out of sitting at the table, but I wasn't trying too hard either. The lust was swimming in the air, and I could feel the pull to jump in.

I went over, to get my drink, and Shadow wished me luck. I sat on the edge of the booth and told the new comers that I never sat still for long because I was a slave to the dance floor. This wasn't entirely untrue. I did, however, leave off the fact I found their intense magnetism unsettling.

As I went back and forth between them and the dance floor, more and more people made their way to the booth trying to get in with the new "cool kids." Raven and Joy were quick to make sure they marked their territory.

Guilty pleasure went through me as David made the crowd move so I could sit and drink. The new people seemed nice enough. They freely bought shots and drinks for Joy, Raven and me. I gave mine away as much as I could to the groupies that had gathered around.

I would hit the floor with every remotely danceable song. All the work to keep a good distance from them was making me exhausted. I began to take some of the ambient energy in the room. I had always had the ability to see and feel energy. As I got older I gained the gift of taking and using it, not a lot, but enough for a boost. It affected me like taking a vitamin energy drink.

As always, when I began to take energy from any source, I would taste copper and salivate just a little. My third eye opened wider to see the colors of the different energies.

I wasn't trying to take any energy from anyone. I was only absorbing what people were releasing. I saw shooting pinks and brilliant blues. I could see the energy of the electronics humming. The gel lights in their own frantic dance with the pounding music played havoc with my third eye. I was unable to tell the difference between auric energy and laser lights.

When I took ambient energy my sixth senses became much stronger. Auras were no longer existed in my third eye alone, but were visible to my physical eyes. I could sense the shadows of thoughts and feel the hum of emotions. It could be overwhelming.

I took in the excess energy and used my own auric shield as a filter so I didn't get anything negative invading my space. It helped sober me up from the forced drinks and also helped my aching knees and feet.

People only seemed like shadows to the energy I was watching and skimming. I looked over to the cave where Joy, her man and his people sat. I was stunned to see that there was no energy at all coming from the new people. I could see Joy's pink aura trying to reach towards Bjorn. Raven's calm blue-green aura was in a holding pattern as it was kept at bay with an invisible wall coming from August on one side and Delphine on the other.

There was no color around them at all. It was not even as if they were cloaked and trying to hide. It was simply that no energy was being given out. They would have been completely invisible if they had not been near my friends. This time all four of them glanced up at me, smiled and went back to working the crowd. August and Bjorn exchanged a few words and backed up Delphine and David's efforts to distract the crowd. *Who are you people?*

As if this wasn't enough, the familiar tug of someone watching me latched onto the back of my neck. I immediately looked up at the balcony that neighbored The Pit on the second floor. Just outside the VIP's glass room stood three guys watching from above.

I matched their eye contact. *What is your problem?* My right eyebrow raised in a challenge. Only one turned away. The other two stood their ground. All three had something heavy weighing on them. A shadow wormed itself through their blood red auras.

I tried to feel them out. I took more control of my aura, letting it go from a harmless net to a probing arm. I could feel a strong ward protecting them, most likely a magick charm of some sort.

When my auric arm made contact with them, they quickly went back into the VIP area hiding behind the mirrored glass, and new harmless tourists took their place to watch the freaks in their natural habitat.

I decided to just let it go. I wanted to have a good time and blow off some steam. *Is that so much to ask?* I finished up the song and tried to make my way off the dance floor to say "hey" to some of my friends that had just come in.

"Hey!" Tom's voice was barely audible through the music. He had his camera around his neck ready to take pictures of the most striking of the girls and costumes. He wasn't alone with his camera; there were many photographers in the scene. Some wanted to be artists, others just wanted to get laid, and still others just wanted to leave their boring lives behind and pretend to be a part of the scene.

Tom was a husky guy with a great, but rather shy,

personality. He used his camera as a way to open up with people. His photos were amazing, and he was always fun to pose for. He had his girlfriend Shelly with him as always, and she gave me a big hug.

Shelly was a very voluptuous woman. One of her breasts weighed more than the entirety of Raven. Shelly was an accountant by day and a hell-raiser by night. Shelly and Tom were one of the happiest couples anyone could know. "So what's new?" she asked in her usual loud voice.

"Nothing much. Just working the dance floor and hanging with some new people." I pointed to the booth with Joy and Raven.

"Damn, those are some sexy-ass guys! What are they doing here?" She instinctively caressed her handmade corset. "Well, honey," She grabbed Tom's arm. "I think we need to introduce ourselves."

"Y'all have fun." I was about to find someone else to talk to so I could avoid the table and its temptations.

"What's that face for?" Shelly asked.

"What face?" I never could hide what I was thinking.

"That one."

"They're hot, but there is something..." I lacked a good word, "weird about them."

"We're all weird, honey, or we wouldn't be here!" She gave a full laugh and her breasts threatened to spill out of her top.

"I don't know. Maybe I'm just being silly."

"They are too damn gorgeous to be unattended."

"So I've gathered." I walked hesitantly over with the happy couple.

Shelly took the lead and pushed the gawking tourists out of the way. The crowd barely took their eyes off the dance floor where three "vanilla" women were making out and a dry humping on the speakers. They were trying desperately to get some men to notice them instead of the freaky girls dancing in fishnets and hardly anything else. "Damn party bi's." Shelly grumbled.

Shelly busted through the ranks of the sloppy drunk girls on girls action. August and Bjorn immediately pushed some girls out of the booth so I could sit. "Thanks." I halfheartedly smiled, but on the inside I was a little giddy.

Shelly introduced herself and Tom and began bullshitting with the other admirers. Everyone was trying to get the newcomers' attention. Tom asked if he could take a few pictures, and the new group happily agreed to a few snapshots.

August whispered something to Delphine and then David. He just glanced at Bjorn. They all three stood up and Bjorn announced over the noise "Who wants drinks? To the bar!" All fifteen people followed the pied pipers. Only August and Raven remained. I began to get up.

"Lydia, could you stay? I am sure Raven would not mind getting us a couple of drinks." He had the slightest accent, but I couldn't place it. He gave Raven a hundred dollar bill. "Raven get yourself a Johnny Walker Blue, I think that is what you called it. Lydia, what would you like?" His tawny eyes reminded me of an owl's. Nothing escaped his gaze.

"I'm good. I think I've had plenty to drink tonight," I lied.

"Are you sure?" I had the feeling he was not the type of man who takes no as an answer.

"Just a Coke." I wanted to keep a clear head. He nodded to Raven to go and she did with a sway of her hips.

"I wanted to talk to you, but you seem to be always on the move." He called me out politely.

"I don't like sitting still. Why waste good music?" I countered.

"Very true." He measured my answer. "Raven and Joy were saying good things about you."

"Oh?" I was interested in what kind of information had been given away about me. Ever since being dragged into court all those years ago, I had severe apprehension about information and rumors being spread.

"That you are one hell of a witch, for one." He was direct; I would give him that. He was a very well educated man. *Why would you believe in witches?*

"I do what I do. I have my strengths and weaknesses like everyone. Joy is excellent with glamours." His compliment made me uncomfortable. I made sure to keep my focus everywhere but on his vivid amber eyes.

For some reason certain people, especially Joy, liked to brag about being around a "real" witch. She has more than once outed me, not that I was in the broom closet; I just didn't want to fly a broom while blowing an air horn. Although in this crowd, every other person here at least owned a tarot deck, if they weren't a full practitioner. After I lost Ember, I was a bit gun shy.

"I might have need of a good witch." His head cocked to

the side and looked towards the crowd seeking out Bjorn. Bjorn noticed his gaze and went back to tending the crowd.

"What for? I'm sure Joy can do whatever it is you need, if not Raven."

"You have a reputation, Lydia. Even those who hate you respect and fear your abilities."

"Hate me? Who've you been talking to?" My brows furrowed. I knew plenty of people who didn't like me for one reason or another. Generally I didn't give a fuck, but it's good to know who your enemies are.

"Why are you talking to people about me?" My gut feeling was settling on cold distrust.

"People love to talk, and you always come up when people bring up southern practitioners or the occult. You wrote a book, did you not?" August's face turned soft and pleasant. It didn't seem natural. His long hands reached out for the last sip of a watered down drink.

The group still waited in line to get their booze at the bar. Raven and Joy were talking politely. Delphine had disappeared in the crowd. David and Bjorn were on the edge, subtly herding the group.

"Yes, I did." I worried that I might have been a little too defensive.

"Called *Hodge Podge*." He read my embarrassment. "A fine little book, but I believe you kept the good stuff to yourself," he said with a wry turn of his lips.

"I don't see you as the type to be interested in beginner root magick."

"I found it interesting, at least some of your recipes."

"Well, if they work, they work." I concentrated on coming across breezy and unbothered.

He leaned in closely, and with a slight guttural accent that tainted his words he asked, "Precisely. I was just wondering where you came up with that symbol for protection against what you called 'tween' creatures."

I knew the one he meant. That one had come to me in a

dream when I was barely a teen.

"It just came to me one day. I've used it for many years."

"Did some one teach it to you? Did you read it somewhere?" His face became more owl-like.

"What do you mean? It's just a little spellwork that came to me in a dream." His questions and body language made me nervous.

"I collect rare books, very rare books. Most of them are grimoires from a few known, but most not, some notorious, but all of them powerful, practitioners through the ages. That symbol you have in your little book is only in one other, and it has not been read by anyone other than myself and my..." he hesitated looking for a word, "associates." His voice had lost all softness.

"Well my *little* book, are all my personal spells." I looked for my exit. "Excuse me, the dance floor calls." His shadow grew, pushing out what little light found the booth. My nervousness was being replaced by defensive anger.

He grabbed my arm firmly with his long claw-like fingers. "Tell me where you got the symbol." Every syllable pushed through sharp clenched teeth but kept a thin veneer of civility. His charms tore away revealing a savage face with severe golden eyes.

"Let go of me!" My armed ached, but the pain pushed my fear away and left only my anger. My blue green eyes met his with the same ferocity. "Let go or I will scream." My energy began to build within me. I wasn't the type to scream, and he knew that; but I'm a fighter, and he knew that as well.

He suddenly lost all viciousness, and a soft alluring smile soon painted his face. He had forgotten himself, and he realized he had made a terrible mistake. Only for the briefest moment did the surprise and regret wash over his face, but he soon recovered his mask with a clench of his jaw.

"I did not mean to lose my patience." He tried to reassure me, his mysterious accent gone completely.

"You're still holding my arm." He was less a great fierce

owl and more a sulking raven. I grabbed his hand and plucked it off my tender arm.

"I have to know. It's for your own safety." It sounded more like a threat than a concern coming from his sharply arched lips.

Enough of this. "I don't think you give a shit about anyone's 'safety,' especially mine. And I have been just fine without you. Good night." I gathered up my things and leaned in close to him.

"If you hurt my friends, I will live up to my nasty reputation." In reflex, I flared my auric shield, and the mirror cracked. He felt my will. I saw the little hairs on his arms stand up, and his jaw clenched again, but nothing cracked his control again. *I will fuck you up.* The dark thought stayed sharp in my mind as I left the booth.

"We will talk again." He looked at me with respect, but not worry. His mind was working, and he looked pleased with himself.

I slid out of the booth and saw the crowd starting to head back to our dark corner. I didn't want to deal with any of them, but I did want to find Joy.

She was walking beside Bjorn when I stopped in front of her. Everyone else went around us laughing and trying not to spill their drinks. "Joy, I need to talk to you." I was grinding my teeth.

"What is it?" She wasn't going to leave Bjorn's side with so many horny hot women around.

"August can be an ass sometimes." Bjorn low voice broke through the nightclub's chaotic hum as he guessed correctly.

"You could say that," I answered him, making no moves to invite him into mine and Joy's conversation. "I just need to take your girlfriend for a second. I'll bring her right back." I lied.

"Baby, I'll be right back." She rubbed his arm and bit her lower lip. Flirting came so naturally to her.

"I can't guarantee I can save your shots from the mob."

His eyes darted towards me. Those weren't the words he was thinking. I believe it was more like "Don't believe a word she says."

I walked past Joy, gently put my hand on her shoulder, and turned her away from the staring eyes of the pack. I pushed her forward toward the hallway leading to the bathroom.

The harsh lights blinded me as I opened the restroom door. The strong stench of cleaner and cigarette smoke began to burn my lungs. The same dirty tiles and graffiti decorated these walls as it seemed to in every club.

Only two stalls were available, one without a door and the other too gross to go near. A tall thin blonde acted like a door for her friend who was trying to pee as fast as she could. "TP!" The thin woman's friend called out. The blonde bent over and picked up a roll of toilet paper, which had been in the middle of the bathroom floor. She reached behind her handing off the paper without looking at the brunette trying to hover over the toilet.

Joy and I both lingered at the sinks trying not to be impatient with the other girls. With a loud flush and the clunking sound of drunken heels trying to find balance, the short chubby girl pulled her layers back on.

"Oh shit, I think... I think I pissed on my leg." The dark-haired one's slurred words echoed against the walls.

"Don't worry. It's too dark to see," the blonde reassured her. They both stumbled over to the sinks.

They washed their hands, and I opened the door for them to leave. "Thank you, you're such a gentlemen." The tall woman's words blended together. The door squeaked as it swung shut and closed with a loud clank. It was time for Joy and me to talk.

"Who the *hell* are these people, and why are you talking to them about me?!" I insisted with the subtlety of a sledgehammer.

Joy face was shocked. "What are you talking about? They're my friends and I talk about you because you're my best friend."

I felt like an ass, but I was still upset. I calmed myself down, but I wanted to know more. I had to remind myself I wasn't angry at her. "August was asking me a bunch of questions about my book."

"Yeah, so? Isn't that the point of writing a book?" She was confused and annoyed.

"No," I huffed, "I mean... yes... but not these questions. Not how he was asking."

"What do you mean?"

"I mean he asked where I got the protection symbol."

"Yeah, and hundreds of others have done the same." She was not getting it.

"Not like this." I was losing this battle. I was flustered. *This is not like me.*

"You never like anyone, Lydia. You always find something wrong with everyone." She said matter-of-factly.

"That's not true, and this has nothing to do with whether I like people or not."

"Doesn't it?" A sign of a true professional drinker, she was still able to make a logical argument.

"Yes. There is something I don't trust about them. My gut says to get away from them. Don't you feel it?" I admitted.

"All I feel is your fear of making new friends. Every since you lost Ember and wrote that book, you've become a hermit. All up in your head... all the fucking time."

"What does this have to do with...?"

"Everything. The Ember thing I get, but it's been a few years. Get over it! And you think you're so *damn special* because you're published. So what! I can be published too. I'm just as good a witch as you are, but everyone always wants *your* advice, *your* help. I know my shit too." I was in shock. *How dare she bring Ember into this! Where is this was coming from and where the hell is this going?*

"Do you know what it's like being your friend? Poor, poor Lydia! How terrible her losing her kid. And August doesn't even look at me for advice. He has never asked me about my practice. He is always asking about you and what you can do. *Bjorn* even asks about you. I'm always second to you. I'm never Joy. I'm 'Lydia's friend.' 'Where's Lydia? What's Lydia up too? Is Lydia doing okay? I need to ask Lydia something.' Damn it! I know things too! I am smart too!"

I stood there still stunned. I felt like I had been slapped in the face. This had been building up. *For how long?*

"I... I didn't know." I was totally off balance and those were the only words I could think to say.

"And so if you did, then what? You would quit being you?" Her face was swollen red with frustration and anger.

"I'm sorry if I hurt you."

"Whatever. Maybe you need to learn to be grateful that people give a shit about you." She grabbed her stuff, slammed the bathroom door open, and stormed out in the chaotic noise.

Chapter 12

Saturday night
15 days until Solstice

The cold, wet sink supported my stunned body. *What the fuck? How dare she bring up Ember! Where the hell... what the fuck...* I wasn't sure what to do next. *I need a fucking drink.* A shock of music hit me as I left the bathroom.

The barely lit hallway was empty except for two young guys standing in the back corner next to the emergency exit. Neither one blended in with the crowd at The Alt. The youngest wore a baby blue polo, and the other, only slightly older, wore a yellow button up. Their conversation stopped abruptly. The blue shirt guy turned pale and began to sweat. *Weren't you one of the guys upstairs?* The yellow shirt had dangerous mischief in his eyes. *Now what?* I had sobered up quickly after my fight with Joy.

Two older men stepped into the hallway and blocked the way back to the bar. They were the same two men I saw with the blue shirt boy on the balcony. *Something's wrong. Thank the gods I am wearing my boots instead of heels.* I took a deep breath. *Okay. Lets do this.*

As I began to walk toward the crowded dance floor, the two older men started to walk forward. The two boys by the emergency exit followed their lead and closed in.

"What's up?" I nervously asked through a polite smile in the hopes to get some kind of read on the ring encircling me. *My knife is in my right boot.*

"Are you Lydia Keening?" The gray haired man's eyes met

mine as the yellow shirt stopped at the emergency exit door.

"Yeah." I cautiously put my back to the wall. I knew if I screamed no one would hear me over the ear-busting speakers. I prayed someone, anyone would come down the hall. I could handle one, maybe two but four was out of the question.

"We're fans of yours." The blond man next to the older leader said contemptuously.

"You don't look the type." My face grew hot, and my chest began to tighten. *Someone please come down this way. Don't show fear.*

"Hey Lydia, what's up?" Shadow pushed through the men blocking my exit. Relief passed over me, and I said a silent "thank you" to the gods. *They won't start shit with a witness.* The leader's second in command, the blond, straightened his back and glared.

My eyes widened, and I forced a desperate smile. *I'm in trouble! Help me!*

"Is everything cool?" Shadows usual laid back physique quickly begin to stiffen, and his slouchy demeanor straightened, making him appear to grow six inches.

"Get lost, freak." The second stepped up into Shadow's face.

"Fucker, who do you think you are?" Shadow's voice dropped in pitch and raised in volume.

"Get. Lost." The blond repeated "This isn't your business."

"If you don't leave, you're gonna get hurt, boy." The leader stepped between Shadow and his partner. The yellow shirt started to edge closer to me.

Can I grab my knife?

Shadow's eyes began to redden with the heat of his anger. "Boy? Motherfucker, I will end you!"

"Let's just go." I reached for Shadow, but the old man's weathered claw of a hand caught my arm. Shadow immediately grabbed the old man's throat, and he dug deep with his long fingernails.

"Let go of her. *Now.*" Shadow sneered. My friend transformed from teddy bear to fierce protector.

The second peeled the corner of his jacket away revealing a gun sitting in a holster tucked against his side.

Fearful sick chewed at my guts. *What's happening?*

"Shoot me, because I'm not letting go till he lets go or his throat's on the floor." Shadow trembled with hatred and adrenalin.

"Shadow, just go..." *Oof!* My feet broke from the ground as the yellow shirt grabbed me from behind. I struggled for my knife in my boot. As I plucked it from its sheath, I heard the second and the blue shirt tackle Shadow against the wall.

The second crashed into Shadow's midsection, breaking Shadow's grip. The old man gasped for breath as he reached into his jacket and pulled out a stun gun. A *crackle pop* rebounded off the brick walls as he flipped the switch.

It rained blood as Shadow punched the second in the head over and over again. The older man snatched his friend out of the way and struggled with Shadow's long arms.

I smashed my heavy boots into the knees of yellow shirt who still was holding me. He dropped me with a cry, I landed on my feet and turned with my knife and fists raised, my back against the opposite wall. "*Security! Someone!*" My scream was lost in the cacophony of the dance floor.

"*Quiet the whore!*" The older man screamed as he tazed Shadow. Shadow crumpled but that didn't stop him from swinging. The second started another chorus of crackling and popping as he brought out his taser.

They both slammed their electric fists into Shadow's body. Shadow collapsed, and the second in command jumped on top of him, slamming his head into the wall and floor till he was knocked out.

"Stop it!" I ran forward and was about to stab my blade into the guy beating Shadow when the old man crashed into me. At least one of my ribs snapped.

I tripped over the second's feet, and my head landed with

a hard crack against the women's bathroom door. My right hand turned white as I gripped my dagger tightly, envisioning burying it hilt deep into my attacker's body.

Crunch! Searing pain shot up into my fingers and down my elbow as yellow shirt seized me with unchained ferocity and crushed my wrist against the door frame. The second tore at my clenched hand trying to sever my grip on my only weapon.

Slam! My wrist was cracked against the doorframe again and again. The stiletto's steel hit the cement floor when my hand could take no more.

The yellow shirt's face was below mine as he had me pinned around my waist. A strange tattoo of a bright red cross on top of a yellow shield marked his neck where his ear lay vulnerable.

I sliced through his ear lobe with my canine, splitting it in two. He screeched, pulled back, and slammed his gorilla hand into my face. My jaw dislocated with the blow and he held me firmly against the wall.

The penny taste of blood flooded my senses, and my fighting rage was fueled on. I kicked with heavy legs.

The hall light flickered, and the leader was tossed aside. Delphine was on top of him holding him against the opposite wall.

My wrists were suddenly freed as another blur met yellow shirt's body with a cracking thud as they collided with corridor's dead end.

My eyes blurred with the pain in my jaw. I turned to run towards the bar, but my head was pulled violently back by my hair as a cold knife was brought to my throat. I wasn't able to get back on my feet. I was being dragged across the coarse carpet.

I looked over at Delphine and saw the second struggling to pull her off of his boss. David's back was to me, and the screams of the man he had in his arms were absorbed into the music of The Cure's "Friday I'm In Love."

The emergency door slammed open. I still fought to find

my footing and grabbed at the doorframe with broken hands and heavy boots.

The alleyway was only a sliver of a road between two brick buildings. A white work van skidded into place, blocking the only way out. Three men stormed out of the vehicle, rushing to overpower me and help wrangle me into the get away car.

I growled and scratched like a feral cat. The driver had turned off his headlights so their violence would go unseen. My savage howls were all but absorbed in the war of sound from both nightclubs.

My hands were clamped on the blue shirt's wrist, keeping his blade from slicing my throat, his own panic surpassing my own.

There was another flit across the lights as something flew by. The white van minions were swept up into the air, scattered by the night wind only to slam into hard ground.

"Stay away or I will kill her!" Strong words said with a weak and shaking voice. My kidnapper's heartbeat thumped against me and his rapid hot breath hit my cheek. He smelled like panic sweat, myrrh and frankincense.

Who are you talking to? The van convulsed as red sprayed the inside of the windshield. It was all so surreal.

I was quickly brought back to reality as the boy slammed me up against the bricks. A brutal tear bit into my skull. Through my tears of pain, I watched as blue shirt's weepy brown eyes grew wide and his mouth gaped. He was looking everywhere but at me.

The chaos began to blur and everything began to move slowly, as if in water. The music faded as my kidnappers' terrible cries burst through the white noise of the night.

Blue shirt was maybe twenty-one, a boy, not a man. He had the same tattoo as yellow shirt. The details of blue shirt's flesh began to fade, and only the colors of his aura endured. A bright, sick, broken yellow-orange streaks gashed through with great gaps of black.

His energy began to engulf me. I felt a fresh sting of fear, not mine but his. A shift happened inside me. A shift of light to darkness. A deep hunger for energy, for life force, brought water to my lips. Instinct became my only guide.

Where our bodies touched, his energy bled into mine, and I absorbed it. My auric arms wrapped around him, and I tasted, savored, his overwhelming emotions. A deeper shift. I had never fed directly on someone. I had always been so careful "to harm none." My primal desires cried out and would not be denied. *This is not the time for mercy. You're mine.*

My phantom arms drew him closer and squeezed him tighter with his every breath. Each finger of my life force invaded deeper. Every heavy beat of his young heart filled me with unquestioned power. It was like nothing I had ever experienced before. Invincible.

He realized too late that something was wrong. Terror and confusion twisted his face. His lips turned deep purple and his skin pale white. He was desperate to find something around his neck. I glanced down to the broken cement where a small brown bag had burst open, regurgitating its contents on the ground.

My head cocked to the side, and his eyes met mine making our bond even more complete. *You are mine. Give me everything,* a dark inner voice spoke.

"Yes." He answered my thoughts aloud.

"Everything," I whispered, my voice raspy and in complete control.

I began to tremble as he pushed his life force into me. I had never gone so far. He had dropped the weapon. I was holding him now. Holding him close; taking what was mine.

Wait...what am I doing? I can't do this... this is wrong!

I tried to stop, but the taste of his energies would not be ignored. The power surged forth. I was whole. I was a Dark Goddess.

"I am yours." I heard his voice in my mind, seducing me, tempting me to take all of him.

I have to stop!

His skin turned cold, and his aura was almost entirely gone.

"Stop!" I yelled as I pushed him away from me. I was drunk, and the world was spinning faster and faster. My eyes blurred and body was clumsy, but all my pain was gone.

The strings of his fading life were still connected to mine, giving me every last drop of energy.

What have I done? I stilled myself but I was still spinning, reeling over my attacker who became my victim. There was no longer a material world, just a world of light, dark and pure energy. I floated within the Aurora Borealis with all details obscured, nothing held form. Only the echoes that took vague shapes of their origins.

A shrill shriek called my attention to the dead end where I could just make out the brilliant colors of my attackers being chased and held down by a black humanoid form.

As I got closer, details emerged from the black cloud that vaguely resembled Bjorn. He was looming over his prey like some great primordial bear. The victim's aura was dull and fleeting. *Is this real? This can't be real...* Bjorn's eyes burned like a torches, but no other features could be seen.

Horror broke through my daze, and I ran hard and fast towards the alley's exit.

The colors of the world blinded me. I tripped over potholes but did not fall. The light drowned my senses, but I focused on the white van.

Another black figure hoisted a pale body against the wall. Two more bodies littered the alley. Including my contribution, the boy in the blue shirt, looking almost asleep on the broken glass and dirty pavement. His life force was gone because of me.

I ran faster, confused and frightened. *Home. I have to get home.* David reached for me and caught my right arm as Delphine appeared, abruptly cutting off my escape. Delphine's jade eyes broke through the cloak of shadow around her. Again, the familiar feeling of being trapped.

"Get away from me!" I demanded. They carefully walked towards me as though trying to capture a wounded animal.

I had to get to my friends inside. I fumbled open the exit door and blundered my way into the club. I had to find someone, anyone. I was drowning in my second sight. I had no form to focus on.

I welcomed the feeling of the sticky cement walls as I used my hands to find my way through the haze of energy. I was thankful for something "real" to focus on. I didn't see anyone including Shadow. *Shadow, where are you? Are you okay?*

I had to get to someone, anyone. My heart punched holes through my chest. I'd taken too much energy. My body couldn't handle it; my legs were walking on a stormy sea. I finally reached the main part of the club. August was among his new disciples, his energy absent among the abstract patterns of vibrant colors of the desperate hopefuls by his side.

I was afraid. Afraid of them. Afraid of him. And I was afraid of myself. I needed to find my friends, but no matter where I tried to evaporate into the crowd, his gold eyes found me. I knew that I couldn't leave the club. I would be even more vulnerable outside the herd.

The stench of the perfumes, cloves, and sweat begin to fill my lungs and burn my throat. My airways began to tighten.

I can't breathe. I tried to take in more air.

I can't breathe! Panic raged through me.

I can't breathe! My heart throbbed and failed to keep rhythm.

I can't breathe! My mind began to close in.

Oh, Goddess help me! My soul, mind, body screamed silently.

Where is my voice? Can anyone hear me? The thunder noise of The Alt threatened to burst my ears.

In the distance, a hundred miles away, "Help me." A small voice, soft voice, a numb voice: my voice.

Rough hands caught me as my body collapsed and gave

up the fight. I saw light, then darkness. I heard muffled roars, then silence.

A blur of red slowly materialized into a velvet curtain wall around me. Soft smells of a sweet garden lingered in the air as the silence gave way to lucidity. *Where am I? How did I get here?* My memory disjointed, I struggled between the twilight of sleep and the dawn of waking.

A sharp knock broke my thoughts, and a slight moan of a door followed. A gentle parting of the velour walls revealed a small, gray and fragile woman holding a silver tray in her gnarled hands. She wore a maid's uniform and a smile that was sincere but reserved.

She motioned for me to sit up. I did so, not knowing what else to do. A sharp pain in my ribs made me keenly aware of my body, if only momentarily. She placed the tray in front of me with its bounty of bright fruits and dark sweets. The sugar tart smell crested a swell of nausea.

She saw the green wave flow over my skin, and she touched my forehead with the back of her thin, hot hand. She gave a nod as if to say "you'll be okay." The greening faded and then came the hunger. I was ravenous like I had never experienced. *Sweet? Yes, something sweet.*

I feverishly groped for the glass of juice like a spoiled child. I was unable to confidently close my grip with either hand. Both were badly swollen and bruised. Perfect. Thick, cool and sweet.

I greedily gulped the ambrosia as the petite elderly lady

went into an adjoining room. I heard the crash of water as she drew a bath.

What's happened? My mind, not echoed by my voice. I tried to pull my thoughts together, but they dissolved as quickly as they came.

The woman motioned to ask if I had finished with the food. I mechanically nodded. She helped me slowly leave the safety of my womb-like enclosure. My body ached from toe to head. My rib screamed, and my teeth clenched.

I was welcomed in the next room by a beautiful marble clawfoot tub. The steaming waterfall created an ethereal rolling mist that consumed the room slowly. Lit candles flickered, gently making shadows cast theater on the walls.

Sharp cold crawled up my flesh from the bathroom floor and I suddenly realized that I was naked. The elderly woman gave no attention to my muted embarrassment. My mind was not yet able to be reflected in my body or voice.

She gently took my hand and encouraged me to test the water. I nodded my approval without thought or reflection. She helped me into the bath carefully as my ribs stabbed me again. The water was delicious, warming me from the outside, in.

Once I submitted to the will of the bath, the little old woman stirred some herbs and flower petals in to brew and left unceremoniously.

I had no desire to make sense of what was happening. I was existing only in that moment. My memories of why I was there were out of my reach. My will was numb and spirit lost.

I soaked in dumb silence, watching the shadows flirt past the forms and shapes around the marble room. My eyes adjusted, and I began to see through the distortion of the fog and the darkness.

The bathroom was very Roman in colors and decoration. There were many statues of handmaidens and servant girls, and a ring of half columns emerging from the golden flecked walls encircled the room.

All focus was drawn to a large arched inlay directly in view of the tub. A statue of Venus loomed hauntingly foreboding as if she had a secret that she refused to share. Fresh flowers and sea shells of all sizes surrounded her. Incense and pink candles burned at her feet. A soft scent of jasmine and rose danced seductively in the air and followed the current to the bedroom.

As my mind and body began slowly to become mine once again, I fixated on the bold red petals that floated gracefully over my pale body. *Where did these bruises come from?* The question left my mind and I fell into mindless action.

I swung a small silver table that was attached to the tub over the brewing bath. It held a razor, a small shampoo, small conditioner, brush, soap, rag, mirror, and a small note: "If you wish."

Do I? I don't know what I wish. How did I get here? Is this a dream? No. Too real. I have had seemingly real dreams before. No... this is real.

I was...

I grabbed the soap and began absently to wash my body.

I was... at the club?

The soap stung my broken and raw skin.

Yes, I was at the club.

I rinsed. My muscles ached.

Who was I with?

I stared blankly at my swollen purple wrists.

Shadow and Joy...?

As I let my body soak, my aches and pains began to lessen.

Something happened...

I slipped down into the water till it was up to my neck.

I was afraid.

I splashed some water onto my face.

Of what?

I submerged myself.

Of them.

A flash of men yelling. I crashed through the surface and

grabbed at my throat as a phantom blade moved across it. I searched my mind.

Their eyes... August's and his crew's glowing eyes.

A tap at the bathroom door demanded my attention. The old crone had towels and a robe piled in her arms. She carefully placed them on the sink counter. *What was I thinking about?*

The hypnotic lights made play with her features. Her eyes had become wicked. Her slight smile edged to more of a sneer. Her once grandmotherly lines had become brutally carved.

It's just the candlelight...

She shuffled over to the tub and grabbed the removable showerhead. Then with a tug at my hair and a burst of new warm water, my sense of self was rinsed away. I had no mind to stop her or to even ask questions.

My eyes slid across the room and locked with Venus's once again. The silent observer's eyes looked more human than those of the woman touching me. I could almost hear a soft sensual voice whisper to me. "Prepare yourself."

What's going on? Why can't I think... What is happening to me! My mind's voice, desperate and determined to make her answer me.

My plea was broken by a rough jerk as my long hair was twisted in a towel with one precise movement.

The servant raised me to my feet. I weighed light on her fingers as if I were nothing more than a child's doll. My body stood naked, submitting to another spray of hot water as she rinsed me.

The maid carefully helped me out of the tub. I wobbled under the regained sense of gravity and caught myself with her shoulder. Like a stone, she did not waver.

My feet were on the ground, and the familiar shock of cold from the marble made my legs feel more real and steady. The plush coolness of a towel patting me awoke my senses enough to notice a large mirror behind the counter top. A blur of a woman stared back at me. My mirror image captured my essence.

She wrapped the robe tightly around my body and ushered me out into the bedroom. She sat me down and began to brush my copper hair carefully and methodically.

A low yellow light coming from a small chandelier warmed the roomed. I got lost in the intricate strings dappled with crystal dewdrops. They drooped and swayed in a spider web design over the soft golden branches of the light fixture. The high ceiling itself was covered with a brassy metallic tiles which encouraged the light to soak into every pore of the room.

The walls were the same garnet red as the velvet canopy. The blankets and pillows were bloated with feathery fillings. Golds swam through the room accented with splashes of jewel tones. Decadence dripped like venom honey.

"Where am I?" A weak cracked voice asked, my will finally breaking through. The little old woman seemed not to hear me.

"Where am I?" My voice was stronger and more recognizable as my own. She hesitated and went back to brushing my hair.

"WHERE AM I? !" I yelled and grabbed her hand in mid stroke. Her hand stopped by her will only, not by my hand. Hard and cold, she stayed still for a moment, she then set down the brush and began to leave the room.

"Where are you going? ! *Where am I?*" I yelled in desperation and fear of losing my voice again. I clutched her again. This time her eyes met mine with a warning. Like a shark's, her eyes were hollow and unyielding. I let go and she walked out, locking the door behind her.

I timidly reached for the iron doorknob. It did not give. It was in this very moment that I looked around the room and saw my gilded cage for what it really was.

As time passed, my body and mind became fully mine. I explored the room and it revealed itself to be a jewel, beautiful yet cold.

My locket!? I grabbed for my necklace, and it still held tight around my neck. I rushed to a mirror and saw it sitting just below the hollow of my throat where it always did. *Thank you.*

My injuries caught my eye. I leaned in closely and watched as the light bruising around my jaw began to fade. *How?*

I dropped my robe and twisted to survey all the damage that had been done. Among the familiar freckles, moles and my strawberry birthmark, brutal reminders of that night screamed out. The alien marks on my body had already began to dissolve. My rib had been silenced. *She must have put something in the water... the juice... both?* I was in awe of the healing magick. I'd done healing, but it was never this bold and fast.

I had lost myself in the magick when I saw a glimmer of light. *Is that a window?*

My heart jumped with hope. I rushed to the heavy drapes and yanked them forcefully to the side. The glass was covered by iron bars, but I tried futilely to open the window.

Maybe I can fit through!

Someone was standing behind me. I turned quickly to see the old woman's face still possessing her soft smile. She had some clothes in her hand. She laid them carefully down on the bed. She then pointedly walked over to the window and politely moved between me, it and my hopes. She delicately pulled the drapes perfectly back into place.

She motioned with her thin hands to the clothes and started to walk towards me. "I can do it myself." Her presence haunted me. Something was unnatural and wrong.

She simply left again. I didn't try to stop her.

The need to cry was choking me, but I refused to let the tears bleed. *I need to stay strong.* I glanced into the mirror and saw my newly healed face. I was afraid but had to resign myself to patience.

I weakly stood up and examined the clothing I'd been given.

A long black satin dress, simple and beautiful, was cool to the touch and reflected the light like onyx glass. Under where the dress had laid were more satin things.

Panties and bra? My face reddened... I felt violated and vulnerable.

Oh gods... My mind imagined them taking off my clothes as I laid unconscious. They could have done anything they wanted to me. My body shook. My stomach churned.

I took in the fragranced air, trying not to become paralyzed in my head again. *Deep breaths. I must be strong and push forward.*

If they had wanted me dead, I would be. I only hoped that my full memory would return soon so I would know what I was dealing with and who "they" were. My stomach convulsed in knots again.

Hot tears began to swell. *No! Stop This! They need me for something or they would not have bothered to heal me.*

My desperate breath turned into an angry rage. My anger gave me strength where fear only made me weak. I sat there on the edge of the bed, hugging the cool dress. I began to ground myself, taking in earth energy, finding my way back to center with every deliberate deep breath.

Breathe in, breathe out.
Calming my mind.
Calming my body.
Calming my spirit.
Calming my heart.

I am here in this moment, and I am okay.

Air, give me clarity and sharp thought.
Earth, give me strength and stability.
Fire, give me courage and inner power.
Water, give me peace and wisdom.
Lord and Lady, bless me and keep through these dangerous times.

So mote it be.

I slid the frigid dress over me while my hair tucked itself within, curls upon curls, still damp against my back. My blue-green eyes looked weary but there were no hints of the damage that had been done to my body.

The bedroom door squeaked open slowly. I held still expecting to see the old maid, but she did not appear. I walked towards the door cautiously.

My room was at the end of a long hall scattered with doors and photographs of lonely trees and old ruins.

As I went towards the light with soft steps, my hands began to shake with the unknown. *Maybe I can run.* Laughing voices tempted my curiosity and urged me forward.

The stairs forked over a large foyer like an ivory serpent's tongue. Timidly, I stood at the railing absorbing the scene. The cream marble floor and neutral tones everywhere else had a quiet sophistication. A faux Old World fresco adorned the high ceiling.

"Hello, Lydia." August greeted me as he emerged from behind the corner. His hair was tightly pulled back which made his features more severe than they appeared at the club. *Golden eyes.*

My knees began to buckle from residual weakness. A strong hand kindly grabbed my arm to keep me steady. The old woman with the small smile and dead eyes held me. She silently conferred with August. He nodded, and she began to help me down the stairs.

Another man stepped out with a girl on his arm, Joy. A mischievous grin lingered on her lips as she looked ready to burst. Her makeup was perfect, and her jewelry sparkled in the light. *Are those my earrings?* Bjorn had his coarse hair braided down his back, his goatee trimmed precisely, and he wore a pressed modern suit. In comparison, Joy, wearing a black Lolita dress trimmed in hot pink that matched her new hair color, looked a bit silly next to the well dressed men. Bjorn's azure eyes focused on me, and he gripped Joy tightly around the back of the neck.

"Hey! What are you doing?!" she snipped at him. Bjorn only glanced at her. A wave of annoyance crossed his face then quickly ebbed into a friendly smile. His gaze locked back onto me.

"Bet you're wondering what's going on huh? OUCH!" Joy smirked then was tightly gripped again.August visually searched my body for something. A full smile softened his edges as I stepped down from the steps to the very cold marble floor.

"You look better. I've got her, Cerbina." *Are those contacts?* He took my hand gently and softly kissed it. His hot breath made unwelcome desire and terror rush through me. I pulled my hand away and steeled myself.

"Welcome."

"What's going on?" My jaw clenched.

"Soon," he answered. Joy giggled.

"Why am I here?" I asked.

He cocked his head and smirked. "You will get your answers. I just ask for a little patience, I have someone who wishes to speak to you."

He placed his hand on my back and guided me into the next room. Joy and her companion stayed outside.

The door opened and revealed a study. A large fireplace bristled with flames and was dressed with a large photograph of sequoias in the morning mist. One large window, hidden by heavy drapes, let only muted light fall on the collections of books lining the walls.

"Please sit," he directed as he closed the doors behind us. Victorian inspired dark leather chairs were turned slightly toward the matching couch. Two sets of sliding wood doors stood like sentinels behind and to the right of where I stood.

"Tell me what is going on." I squared my shoulders.

"Where am I?"

"Have a drink." His face was soft but not friendly.

"No."

August placed two glasses of wine on the table and then made himself comfortable on the couch.

I sat down reluctantly. *They did help me... I think.*

"Do you remember being at The Alt?"

"Yes. Last night..." My memory was a patchwork coming apart at the seams. *How much did I drink?*

"What happened to me?" My brow tightened.

"I asked Joy to help us to meet you."

The fire crackled and I welcomed the warmth hitting my face. I readjusted myself as my rib pulled. *Another flash of the night the fierce eyes. Impossible.*

"Your friends... they killed those men." I tried to stitch together the details of the night in some sort of understandable pattern.

"Yes, they did. They were protecting you." He was controlled and measured.

"Shadow?" Worry drained my face.

"He is fine. He is currently at Huntsville Hospital."

"Oh God." I grabbed my stomach as I recalled the boy who held me. "I think *I* killed someone..." My body flushed cold as I relived my attack on him. I bent over in disgust.

And then I stumbled into the club...

"Yes, you did kill him," it was a a woman's voice who replied, "but you were defending yourself." I looked up from August and saw an exotic beauty. She exuded grace and elegance. Her dark black hair was pulled up with a bouquet of peacock feathers framing the face of a goddess cast in bronze with vivid ebony almond eyes. "The others did what they did to save you and Shadow. We brought you here to protect you. Unfortunately, they were a bit hasty, and we did not get a chance to question the would-be kidnappers." She shot a look to August.

"Thank you, but I would like get my stuff and go." I stood

up to take some kind of action, any kind of action. Frayed memories snarled within me. I couldn't tell what was real and what wasn't. *What did I do to that boy?*

"I am sorry, but I can not let you. You are still in danger, Lydia." She walked over to August and placed her hand on his arm. He nodded in answer to a secret request.

"Lydia, I hope you decide to stay with us. We rescued you at great risk. Please do not make our efforts be in vain." August slightly bowed his head towards the woman, and made his leave. After the soft click of the door she motioned for me to take a seat once again on the couch.

"My name Anna Belle, and this is my house." She introduced herself and opened her arms in gesture of welcome.

"I appreciate all that you've done..." *I think.*

"You are still in grave peril." She handed me my glass of wine.

"Shadow, he is at the hospital, but...?"

"He is safe." She answered with a knowing twinkle in her eye.

"The police? Are they looking for me?" *What am I going to do?* Panic and confusion cut into me.

She reached for my hand, her skin so soft and her hands so long and feminine, and guided me down to the couch. "No. They are the least of our worries. We took care of any evidence and loose ends."

I found air again. "Oh shit, my cats! "

She kept patience with my lack of focus. "They are fine. I had Joy look after them."

"Joy?" *Can I trust her?*

"I can find someone else if you like, but you would need to take down your wards first. I don't think either one of us want that." She comforted me. There was a strange spark of desire lingering in the undercurrent of our conversation.

Her eyes, like the others, held an unnatural glow. I tried to not be distracted, *but her eyes...* I centered myself. "Do you think those rednecks are going to come after me again?" *How does she know my wards?*

"They were no rednecks, and you know that. And yes." She had beautiful smile. She was right, I knew they weren't the usual backwoods rednecks. They were organized and prepared.

"Who were they? And what do they want?"

"They call themselves the Hounds of Heaven." Her face looked pained.

"Why does that sound familiar?" The named scratched at the back of my mind.

"I assume you are familiar with The Inquisition."

"The Spanish Inquisition?" I had done a lot of research on the subject, being the witch that I was.

"Yes, Torquemada's helpers were called the Hounds of Heaven. Of course, his lot were focused on crypto-Jews and Muslims. This particular group is held over from then and many of the other Inquisition's incarnations spanning through the Christian theocracy's time line. They went the way of focusing on witchcraft and the occult," she answered, and my heart sank. *I have fucking zealots after me.*

"They're *witch hunters?* You have to be fucking kidding. This is insane!" I stood up in rage, confusion and dread. "What the hell? This is the fucking 21st century, right? We're in the fucking United States? !"

"I know this must be unsettling." Her ladylike decorum never cracked.

"Unsettling? That I had witch hunters trying to kidnap me? Coming after me for a silly little spellbook."

"It's not about your book." Her eyes, large and warm, watched me begin to pace.

"Then what? I won the raffle?" I quipped.

"Something like that." Her faced grimaced into a cynical smirk.

"I can just call the police. You know who they are, and we were just defending ourselves."

"I can not explain this all to you right now; we must wait for the Elders. I just wanted to assure you that you are safe here, but you are in very real danger out there."

"Did I do something wrong?" I sat down on the uncomfortable couch.

"Your sin is just being who you are meant to be." She raised her hand and softly stroked my cheek. I closed my eyes and lost myself in the moment of her comfort.

There was a crisp knock at the door.

"Yes?" Anna Belle answered sounding a bit annoyed as she lowered her hand back to her lap. I missed her touch.

The door cracked open and Delphine peaked in. "They're arriving in about an hour."

"Thank you, Delphine. You will soon have all your answers, Lydia. Please just stay with us for the night. Can you do that for me? You are already dressed for the occasion and looking beautiful." I could not have said no to her charms.

"Will you tell me what's going on and why you care?"

"We will tell you what we know, but we must wait for the Elders. I also need to finish getting ready."

"I can't imagine how you could make yourself any more beautiful." I blushed as the words slipped out. She stepped closer and kissed my cheek. Her cold skin and hot breath sent a quivers through me.

She whispered, "Thank you."

My face went a shade of crimson. She made her way to the door showing that the back of her dress dipped scandalously low, just hinting at the perfect ass underneath. She turned slightly back, caught me staring, and was pleased.

"Enjoy my home, and if you need anything, just tell Cerbina."

Cerbina escorted me back up to my room before I got to see Joy or the others. I wasn't sure what to think and was hoping I could talk to her. I was still confused but thought I was safe, at least for the moment. I would keep my eyes open. They, after all, were not the ones who broke my rib and tried to drag me into a windowless van.

My guide was kind enough to unlock my window and give me back my purse that I thought had been lost at The Alt, maybe as a sign of good faith. I found my phone at the bottom of my bag, but the battery was long dead.

I decided to go along with my host's requests for now. I quickly made myself presentable with the emergency makeup in my bag. I tried the door but found it to be locked once again. There was something behind the veil of niceties they didn't want me to see. I took a deep breath, walked over to my newly liberated window, and watched as a motley collection of people begin to arrive.

The grand driveway ended in a great circle in front of the house. I couldn't see the main street from my window because a great grove of trees stood guard and bordered the driveway up to the allotted front yard. I wasn't even sure that I was still in Alabama, but the house and yard were certainly antebellum in style as was the interior layout.

Limos, motorcycles, sport and eco cars were parked carefully around the fountain circle, and people unrelated in appearance made their way inside.

The click of the door told me I was free to leave my beautiful bastille. I slid on my new heels and gracelessly made my way down the stairs. It was time to meet this curious mix of people. No matter how unreal this all seemed, I had only one choice and that was to go forward.

I walked down the hall and counted six doors. Mine on the end was mirrored by another at the end of the hall. The four other doors took their place along the right side as balcony and stairs opened up on the left. I couldn't help but wonder what was behind each one. The echoes of my clumsy heels off the walls was lost in the blur of party voices.

I peered over the balcony. A slight feeling of falling made my grip stiffen. I could see little groups of people huddled and moving to this room or that room. A group of four kept to themselves: two very rough biker men, a young teenage boy and a woman with chiseled features.

The teen was tugging relentlessly on the collar of his button up shirt. All four were dressed down compared to the other guests and were noticeably uneasy in their company. The three guys all wore utility-kilts with leather vests, and the woman had on a very pretty plain cotton dress. They looked to be people I could relate to.

A few of the guests were politely regarded then avoided by everyone. Unlike Anna Belle and her people who had no energy and the biker's whose energies were radiating heat, those few who were being avoided had a heavy slurry weaving around them.

"Lydia, won't you come join us?" Anna Belle had silently come up behind me. *How are you doing that?*

"Our special guests will be coming in shortly." She glanced through the large windows at the front of the foyer at the pink sky. "Let me introduce you. Everyone is very excited to meet you."

"Me?" I would rather have just blended in. I debated if I should even mingle. Joy was working the crowd hard.

Delphine, Bjorn, and August were hurriedly organizing something. David, with his spiked orange hair, stood outside the front door shifting from one foot to the next.

"Let me show you around." She took my arm. Even under her cool calm there was an air of unease.

We stopped midway down the steps so we were still above everyone. Cerbina had quietly come up on my lower right and offered Anna Belle and me a glass of champagne. Anna Belle took both crystal glasses and handed me one. *Please don't let me drop this.*

She gently tapped the crystal with one of her rings and a hush fell over the visitors. Most of the guests had the eerily quiet focus of a predator in wait. I instinctively braced my auric shield. My hands began to shake out of embarrassed nervousness.

"Ladies and gentlemen, I would like to take this moment to introduce you to our VIP this evening, Miss Lydia Keening." I felt a shift in energy amongst the onlookers. An ocean of eyes crashed into me. Some searched out with auric arms, practitioners. My aura was being pressed and pulled as they tried to read me.

"I know that you are all here to meet her, but please do not overwhelm her." She was charming but her tone was not that of a light hostess, but of heavy warning. "Lydia, this is everyone." She turned to me and gave me a confident smile.

Everyone lifted their glasses in welcome to me. I was awkward but polite.

"Lydia," a patron from the crowd called out. "*Ena te noct prak üt, ish üt prak te noct!*"

A chorus of one word salutes drifted my way. "Cheers!" "*Salut!*" were the only ones I recognized. I tried to maintain a civil smile, but my confusion surely showed. *How did I get here, and what the hell is going on? What are we drinking for?* But I had promised to wait till the Elders arrived. Anna Belle gently touched my hand in reassurance.

I sipped my glass of very dry and harsh champagne as we

made our way down to the man who made the toast, taking some time to quickly greet some of other guests along the way.

The gentleman who offered the unique toast was a very tall, thin, older looking man with thin hair slicked tightly back, but greeted me with a joyful smile. Next to him was a short, built, clean-shaven, intense bald man. Both wore a fitted all black uniform-like suits with no tie.

"I am Otto, and my esteemed but serious friend is Varrick." Otto's voice was so thick with a German accent that I could hardly understand him. Otto held out his gloved hand to take mine. I reluctantly yielded. He raised my hand to his mouth for a very polite kiss. *Real Old World charm.* I was beginning to enjoy myself despite such odd and stressful circumstances.

"Lydia," Varrick's voice was such a deep tone that it was more felt than heard. He was not congenial, nor did he seem the type to be polite for the sake of civility. He surprised me by taking my hand almost before I had offered it. His eyes were a strange silver, and those silver eyes did not move from mine as he gave a firm kiss on the top of my hand. I sensed he was challenging me silently. Why and for what I had no idea.

"Thank you, Otto, for such a welcome for Lydia. She is a bit nervous. I would be with people like Varrick around." She jabbed politely. Varrick grimaced a smile.

"May I ask, what was the toast?" I was timidly curious.

"Oh my, of course!" Otto gave a full laugh, and I couldn't help but like him. "May the night protect you, as you protect the night."

I didn't want to be rude and ask what that was supposed to mean or even what language that was. Maybe it was some old German colloquialism.

Varrick watched me intently as Anna Belle and Otto made small talk about the gathering. I tried to not show my extreme discomfort. He was a very attractive man even with his permanent scowl. His strong jaw and pouting lips clenched repeatedly as if to stop himself from blurting out whatever it was he was thinking about me.

I decided to focus my attention on Otto, who was telling a story that he and Anna Belle found very funny. I could only understand every third word. Varrick's stare began to dig deeper. I was tired of being polite and directed my unflinching gaze his way. My jaw tightened. *Are we going to have words?* My energy built and swirled protectively around me. Joy suddenly bumper carred her way into our four person circle.

"Sorry to interrupt, but y'all sounded like you were having a good time!" Otto was pleased to see the bubbly pink haired girl. It gave him another chance to tell one more of his favorite jokes. Anna Belle smiled, a bit put off by Joy's intrusion. Varrick had a sneer of disgust roll across his face as if he smelled something very foul. He withdrew himself tightly into his noble demeanor.

He looked back to me, and I glanced to Joy and back at him to let him know I saw his reaction. My eyebrow raised in question. I wouldn't get any answers from him, and it was probably better that I didn't. Joy, thankfully, hadn't noticed him.

"Lydia, I have a few more people for you to meet." Anna Belle pulled me away from my silent staring contest. She led me to the four people who, I had noticed earlier, were just as uncomfortable as I was.

"This is Bill, Sky, Grey, and Rummer." Anna Belle kept a bit of distance between herself and them. "Sky was kind enough to give us the herbs that have helped your healing."

"I guess I owe you a big thank you." I meant it. She had beautiful strong features accented by long straight chestnut hair that had feathers and stones sewed into two braids that fell from the nape of her neck. Her high cheek bones, square face and accessories made it no secret that she was Native American.

"Hello, I'm glad to finally meet you, Lydia." Sky shook my hand with a caring smile and bright brown eyes with flecks of shimmering gold. The only age she wore was around her eyes.

"I'm so glad it helped. It will be a few days before you're back to full health." She had an overpowering energy of "Mother."

"We are thankful that August and his friends were there to help you." Bill's gruff voice was genuine. He looked to be a very fit fifty-something with a prominent long goatee. His numerous tattoos were faded from many years of sun exposure. He cleaned up well in his leather utility kilt with matching vest and plain white t-shirt.

"Hey," Rummer grimaced. He was very restless. Rummer was at least six and a half feet tall and very broad in the chest. He had a long, frizzy, dyed black hair and a matching goatee. He had his own tattooed sleeves and kilt. It seemed to be the unspoken uniform of their group. Even motherly Sky was covered in tattoos, but they were better taken care of and were very earth centric.

"Hey, nice to meet you." Grey's voice cracked anxiously. He was a lanky goofy teenager. He was the one who was tugging the most at his shirt collar. He had no tatts yet, but he did wear the kilt uniform, only his was made from black canvas. Grey reached out his hand.

"Nice to meet y'all," I gladly met his sweaty palm. They weren't the type to go to this kind of affair.

As our hands touched, a rush of hot air flowed around and through me almost knocking the breath out of me. I saw the red-orange auras of the bikers more clearly than I saw their faces. My eyes were on fire and my jaw violently cracked as a ball of fierce heat grew within my abdomen. My ears flooded with the sound of rushing pulsing beats. A primal song called...

I dropped back from Grey. Anna Belle and Sky had both caught me. Sweat pooled all over my body. I found my breath again as the heat fizzled away.

"Are you okay?" Sky asked. Grey looked frightened.

"Y...yes." I stuttered. My eyes still burned, but I could now see that the faces and the colors of the energies were fading into the background once again. "Hot flash!" I joked.

"Cerbina, get me some ice water." Anna Belle ordered.

"Rummer, get me that chair." Sky pointed to a simple chair that was against the wall.

Both Rummer and Cerbina jumped into action. Embarrassment reddened my body. Everyone was looking at me. *Please stop, it was nothing. Go about your party. Please stop looking at me.*

The chair slid into place, and I was promptly seated. Sky and Anna Belle exchanged a quick look. Sky squatted in front of me. "Are you okay? What happened?" She looked into my eyes.

Anna Belle put her hand on my shoulder and said something in a hushed voice to August. *There's that odd language again.* He began to work the crowd and so did his friends. Everyone soon started hastily chatting to each other. Varrick stood very still in his corner and watched silently.

"I... just got hot. So very hot." I squeezed my hands together, and my knuckles popped like a string of firecrackers.

After I had sat for a minute, I regained myself and began to walk around. Grey had come up to me and apologized if he had made me sick. "I'm fine," but even as I said it the raw heat coming from the boy threatened my senses.

"I hope you feel better," he paused with some sadness. Rummer called him over and Grey gave me a quick smile as he walked away.

"I hope I didn't scare Grey," I told his mother.

Sky's face crinkled with a smile, "My son is a tough one, he will be fine. You seem a lot better." I noticed the resemblance among the three of them: Bill, Sky and Grey. Rummer wasn't related but acted as a close uncle.

Bill joked, "My boy has quite an effect on the ladies." Grey heard him from across the room and blushed hard.

"I feel better."

"You look better." Sky comforted me. She had wisdom in her eyes but she held her tongue. She simply watched me and waited for my next move.

"I think I am going to go upstairs and rest a little."

"I'll tell Anna Belle." Sky offered. "I believe the Elders are going to be here in about another hour."

"I'll be back before then." I wanted answers.

Chapter 16

Sunday
14 days until Solstice

This time the room had not been locked, but I took some
time and enjoyed the quiet isolation from the building crowd
down stairs. As the sound of music hummed throughout the
house, I watched the night soak the world in shadow from my
window. *Why am I not running away?* A part of me thought
it would be rude, and admittedly, I was curious. *They have
been very welcoming. They saved me... well... helped me save
myself.*

I played out how I could squeeze through the window and
hazard a fantasy escape. *If I fell, I might not break my legs or
my neck. It's only two stories.* The cement statues and prickly
bushes that encircled the house made me rethink my plans.

*I will stay and listen to what they have to say, but if
anything gets weird I'm out of here. I'll have to look for a
better exit.*

*And what the hell was that with the kid? I have never felt
such radiant heat from someone's aura. I've never been so
overwhelmed... except with the guy in the alley but that was
different somehow. Grey's energy made me feel raw, not
drunk like the boy in blue. What the hell is going on with me?*

I knew it was getting close to time for their honored guests
to arrive. The tension proliferated through the walls.

I walked down the stairs once more, but this time I went
unnoticed. I mingled politely but did not linger with any one
person. I wanted to check out the rest of the house without

someone looking over my shoulder. I walked under the dual staircase and into a small ballroom type space with a gigantic fresco that wrapped around the room. Gods and goddesses from all the world's corners mingled on the walls in a fabricated faded glory of chipped paint and pallid colors. It was classically beautiful.

In the side corner of the room from a slightly raised stage, a warm melody of a solo cello melted through the space. The magician who played was dancing and wooing his instrument to cast the enchantment. His dark curly hair and beard vibrated with the rhythm, and his sullen Russian features looked as if he were seduced by his own spell.

I silently enjoyed the elegant room as I watched the others. There was still an unusual mix of auras, from the dark and twisted to the absent. There were more natural, typical energies, like Joy's, mixed with the crowd now. Many were checking their phones and watches, growing more anxious.

Grey and Rummer had the most vibrant auras in the room, reminding me of a sunrise after a fierce storm. I joined them at the buffet table as Grey was eagerly loading his plate, and Rummer was sipping out of his wolf's head flask.

"Hi, Grey, Rummer." I smiled passively.

"Hi, Miss Lydia." Grey raised his dish to me. "Want some?"

Rummer watched me for a second, checked his phone for the time, and scanned the crowd.

"No thanks. Where are your mom and dad?" Bread skeletons laid discarded on his plate as he plucked out the marrow of ham from the finger sandwiches.

The same fruits and treats that I had been fed earlier that day were flamboyantly displayed on silver plates. I grabbed a few pieces and tried to be ladylike as I scarfed down some sweet fruit and cheese.

"They went out front with Miss Anna Belle and Mr. Varrick." He stuffed a few more bits of food on his little plate.

"Is everything okay, Rummer?" I asked as his hair bristled.

"Yea, thanks, these... people," he shook his head and

shifted his gaze around the room. His dark eyes reflected the yellow light of the huge chandelier, which dwarfed the one in my room.

"You'd never see a Black Paw put on a show like this. It just proves they think their shit don't stink." Rummer loathed the high society circus.

"Do they shit?" Grey looked up at Rummer. Rummer snorted to himself.

I didn't get the joke. "What's a Black Paw?"

"The Black Paws is the name of our pack." Grey answered with great pride.

"Oh?" *Pack? Does he mean a biker club?*

"Our blood and chosen family." He saw the question on my face. Grey was a smart kid.

Rummer gave Grey a look of warning and began to pace, growing more agitated. *That would be my cue to leave.*

"Well, I'm going to go be social. Talk to you later?" I playfully took a piece of food from Grey. I had so many more questions, but this wasn't the time nor the place. Grey nodded with a newly full mouth and a chipmunk cheeks.

I found my way to the great windows that faced out to a dimly lit fountain and garden outside. Beyond that was a mystery hidden in the moonless night. *This is another way out,* I noted.

Otto's full laugh mingled with the cello and called my attention. He was chatting up some people I hadn't met yet, two very odd women who looked to be twin sisters. He noticed me glancing, and he waved me over excitedly. The two ladies turned simultaneously and their haunting overly large eyes chilled me. *Heroin chic.* The image of emaciated models haunted me.

Rummer slightly touched my hand from nowhere and startled me. "Be careful, girl, there be monsters here." His own features hinted at something unnatural. I nodded that I understood even though I didn't, and I walked over to Otto and the ladies.

"May I have the honor to introduce Lydia to you fine ladies? Lydia, this is Mab and Mildred, twin sisters." A hopeful perverted leer crossed his lips.

"Hi," I greeted them. They were no more than flesh wrapped around a bundle of stick-like bones, but they weren't fragile.

"Hello," both spoke in stereo. Their angular faces moved in unison to greet me with a tight pulled smiled.

"We are so glad to meet you." They alternated finishing each others sentence.

"I hope I don't mix you two up." Their dead eyes met mine as I tried to lighten my apprehensions.

"It happens all the time." One mind, two mouths.

They both grabbed my same hand. My blood ran cold, "Sisters of the mist..." the words fell out of my mouth. They both let go, glided back and twisted their heads in curiosity and shock.

Warmth began to fill my body again. "I'm sorry... I don't know..." I couldn't control my sixth senses anymore. I was blurting out my thoughts like I had Tourette's and tapping into people's energies when I didn't want to.

"How do you know this? Have we met?" They hissed with whispered voices.

"I'm sorry, I don't know. No."

The entire party dropped into silence. The cello rested against her master quietly, and the guests became motionless.

Cerbina came into the room and stood patiently at the door. Anna Belle solemnly stepped into place. *She is breathtaking.* I had to look away.

"Ladies and Gentlemen, I would like to announce the arrival of our dignitaries." She paused as a six foot tall man stepped through the archway. He looked like the male version of Sky.

"First son of the Dark Spiral peoples of North America, Laughing Dog." Sky and Bill followed behind as he entered the room. His name didn't represent his stern demeanor.

"And High Vizier Telal of the Holy House of Lilitu." She spoke proudly and clearly.

Telal entered, bringing with him a heaviness that pressed into my heart. I'd never seen anyone like him before. He had ghostly ivory skin and long straight white hair. His eyes where surrounded by shadow and yet, from across the room I could see the orange orbs. I was stunned and was only brought back to life as the guests clapped to their arrival.

"Thank you for your warm welcome." Telal's voice wove a demonic harmony.

His darkened eyes found me with such force I lost my balance. He withdrew his gaze and turned his attention to Laughing Dog. They both respectfully acknowledged each other.

"I would like to thank Laughing Dog and his family for joining us tonight. This is a gathering of goodwill and purpose." Telal addressed the party.

Laughing Dog smiled, showing his unusually large teeth. "Yes, I would like to thank the House of Belle and of course Anna Belle herself for hosting this eclectic gathering of Cthonians. Also thanks to Telal, elder speaker of the People of Lilitu, for welcoming us." They both bowed slightly to each other. The crowd clapped and welcomed them both once again.

"Please." Telal waived his long fingers to the cellist to begin again.

The curly haired man gave a deep bow to both men and began his spell again.

Telal and Laughing Dog walked directly towards me with Anna Belle and August in tow. A primitive fear took hold within me. Telal was unhindered by gravity; he tolerated its pull out of polite indulgence.

In contrast, Laughing Dog's steps struck the ground with power and strength. He, too, was wearing a kilt like the Black Paws. *Why?* He had strong, fierce eyes, but they softened with friendliness.

A dark thing, Telal ended his phantom steps only a few feet from me. His eyes burned down, and the air around him grew cold. He put out his hand as Otto had earlier in the night. I dutifully gave over my hand. He raised my hand, and his cold lips brushed against my flesh. A sense of *wrong* filled me. I was over full and empty at the same time. *I taste pennies.* At that moment something in my nose popped and broke away. A gush of red splashed down. My sight went blurry.

My voice a harsh whisper, "Alal! Alal! Alal!" I tried to hold my tongue but it repeated angrily over and over in my head till burst out again, "Alal! Alal! Alal!"

Telal's expression was unmoved. He softly let go of my hand. He looked to Anna Belle, "So it is true."

Cerbina reached up and carefully cleaned the last of the blood drops. She held the same indifferent expression. *What was that?* A shimmer of gold flirted across her harsh thin lips. She turned away from me and rinsed the red-splotched rag in the already pink water.

I'd lost all control in my life, my freedom, my self-restraint, and now, command over my gifts. Doubt and trepidation held me hostage. I was caught up in a maelstrom of unknown power and destination. Silent tears broke free.

My ears ached with the sounds of battle as the caterer's battalion maneuvered into position and set out into the field of the ballroom. I sat isolated from the soldiers and generals on the far end of a large stone top island.

I am going to be okay. I will be okay. I filled my lungs with measured breath and pace. I didn't believe my words, but they were all I had.

I kept my focus steady on the double sliding doors that led into the study. Anna Belle, Telal, Laughing Dog and their people had gone into the room to, no doubt, talk about me. I was at the center of this storm.

When Cerbina went to wash the bowl, I took the opportunity to eavesdrop. I leaned in close, my hot ear caught a chill from the chocolate wood door. Heated muffled voices found form as my ears adjusted.

"We should have left her at her home and guarded her

there." Bill was growling. "She would never have known we were watching her."

"We could not take that chance. We needed her here first and foremost to protect her from a world she doesn't even know exists!" Anna Belle's voice was hard as stone.

"You mean this world?" Bill's voice countered.

"What world?" I opened the door leaving behind my fear. *I won't be a pawn any longer.*

"Lydia, how are you feeling?" Anna Belle quickly changed from heated anger to soft concern.

"Don't change the subject. What were you talking about? You were talking about me?" I eyed everyone in the room, trying to gauge their energies. "You know what's happening to me?"

"Yes, we were talking about you and your situation." Telal spoke frankly.

"And what is my situation? Why am I here?" I wasn't sure I wanted to know, but I had to find my strength.

"Yeah, what's going on with her?" Joy's voice surprised me. She had followed in behind me.

I didn't need to be psychic to feel the annoyance in the room directed toward Joy. Bjorn grabbed Joy by the arm and started to walk her out.

"No, she stays," I demanded. I needed a friend I knew and could trust by my side. Anna Belle waved her hand towards him to do as I said. Anger held in Joy's face as she glared at him to let go.

I turned back to the room in front of me. I took notice of the people who had made it to this stolen conversation. Varrick, August and Bjorn stood on the edge of the room; Laughing Dog, Telal, Anna Belle, Sky and Bill held court in the center. They all had stress scratched across their faces.

"What do you think is happening to you?" Telal's pale skin was a startling contrast against the sun-kissed skin of the Black Paws. His eyes were more hollow than before.

The door shut behind me, and I turned to see Cerbina

standing quietly by. Everyone awaited my answer intently.

I stood still for a moment while I gathered myself. I stumbled through my words, "I'm doing things out of raw instinct, like when I first had the calling." The calling was sometimes called the awakening by people who came of age and realized they had been cursed or blessed with talents. It was always chaotic, painful, and, many times, dangerous to everyone around. It took years to understand and to find balance. I tried to organize my scattered thoughts. "It's just happening, and I have no control. I'm reading and channeling with no filter or choice... and I killed someone."

"The boy at the club," August confirmed. A worm of guilt burrowed into me.

I caught myself fiddling with my locket and my mouth was dust. "The boy," I stuttered, "the boy at the club." I took a deep breath, "I'd never..."

Telal raised his hand to stop me, he had no patience for guilt or excuses. "There is a reason you are going through the calling again. You are on a precipice of great change. A reawakening is upon you and those like you."

"And why do you care?" I asked.

"What happened when you killed the boy?"

"No. Why do you care?" I pushed.

"What happened?" He held firm.

"I just... tapped into him. I connected to his life force, and I took it all." I wanted to cry for the boy in blue but wouldn't dare in front them. "Then I saw things... My third eye was punched open, and the world was a blur of color."

"What kinds of things, Lydia?" Laughing Dog's smooth tone and strength gave me the confidence to continue even though I felt like I was going crazy.

"I saw... August's friends were helping get those guys off me..." I watched Laughing Dog's dark stern demeanor and my conviction wavered, "but my mind made them into... monsters."

Everyone but Joy smiled slightly like I had just told a

child's joke.

"You saw nothing of fantasy, only a glimpse of the dark truth." Telal's voice had lowered to a growl.

"What?" I shook my head. Anna Belle walked me over to the leather couch and sat me down.

"I just saw glowing eyes in shadow. Moving so fast..."

"In your vernacular we are called vampires; it is the closest definition. That is what you saw: our true face." Telal answered as if he had no idea how insane he sounded.

"There are no such thing as vampires... at least not like that." I once again saw the flashes of claws and teeth attacking with blind fury my would be kidnappers.

I started to wonder if the "Hounds of Heaven" and "vampires" were part of some new live action role playing group, like Vampire the Masquerade or Dungeon and Dragons, and they had lost total touch of reality.

"Are you fucking with me? Did you drug me?" I accused August. "You dosed me didn't you?!"

"No, we are not 'fucking' with you. And no, August did not drug you." Anna Belle was enchanting.

"Liddy, I told you that they're vampires." Joy chimed in. This time the crowd seemed to appreciate her help.

"But this can't be real..." My body began to shake. "Auras are one thing, but fucking vampires! Are you fucking insane?"

"Look into Anna Belle's eyes." Telal walked over and motioned to her sitting next to me. I looked up at Telal into his own red-yellow eyes. *Clearly contacts*, I reassured myself.

I leaned closer to her and looked into her beautiful eyes to see if I could find the tell tell ring of a contact.

"Closer if you wish." She welcomed me with her hand on my leg.

I moved closer. I was nervous, and part of me wondered if I was the butt of a joke. *What if they are telling the truth? I am locked in a room with vampires... a house full of vampires.*

I studied her eyes closely. Her deep black iris blended seamlessly into her pupil. Along the perimeter of what should have had some color, was a thin line of golden-red. Her eyes were still beautiful but now held the menacing familiarity of a unflinching predator's eye.

"Closer if you like." She leaned forward. I squinted hard to find the contacts. She did not blink.

"Those could be contacts," I defiantly argued, but I wasn't so sure anymore. She blinked and sat back.

"Don't be like that, Lydia." Joy chastised me.

"Then look into mine." Telal jerked me up with one hand, and his other hand found the back of my head. He held our bodies close. My hands landed on his chest over his tailored black suit. *No aura.* He gave off no signs of life but the strength in his body.

Anna Belle stood quickly beside me. "Sit," he ordered her and she did so reluctantly.

"Look into my eyes, Lydia," His teeth peeked through his thin harsh lips. They were the teeth of a killer, knives ready to slice. I saw the dark truth.

Oh shit. Frigid fear struck my soul. His deep inset orbs held the secret of Hell; the black circlet faded into rivers of lava flowing towards the inner abyss.

I started to push away, trying to find freedom again. He pulled closer to me. I couldn't move. Our faces, only inches apart.

"Do you believe, or do you need more? I would be happy to show you." He revealed his teeth with a sinister sneer: six razor sharp canines, two on bottom, four on top. He gave me no doubt.

"No please, let go. I believe." I was terrified. Telal kissed my cheek just as Anna Belle had, but it felt as I would imagine having a viper do the same. "Let go. Please."

He let go, and I fell back onto the couch. Anna Belle caught me. She tried her soft touch, but I looked into her face and knew she was just like him. They all were, except for the Black Paws.

"Lydia, it's okay, they wont hurt you. They don't kill

humans." Joy reassured me but what I saw in Telal didn't let me believe that. Bjorn held Joy in unbridled contempt.

Sky and her men stood with raised hackles but were very still. Their heat had turned into a flame.

"What are you then?" I asked my mouth quivering.

Laughing Dog stepped forward. He knew I saw something that set them apart. He didn't question it. "We are shapeshifters. Sky and I are skinwalkers, and Bill is a lycan."

"Werewolves?" This was too much so I started to laugh to myself. Sky started towards me, and I jumped back into the couch. Anna Belle steadied me. I jerked away, stood up and started slowly to the door where Varrick had been standing quietly. Cerbina was at the other.

"I want to go home now. Right fucking *now!*" I demanded, my aura picking up force like a gathering storm. *I don't know what I am capable of, but if there was ever a time…*

Telal smirked. Laughing Dog held Sky back. Everyone else was simply waiting.

I went to the sliding door but Varrick didn't move. "Move!" I demanded, faking bravery.

"Or what?" Varrick challenged me.

I didn't know how to will my power like I had at the club. I tried to feel out for his energy, but there was nothing there. My unease and confusion turned into familiar anger. I turned around and looked back at the faces calmly staring out at me.

"Why are you doing this! I'm nobody," my mouth snarled. "I am a mediocre witch at best. Hell, I didn't even believe things like you existed!"

"It is time. Tell the sisters to join us," Telal told Cerbina. She immediately left the room.

How can I get the fuck out of here?

Shortly the old woman came into the room with the weird sisters, animated scarecrows, following.

They both bowed to Telal. "How may we help you, Vizier Telal?"

Anna Belle went to the bookshelf to the right of the

fireplace and pushed a button under the one of the shelves. A small click was heard, and she pulled the shelf system out of the way.

Everyone started down some steps into the darkness. I lingered as Varrick did not leave his post and neither did Cerbina.

Anna Belle looked at me playfully. "Cool huh? Left over from Prohibition." She reached out her hand for mine. She was so beautiful. *How could she be a monster? Maybe they don't kill.*

She took my shy hand and led me to the stairs. "Come with us, we don't need anyone else overhearing." I hesitated. "You are safe. Who better to protect you than the devils themselves?"

Iron steps curled like a screw into the depths of the house.
Anna Belle turned a knob and a dim light scattered the
darkness.

I made my way down the antique stairs with timid steps
following Joy's overly excited voice. A large wooden door
and its iron sister had been already opened by the time I had
left the last step. My eyes had a difficult time adjusting to the
tawny orange of the century old lighting. Beyond the entryway
was a long, red bricked, warmly lit room. The entire space had
stepped out of the 1920s.

Beyond the bar and lounge area at the very back of the
room was an ebony wood table with eight very intricately
carved chairs.

"This is all original. The table was upstairs, of course, in
the dining hall, but it could be better used down here. I spent
a lot of money to repair and restore, but I think it was all
worth it." Anna Belle was very excited to have someone to
show her hidden room. "This room had been forgotten and
was only discovered when workers were installing new shelves
in the study."

She pretended that I hadn't just had my view of reality
turned upside down. My dread and anger melted into
numbness. I was outside of myself just watching my body go
through the motions.

Joy playfully tugged at me to not look so grim and to enjoy

the moment. I followed her to the table in the back of the room where everyone else had gathered. The three walls that surrounded the meeting table were floor to ceiling books, shelves behind a glass guard. These were not your off-the-shelf books from hipster store fronts. These books hummed with power. I instinctively held up my hand to feel their heartbeat.

Laughing Dog and Telal sat at each end of the table. I was placed in the middle chair on the right side. Anna Belle and Sky stayed close to me.

Varrick leaned back against the door on the left wall across from me. Joy was being held close by Bjorn to one side. Bill placed himself next to Laughing Dog.

August had gotten something from a locked drawer. The strange sisters stood on either side of me, barely able to contain their excitement. They had the strong aroma of swamp and salt. August placed in front of me a large, heavy box which had been decorated to look like a book with strange symbols, marked in gold and red across the front and spine. He took a key from his pocket, unlocked the box but did not touch the lid.

"Open." Mab and Mildred pulled the box towards me.

I popped the top open, and a wave of prickling energy crawled over me. The smell of sulfur and musky herbs smothered my senses. A leather book, length from my elbow to finger tip, rested within the plush velvet surroundings. The milky leather was intricately colored with blue pigment which had bled and faded over time.

All eyes in the room rested on me and this mysterious book.

"Is this?" *human?* I couldn't look away.

"Yes," both sisters answered.

I stroked the face of the book. Its power was intoxicating. It called to me. It wanted me to open it. It wanted to share it secrets with me.

No, I shouldn't. Nothing good could come of this.

The flesh felt no different from any other leather except for the stinging electricity that pulsed through my fingertips like touching a live wire.

"Should I be wearing gloves?" I kept tracing the map of blue lines with my bare hands. Both August and Anna Belle shook their heads "no." I opened the cover with the sticky sound of a book that is rarely used.

The pages were made of vellum, a very high quality parchment. "Is this made of human too?" I held the first page in my fingers looking over the very intricate painting on the first page, a dark-haired woman calling down the moon.

"Yes," the sisters answered happily.

"This was a very old grimoire. Who wrote this?"

"You tell us." Telal tested me.

"How would I know? I can't read objects. I don't have Psychometry."

"We feel that you two are connected." August had gotten up and placed *Hodge Podge* on the table. Its brightly colored cover and silly font looked absolutely childish next to the book in my hands.

"I don't understand."

August opened the page in my little book to the protection and ward spell. My personal sketch had been scanned and put into publication. It was a fairly complicated glyph. If you drew and anointed it with certain oils and then called to specific energies, it was a powerful protection spell.

August reached over and opened the grimoire to the exact page he meant. Before me was my exact glyph down to the very symbols. I didn't even know what they meant. It was how I had dreamed it so many years ago.

The writing that surrounded the drawing was in a language I didn't recognize, but on the periphery of the pages I saw crude drawings of the parent herbs I used for my oils for the spell. *This is my spell.* I knew it without any doubt.

All their eyes focused their will upon me. They all wanted something from me, but I didn't know what.

So I asked a question. "What is this book?"

"The Codex." August sat back down in his chair. "A gathering of what we believe to be a Book of Shadows of many different paths and beliefs. Some works from as far as India, some all the way from the south tip of Africa.

"And what language is this in?" I thumbed through the pages delicately.

"It is a hybrid, we believe, of at least twelve languages." Anna Belle's breath brushed my face.

"Five of them can be spoken by at least one person at this table. The others we are not sure of." August sat stiff.

"So okay..."

"Heaven's Hounds sniffed you out," the twisted voices of Mab and Mildred whispered in my ear.

"Will someone please be straight with me? What the fuck is going on?"

"The Hounds of Heaven believe you're connected to this book."

"I didn't read from this book. Like I told you at the club, I dreamt it. How could they know? Do they have a copy?"

"The Catholic Church has their own library of copies of occult books they took during the Inquisitions, and apparently they have a copy of the Codex, which means you are a very real threat. You are a real witch. You are a monster like the rest of us." Varrick added.

"Monster? Real witch? What is the difference between a 'real' witch and 'fake' witch?" I was offended by the very statement.

"You are not human." Varrick spoke as if it were a compliment. "You're like the Sisters."

"What?" I was shocked. The Sisters only smiled at me.

"Lydia, a witch is something more than a human. A witch is like us, something beyond the borders of humanity." Sky interjected, "It doesn't mean you are a monster, and to be fair you are not like the Sisters. They are witches, yes, but not of the same path." She glared at Varrick.

"You give me a book you think I have some connection with just because I happen to draw the same picture in my book? The Hounds of... whatever are after me for the same stupid ass assumption. This makes no fucking sense. And why would they go out of their fucking way to track me down to kill me or whatever they have in mind?"

I could see Joy squirming in her seat wanting to say something, but Bjorn held her back.

"We don't know. Witches are fairly rare now days but we don't know why they had the need to track you down." Varrick clenched his jaw.

I lifted the amazingly heavy book out of its box. I focused on the tattoos on the Codex in the low light of the room. The knotwork that had lost its detail over time. "Is this Celtic?"

"Yes, around thirteen hundred." August answered.

Who was this poor person damned to be skinned for this book of magick and why? This was a lifetime's worth of work. Who wrote you?

"Explore; let go." The sisters whispered.

The electric feel at my fingertips climbed up my arms and quick started my heart. A name buzzed in my ear. "Thomas, Thomas Chandler. He wrote this." I had answered my own question.

"Yes, he did." August stacked his notes.

"Have you been having the dreams?" Laughing Dog interrupted.

"I have always had dreams, but they're getting worse." I answered honestly.

"Your sixth sense is what separates you from the rest. You have gifts that stand out. You can see, hear, touch and even dream beyond the veil. I believe your natural skills are becoming stronger. Yes?" Laughing Dog placed his hands flat on the table.

"A divine witch among blaspheming neophytes." The Sisters of the Mist growled.

I looked down at the floor and exhaled deeply. I knew he

was right, and this realization made everything suddenly real. My body became heavy and constricting.

I looked up at each person there, and then my eyes rested on Telal. "Why do you care what happens to me being what you all are?" I swallowed hard.

"The Hounds of Heaven are after our people too." Telal waved his hand to include the Black Paws.

"We have heard rumors that they have been kidnapping Cthonic individuals," Varrick took over the conversation. I was even more confused.

"Chthonians are people who are not human or, at least, not fully human. They are creatures of the night and underworld who exist between this world and the veil." I could see Varrick clearly for the first time. He was a warrior. He was a General.

Silence possessed the room. "Why?" My voice cracked. My head began to swim, and air was hard to find.

"We are not sure, but we feel it is somehow linked to the Codex. Just as we believe you are linked to the Codex." August spoke plainly. "It is time for a great awakening. There are many events unfolding and making the veil thinner. People like you who have some gifts are being overwhelmed because you are sensitive to the changes. Even mundanes cannot escape its effects."

This was becoming too real. "I don't want this. I'm a nobody. I can't do... this... whatever this is. It's all too much." I stopped to catch my breath. "I just light candles and see shadows. And everyone dreams." Panic swelled within me. I was trapped. In desperation I yelled out, "I made it all up! I just imagine I can see things! I am crying out for attention. I am a fantastical."

"Fantastical?" Laughing Dog was confused.

"I'm just crazy," I pleaded to the room. Tears streamed, and my stomach turned. I looked to everyone once again, begging to be told "you are not the one."

"Lydia, the people sitting at this table are here to protect and help you." Bill finally spoke. "This fucked up mix of monsters are here for you."

"I can help, Liddy!" Joy finally burst. She revealed her envy. If I could, I would give it all to her.

Bill ignored Joy and continued. "This tentative union is called the Bahlael. We are many and varied. This small group represents some of the top brass of the southeast. You can trust us. We need you as much as you need us. I swear by the Blood Moon I will not harm you, and neither will any of the Black Paws." I searched Bill's face for the truth. His aura was still fire but with the mellow blue-white of honesty in its core.

Telal and the others all nodded in agreement. "You can trust the People of Lilitu to stand with you against the Hounds of Heaven." Vizier Telal added. I didn't have the ability to see his energy and his startling features gave no relief to my worries.

I wanted to know more about The Codex, and what choice did I have?

Chapter 19

Anna Belle and I silently watched her guests from the edge
of the small ballroom. Some danced and others gathered for
polite conversation. The group had decided to rejoin the party
after they realized I had reached my limit. It was difficult for
me to leave The Codex behind, but I was reassured I would be
allowed to work with it as much as I wanted.

Telal and Laughing Dog were just beyond the glass doors
in the garden in unheard deep debate. They were both more at
home in the night air than with the socialites. Laughing Dog
wasn't as shocking to look at as Telal, but something in the
way he held himself made his strangeness equal to Telal's.

"Anna Belle?" I had so many questions but I didn't know
where to begin.

"You can call me Belle." Her soft beauty gave me sanctuary
in this alien world.

"Belle," I savored the name on my tongue, "what does all
this mean? What are we doing?"

"Tonight, we drink and rejoice new friendships and
alliances." Her pink full lips curled.

"Ladies." Sky joined us, bringing with her three glasses
of wine. I took my drink a little too eagerly. That was the
first time I had really taken notice Sky's eyes. I had taken for
granted that her eyes were normal; they weren't. Her iris was
twice as large as the average person's. She barely had any
white showing at all. *We assume so much. What else have I*

not seen?

"The wine will help, Lydia." Sky playfully crinkled her nose.

"I don't think there is enough wine in this room to help me process all this." I took a gulp.

"Do not worry, I have more in the cellar." Belle winked.

"I know it's a lot, but you have us. I know the men are a bit off-putting..." Sky attempted to make me feel better. "They may be monsters... but they're still only men."

We cackled to ourselves. Bill looked up from Rummer and Grey. Bill's gruff features softened with a knowing smile and pointed our way as if to say, "Stay out of trouble ladies."

"Bill seems like a good guy." I didn't lie. "Grey is a great kid." I wanted to learn about all of them.

"I'm proud to have Bill by my side. Don't get me wrong, it hasn't been easy." She was like any other normal woman. "Being a skinwalker and him being a lycan has made for some severe adjusting. Grey is a wonderful boy. I was blessed with him. He's having a hard time though."

"Blood moons?" Belle confirmed. Sky nodded.

"Blood moons?" I wasn't sure what they were talking about. Bill had used that term before.

"It is like..." Sky searched for the words, "a primal awakening, especially for lycans. For Skinwalkers it's different, but poor Grey has gotten traits from both sides, good and bad. The Blood Moon is a sacred rite of passage for shifters."

"Do y'all really change?" Images of B-monster movies passed through my mind: stretched and popping latex pulled over plastic snouts and grotesque bodies bulging.

"Yes, but it's hard to explain. It's not a full moon thing... well in the beginning it is, but you learn control."

"I guess learning control is a necessity of all 'gifts'." I took another sip.

Sky watched her son with worried eyes. "Do you have children, Lydia?"

"Yes, a daughter, but I haven't seen her in years." My heart ached. I answered the question before I had thought better of it. *Maybe I shouldn't share too much of myself.*

"I'm sorry." Sky's mother's heart ached in sympathy.

"It's okay. Being a freak in the South... Everything happens for a reason, right?" For the first time I almost believed those words, thinking of where I stood at that very moment.

"This world cannot and does not want to understand us." Belle held my hand softly with delicate fingers. "Maybe it is best for both sides." Belle and Sky both had a unique cultural beauty, something that is lost in the homogeny of pop culture.

Anna Belle's features came from somewhere in the Middle East. Her frame was small and delicate, giving the false illusion of feminine frailty.

Sky was of medium build and nothing much seemed delicate about her, however, she held the other side of the feminine coin of beauty, being a fierce protector.

The Russian cellist stepped down and was replaced by an all woman quartet. The romantic goths were bewitching and so was their music. The sirens began to sing of unearthly delights.

"Dance with me, Lydia." Belle gave our glasses to Sky and led me to the dance floor. Sky waved playfully at us as she rejoined her family and kissed her husband "hello."

"I don't know how to dance with someone else." I awkwardly tried to follow Anna Belle's steps.

"Just follow me. How do you dance by yourself?" She placed her hands on my hips, and I rested mine on hers.

"I don't know. I don't think about it. I just lose myself."

"Then don't think, and lose yourself with me."

We began slowly finding the heartbeat of the music. Her ebony eyes locked onto mine. I tried to look away, but she wouldn't allow me. Her cool hands stroked my skin like a whisper. Our bodies found each other between each pulse. *Are we doing this?*

Our serpentine dance was watched by all, but she and I

were all alone, hypnotized within the song and ourselves. Her hand moved to my back, and she pulled me forward. I stroked her face, letting my hand follow the line of her deep cut dress. She smelled of jasmine carried on a light breeze.

I pulled myself back to watch her. Her cold skin began to warm. Her full pink lips dared me to taste them.

My eyes drifted to her perfect skin and to her perfect breasts teasing through her dress. Her necklace cast a trance as it caught the light with her sway. It was an odd stone with striking circles diving deep within itself. "You like it?" Belle didn't stop moving against me.

"Yes, it hums." It was the only sense of a energy signature that came from Anna Belle.

"It is petrified redwood." She was sparkling. She touched my locket around my neck, "And this..."

"It reminds me I once had a heart," I answered with a sad smile. I didn't understand the power Belle had over me. I mused that I was young and new, and I could not help but share my truth with her.

"Don't give up faith. You heart will never be the same, but you will find happiness again." Her dark eyes penetrated me. I believed her. "I should show you around."

"Okay." I was lost in her.

I followed her into the foyer. Her green satin dress slid across her body. The sway of her hips led me deeper into her spell.

She opened the door to the empty study where the secret panel once again lay dormant.

"The photograph is of General Sherman." She stared at the black and white photograph that hung above the fireplace. A mist blanketed the floor of an ancient forest. "He was named that in 1879. He is about two thousand five hundred years old, one of the oldest living organisms in the world. He was starting his life about the same time Socrates was born and the Greeks were coming of age."

"Persian wars. A new understanding. Well, at least a

rebirth of understanding." She was lost in thought but found her way back to me with a mischievous curl to her lips.

Did you know Socrates? I dared not to ask. She silently led me to the next part of my journey with that delicious swing of her hips and a brush of her hand.

Chapter 20

Anna Belle brought me into her room, still leading me gently by my hand. She put me at ease. The Codex, vampires, shifters, and witch hunters fell away like some absurd dream as her dark black eyes begged me to trust her.

Her room was decorated similarly to mine but larger and more open. Her furnishings were a beautiful mix of Victorian and Bohemian. The colors were bright and powerful trimmed with gold. It reminded me of the peacock feathers she wore in her hair.

"And this is Methuselah." I could see the reverence on her face as she stood in front of large photograph of the ancient tree. "He is the oldest living creature on earth other than certain microbes. Well, as far as the humans know." She winked at me.

She stepped into my space, "He was born when Stonehenge was little more than a ditch."

"There was Prometheus, who was older by only fifty years, but he was cut down in the 1960's. I didn't get his picture." Sadness melted her smile but it was quickly found again. "There is rumor they have found an even older tree in California. Of course there are clonal trees but..." She paused. "I am boring you. I am sorry."

She brushed her hand across my body. I suddenly noticed how alone we were. I was lured here by talks of trees for a reason. "You may wonder why I love them so much." She thumbed her necklace. "They make me feel young and not alone." I understood completely because that is how she made me feel.

I wanted her. I wanted to taste her. I wanted to lose myself within her.

Her lips found mine with no reservations, and I equaled her passion. She had wanted me from the first and I her. I was nervous like I had never been with a lover before. None like her. Vampire was still just a word to me, but I knew she was something more than human.

She gently pushed me down on her golden comforter. Her eyes were the color of the deepest darkest ocean, endless blackness. Her full lips curled with deviltry on her mind.

"Trust me, I would never hurt you,"Her voice was like dark chocolate on strawberries. "without your permission." She smirked. The opiate of lust and desire turned my worries to dying phantoms.

She stood above me as I lay down on her bed. Her dress fell to the floor with the grace of autumn leaves. Her onyx hair, undone and wispy, fell across her back. Venus stood before me, and I trembled. *How can I ever please a goddess? How am I worthy to worship her?*

"Do I please you?" She asked simply. I couldn't find my words, but by the look on her face she knew. "Your turn, my beauty." My heart skipped. *How could my body ever be pleasing to perfection like her? I'm a wilted flower compared to the rose that offered herself.*

She took my hands and stood me up once again. She gently brushed a stray curl away from my face. "Those ever changing eyes can see so much, and I could get lost in their depths forever." Her sultry voice lingered, giving a new depth to "forever."

"As I yours." I clumsily answered in a half whisper.

"Your copper curls remind me of the wild flames of ancient bonfires." She stroked and freed my mane. "You are beauty." She kissed me, her lips like the softest flower petals. She kissed me again, fuller, deeper. And again, pushing her way in as my lips parted, welcoming her.

My heart beat in the tips of my fingers. She skillfully undid my dress' clasp with one snap of her long fingers. My dress now too was on the floor, like a Selkie's skin discarded.

"Your skin is like fresh milk," I had never felt so naked before. She firmly guided my hands away, revealing my breasts. My nervousness grew as I revealed my strawberry birthmark that cupped my breast and trailed lightly down my right side, but all the worry fell away as I saw her body respond to mine as much as mine did to hers.

Her fingers teased across my reddened breast skin. Her eyes focused on my freckles on my chest and arms, "Milk with cinnamon sprinkles, and let me not forget those sweet cherries." Her hot mouth surrounded my nipples hungrily. Her feline tongue softly caressed them, and her teeth skillfully nipped.

She brought me to her pillows and pushed me lovingly back down. Our mouths found each other again and again. Her hands followed the curves of my body. I knew I was hers.

Her dappled kisses trailed to my neck. A bolt of alarm shot through me but was washed away with her desire. She moved further down to find my pert nipples once again. Her hand massaged one, her mouth hungry for the other. "I love your breasts, so soft and full, like touching Mother Goddess' breasts."

I watched her slink further down, my body tingling and wanting what was to come. I was helpless against her passions. I could do nothing but stroke her silken hair. "I should be worshiping you, Anna Belle." I told her.

"You will, but first I want to drink from your cup." Anna Belle nuzzled my little tuft of red fur, and her hands spread my thighs roughly. Her true strength showed because my thighs' clenching shyness gave her no pause.

She slowly leaned in, and her obsidian eyes locked on mine. Her hot breathe teased me. She kissed gently and

117

consumed me, her purr vibrating within me. The mirror behind her revealed her perfect hips and thighs moving, as if she had an invisible tail. She was glistening for me.

Her eyes closed and her fingers pushed within. I gasped with pleasure and pain. There would be no denying her. She found the secret she was looking for, the one so many never find. My body began to twist, and my cries grew louder. With each moan she grew more excited, and her purr grew deeper. I was hers to take.

Her mouth full and hand thrusting, my eyes squeezed shut, feeling every movement with her tongue and her fingers. I was lost in her skill. My breath held fast. As the crashing wave of ecstasy enveloped me I cried out, "BELLE!" She did not relent. Ecstasy found me on the edge of insanity over and over again till there was nothing left of me.

My body lay still vibrating under her touch. Anna Belle's dark eyes found me once again. She licked her fingers which tasted of her victory and moaned, "tastes like heaven."

Chapter 21

My body was bare of everything but mud and blood. The cold bit into my skin with every wet sticky step, but this wasn't my body, my flesh. My new form was still pale, but absent were my familiar spots. Now I was adorned with permanent blue designs. Long, dark black hair fell in front of my eyes and stuck to my frosted face.

The slicing wind crashed through the towering trees. The new moon, my trusted friend, would not betray me, and her sister mist had chosen sides and veiled my tracks.

I knew this was a dream, but I could not stop the habit of these steps, these thoughts and this fear. This nightscape was not unknown to me. It was familiar but without detail.

Death in the form of light silently and relentlessly followed over the hills behind me. I had stood still for too long. My feet had sunk in deep into the earth, and the cold had crept further up my spine.

With a disgusting slurp, I broke the suction of my feet from the muck. I would not be able to go on much further. My body ached with exhaustion; I had to hide.

A tree, like a giant insect, had fallen into the glue trap that was the forest floor. It was my only choice. I crawled within the tree's exoskeleton and held my breath. The creepy crawling things began to explore my body. I stayed motionless so not to invoke their wrath.

The light crashed over the hill with furious voices following behind. I willed my cold numb body to stay still despite its need to shiver. I was deep within the husk of the tree, but still half my body showed. I rubbed the filth of decay onto my white skin with a prayer that their eyes would not find me.

The ambient glow lost its grace as it reached the pinnacle of the mound. It now quaked with the fevered steps of its keepers. The flickers of flames were quickly followed by the shadows of men.

Unknown words were spit out like rabid foam. Most of the ten men moved on, but three men lingered. They stood in tight congress.

Blood drunk dogs began barking in the distance. Howls and bellows echoed and rung in the forest night. They were coming to serve their masters' will. If they found me I would know pain and suffering unequaled in Hell. My shivers of cold had turned into shivers of tearful panic.

I was not going to survive this.

I woke up to phantom howls of hungry dogs. In the hush of the morning the weight of this new world began to crush me. I needed to get up and move. Anna Belle's ankle laid across mine, holding me captive in the memories of the night before.

I left the warmth of the covers and Belle's touch to seek the distraction of a new day. Her tousled raven hair hid her from the growing morning. I began to relive our shared night to help me forget my foreboding dream.

Only hours ago our spent bodies nestled close under the covers, and the lullaby of pillow talk had begun.

"So do you sleep during the day?"

"Well, don't most night people?" she giggled.

"Coffins? Avoid the sun?" I was half joking but really wanted to know.

She snorted to herself, "We don't burst into flames, if that is what you mean. It is like a sun allergy. A rash, swelling, sunburn... nothing that sunscreen can't prevent."

"Sounds like you just got a bad case of the Ginger Irish to me," I chuckled.

"You would know..." She started nibbling my neck.

"Are you going to..." Her hot breath banished my thoughts as goose bumps marched down my body.

"What? Taste your blood? Drink you down? You want me to?" She nipped.

"Is Joy right?" I was asking whether or not Joy was right

in her assumption that these predators drank animal blood or donated blood.

"Are you talking about another woman while in my bed?" She teased, narrowing her eyes. Her hand sliding over my breasts. "If you want another woman in bed with us I can find someone, but not Joy."

I was shocked by her bluntness. It was refreshing.

"Would you prefer a man? August is very fun."

"You and August... I have a hard time picturing that."

"You're not jealous, are you?" She was concerned.

"No," I chuckled. "Monogamy doesn't make sense in a mortal's lifetime. How could it possibly make since in y'all's?" Her worry left her face. Our lips pulled and tugged at each other's.

"I knew we made sense together." She devilishly licked the tip of my nose with her long tongue.

"So where are y'all's coffins?" I said this with my worst redneck accent. She pinched my inner thigh in answer.

"Ouch!" She followed with another pinch to my ass. "Ouch! You *are* evil! Ouch!"

"I will show you evil!"

I could still taste her sweetness on my lips as I watched her sleep. Her mocha body surrounded with creme satin sheets beckoned me to join her once again, but my stomach growled and demanded food.

The house was so still. There was no hum of music. There was no chatter of guests. It was museum quiet. I went to my room for a quick shower. The long hall was less foreboding in the morning light. The eerie pictures on the wall of dark forests brought pleasant reminders of Belle's passion. Each photograph had a brass tag with a name and an estimated birthdate. *Did she take all these pictures?*

The windows in my bedroom had all been opened wide, and the morning breeze freshened the room. Everything was brighter and more inviting.

On the bed was my old suitcase from home. *Joy must have gone to my house and packed me a bag.* I was elated to see my favorite torn blue jeans on top. I took a quick shower and headed down to the kitchen.

The ballroom had already been cleaned, the buffet table folded and leaned up against one wall. Skewed patches of bright light from the large windows floated over the classic mural walls.

The courtyard's fountain blissfully rained down into its concrete pond as it basked in the sunlight. Green grass and manicured trees framed the oasis. The roll of the Appalachian foothills in golds, reds and oranges heralded autumn's passing to winter's arrival.

I opened the French glass doors to the cool morning air. *Where the hell am I?*

"Cerbina!?" Joy's high-pitched voice broke my peace.

It came from the kitchen. *I'll just ask her where I am.* I walked in to see Joy opening all the cabinets and angrily shuffling things around. "Cerbina?" She called out in frustration. She looked rough in the mornings. Joy without her accessories, shiny distractions, or hours spent on her hair, was very plain, even with her neon pink hair.

"Morning. I think everyone's asleep," I half whispered.

"Oh hi, morning. I can't find any real food, but I guess I shouldn't be surprised sense they really don't need to eat." She opened the fridge and pulled out one of the left over platters from last night's buffet, assorted cheeses and cocktails weenies.

"This looks good to me." I sat on the same bar stool as I had last night when Cerbina was cleaning blood off my face. I grabbed a toothpick and started loading up on the cheese squares.

"I guess." She sat next to me and used her fingers to pick up some slices of apple.

"So how long did you know about all this?" I popped a cheese cube in my mouth. I wasn't afraid of her, so I didn't have to hold my tongue from the questions I wanted to ask. Plus, being so direct offsets most people into giving honest reactions.

"I knew they had wanted to meet you for about a month," she paused, "but I didn't think it would be anything like this." She beamed and looked around the exquisite kitchen. She loved being in the house and enjoyed the lifestyle.

"Did you know they were going to kidnap me?" I continued eating the leftovers calmly.

"Stop overreacting. We saved you. Those dog guys were the ones trying to nap you. And you seemed to have a good time last night." She knew Belle and I hooked up.

"You could have taken me home..."

"And you could'a gotten hurt." She didn't care about that. She wanted this. She wanted to be here.

"Could you at least tell me where the hell I am?" I changed my line of questioning.

"Just over the state line, less than two hours from your house. You okay with that?" She was getting pissy with her food , pushing it to one side and then the other. She was growing impatient with me.

"What choice do I have?" Having some vague notion of where I was did put me at some ease.

"You don't have one. We are out in the middle of fucking nowhere. I guess they feel safer that way." She was becoming more and more uppity.

I gritted my teeth. "So you're not worried at all that we are in the middle of bum fuck in a house full of potential killers who could EAT us?"

"Don't be stupid. They have many options besides killing people. Why would they? They are higher beings." She was so sure of herself. Maybe she did know more than me since she had been in with them this entire time. *Of course, then I slept the mistress of the house.* I was conflicted.

"So if I took Bjorn out in the sun, would he turn into a disco ball?"

"Well now you're just being a bitch." Joy had changed since she began getting to know these people, and I don't think I liked her as much as I used to.

"Have you seen them feed yet?"

"I've given some of my blood to Bjorn if that's what you're asking, and he was gentle as a kitten." She poured us both a glass of sweet tea.

"What about the lycan?" I wondered if they were in the rooms across the hall from mine.

"The werewolves? Nope, but I don't really care about them anyway." She seemed very unimpressed by people who could physically transform into wolves, but I was extremely curious. "And by the way, you're welcome. I had to go into the mess you call a bedroom and dig out your clothes. Actually, I just went to your dryer. You really need to learn to separate your colors."

"Oh, thanks. I'll keep that in mind as I am getting stalked by witch hunters and having sex with vampires." I sipped my tea and stared out the bay window across the room.

Jealous green flashed across Joy's face. That hadn't been my intention, but I enjoyed the reaction anyway. She had the bad habit of bragging about her sexploits while she knew I was alone and struggling. Plus, I just wanted to hear the absurdity of it all out loud.

"So what do you think of all this?"

"I think it's fucking amazing. Look at us." She recovered quickly and was back to beaming. "The dog people won't find us here, and we get to look at that cool book. Goddess knows what kinda spells and shit are in there."

"Dog people? Oh, you mean the Hounds of Heaven." I looked up at her. *We get to look at the book?*

"Yeah, duh." Sometimes she lost the look and manners of a freak and channeled her inner snotty cheerleader. Once in awhile, I wondered if she only became a freak because she thought she would be the pretty fish in the ugly pond.

I didn't want to be alone in this. I needed a friend, even

a dubious one like Joy. "So you wanna show me all the cool things about this place?"

Her face brightened "Okay! This will be awesome."

Chapter 23

Joy and I explored the house as much as we could. She told me that she was staying in one of the rooms across from mine, but Bjorn was currently sleeping off the night before.

We chatted like we used to, making silly jokes as she talked endlessly about how much she and Bjorn were in love. She finally asked about Anna Belle and me.

"Anna Belle is very..." I couldn't express how I burned for her.

"She seems pretty... nice. You know this is her house. She runs everything." She was proud to think I didn't know this but I could tell just by watching Anna Belle walk across the room. "What about Telal?"

"He is like some kinda representative for... I forget what they call it." She and I admired the fresco on the wall. "I think they call him Vizier, like from Aladdin. I think Anna Belle is the archduchess or something."

Archduchess? "So who is their leader?" I could see the wheels turning in her head.

"Why do you have to ask so many questions? Why can't you just enjoy this?" She opened the doors to the cool afternoon, and we sat on one of the benches beside the three-tiered fountain as it lazily cycled water. A mosaic of flat stone lay under foot, and decorative plants hugged the edges of the oasis softly. Out past the blanket of fall flowers and leaves, guesthouses stood watch on the dense forest's edge.

The breeze played with my long curling hair. The November sun caressed my pale freckled skin. My eyes closed to absorb every atom of that moment as she rambled on.

"Hey, Lydia." Grey had come around the courtyard's side. He was enjoying the day too.

He was all of maybe fifteen. He was in the awkward stage of growth where his head looked too big for his very skinny body. I could see both his mother and his father in him, her beautiful skin and his father's cobalt eyes with long thick lashes. "I don't think we really met." He stuck out his large hand towards Joy. She shook his hand politely but it came across forced.

"I'm Joy." She squinted against the sun.

"Grey. You mind if I hang out? The parents are talking and it got intense."

"Sure." I was happy to see him. Facial peach fuzz caught the light as he sat down on the ground in front of us.

"Grey? What kinda name is that?" Joy rudely demanded an answer.

"My family started calling me that cuz they think I look like a greyhound." He rubbed his chestnut head of hair in embarrassment. I could see it with his long face, big hands and feet. He pulled out a laptop from his book bag and opened it. "Hey you wanna see something I've been working on?" He cheered up and turned his laptop screen to me and Joy.

It was a digital comic strip. Animals were fighting with blank thought bubbles hanging overhead. "This is Stinky, the were-skunk. He fights crime one stink bomb at a time!" He chuckled. A soft laugh escaped my lips. Encouraged, he went on. "And his friends are the were-ferrets, Razzle and Dazzle." *I wonder what he looks like after he changes.*

His sharp eyes, irises just as large as his mother's, looked up at me with youthful glee. He was a handsome boy. *He will be a heartbreaker when he grows up.*

Joy rolled her eyes and went back to her texting. Grey took the hint and closed up his computer. I was disappointed; I wanted to see more.

"So your head hasn't exploded from all this..." He squinted up at me. He held himself with more maturity than his age would suggest.

"Not yet." It still didn't feel real to me. This boy sitting in front of me was a fucking werewolf, and I woke up cuddled to a vampire this morning, but still... *This isn't real.*

Joy was completely engrossed in her text conversation. "Hey Joy, can I borrow that? I wanted to call my neighbors to see if they could watch my cats, so you don't have to keep going down there." It was a thin ploy. I just wanted to touch the outside world to make sure the real world hadn't fallen away.

"Oh, I already asked them when I was down there. They said 'sure no problem.' They even took them into their house. Besides my battery is almost dead." Joy didn't look up from her phone.

"What did you tell them I was doing... and how long did you say I was going to be gone?"

"Oh, I told them you had family emergency, and I didn't know when you would be back."

Not having a date when I was going to see my cats or my normal life again made a hard knot swell in my throat. My face flushed.

"So what did you think of the book?" Grey saw my face, and he decided to try to change the subject.

"Overwhelming." I wasn't sure what he knew, and he was barely a teen, so I kept my answers vague.

"I heard my mom tell my uncle you took it pretty well." He jerked his head to the right suddenly. "Look, a deer!"

Joy and I both scanned the wilderness' edge. A doe and her fawn were riding the border of the pines and field. I could barely see them.

"It's so nice here. I miss home, though."He propped himself on long arms and flung his huge feet out in front of him.The deer soon scattered back into the maze of autumn winter trees.

Sky and August walked out from the house. August was a bit out of place in the daylight. He had dark sunglasses to hide his sensitive eyes, but his skin was eerily flawless. *At least he doesn't sparkle.*

"Honey, come on. We got some things to do," her soft mother tone called his immediate attention.

"We should do this again." Grey picked up his book bag and stood.

"For sure." I didn't think Joy even noticed he was leaving.

"You feeling okay?" Sky, the constant caregiver.

"I am a little tender. My ribs still hurt a little, but other than that I'm good. Thank you."

"Those herbs are mainly for superficial wounds, but the rib will heal with time. And of course you're welcome." Sky motioned for Grey to follow her back to the mother in-law houses. Her long onyx hair caught the wind as they left the cove of the fountain.

August stood at the door, and Bjorn appeared beside him sporting his own dark shades. Bjorn's skin had the same flawless quality. I had a suspicion that most people who passed them in the street would get the feeling that something was 'off' with them, but wouldn't put their finger on too perfect skin.

"Lydia, you ready to work on the Codex?" August was wearing leather pants but somehow maintained a studious air about him.

"Yes!" Joy answered for me.

"Lydia?"

"I guess." I had forgotten myself in the beauty of the day.

"I will be waiting downstairs." August patted Bjorn on the shoulder and left.

"Joy, how about you come with me?" Bjorn's hard chiseled face was cracked by a wide smile.

August and I were alone in the hidden depths of house where the Codex was laying open and waiting. I was slightly distracted as I watched him organize and pull his records and research materials together. I could easily understand why Anna Belle would choose him to join us in the bedroom. Suddenly his eyes met mine, and a faint blush crossed my cheeks.

I forcibly focused my eyes down to the ancient book. It wasn't too difficult to forget about potential encounters because the Codex commanded my attention.

I eagerly began to thumb through it as August pulled more books, scrolls and notebooks from the locked shelves. Most looked to be around the same age as the Codex.

"As you can see, I have been working on this for a while." He placed a large pile on the table.

"How long have you had the Codex?" I traced the broken edges of missing pages. "And were these pages already gone when you got it?"

"I believe the Codex came to me around," he waded through his papers, "1705." August looked around my age, but his mannerisms were of someone who had been tempered with time.

"So you're at least three hundred years old?"

"At least." He chortled to himself.

"So, how old are you?"

"If I tell you, can we get to work?" He raised his amber eyes from his collection.

"Yes." I was pleased.

"I was born spring, 1497."

"Wow." I tried to imagine the world he came from. My mind could only see cliched Renaissance paintings. "When did you become a vampire?" It came out more blunt than I'd wanted.

"I thought the deal we made was that if I told you how old I was we could get to work." His sharp cupid lips bowed.

"Hot cocoa!" Anna Belle announced herself into the room. She placed the tray on the table as three mugs let off wisps of chocolate steam. "I hope I am not interrupting anything."

August gave a dramatically loud sigh and leaned his head back on the chair. "At this rate it will be another 300 years..."

"Do not be grumpy, August." Belle kissed him softly on his mouth. She glided over and shyness captured me. "Has he been mean to you?" Her nose crinkled and her black eyes narrowed.

She kissed me, playfully pulling on my bottom lip. Her pert breasts teased from under her white sun dress as she leaned over. August admired her heart-shaped ass with appreciation. *Belle, you did that on purpose.*

"How long have you two known each other?" I sensed a long history between them.

"Here," She handed me a specific mug, "You don't want our cocoa. It would be a nasty surprise." Anna Belle sat down and handed August his mug and took a sip from hers. "I met him when he was just an initiate."

"Initiate?"

"Anyone who is chosen to join the Houses of Lilitu has to prove themselves worthy." Anna Belle stroked my hair.

Varrick's voice crashed into the room. "It's not like in the movies. It's not some fucking STD passed from one person to the next. It takes years of dedication, preparation and perseverance. And even then..." Varrick was more cross than usual; his hard accent was running deep.

"Though most do not make it." sorrow tightened August's throat.

"Don't make it?" My voice softened as I noticed August's pain.

"Yes, most die. Permanently." Varrick had no soft qualities about him.

"Or worse." August retreated deeper into his collection.

"Varrick, what do you want?" Belle's charm fell away to steely gaze.

"Lydia's friend is causing a scene up stairs. She wants to come down here and I think Bjorn is about to lose his patience." Disdain dripped from his lips.

"What's your problem with her?" I could no longer hold my tongue.

"My issue is that she is here at all. Humans have no business being here."

"What's wrong with humans? I'm human."

Anna Belle began to speak but August stopped her.

"How would you feel if wild monkeys lived in your home, their smells and filth."

"You've never had sex with a human after you became a vampire?"

"Would you have sex with a cow?"

"Varrick, may I speak with you?" Anna Belle pointedly told, more than asked, Varrick.

Varrick and I weren't finished, but Belle finished for us. They walked to the door and whispered between themselves. They were speaking in the same language I had heard before between the vampires.

"He doesn't like humans much, does he? He only puts up with me because he has to." I watched Varrick's thick muscular arms fold over his chest as Belle stood firm and showed absolute control over her emotions.

"Varrick's an asshole." August's words were delivered with an undiluted potency. Varrick heard him and met August's glance with a bold smirk.

"You two get back to work." Anna Belle jokingly wagged her finger at us as she followed Varrick out the door.

"Okay, let's get to work. Stop stalling, August. What about those pages?" I picked on him as I sipped from my mug, trying to lighten the mood. *I don't give a shit what Varrick thinks. He isn't the first person not to like me, and he won't be the last.*

August took a sip of his drink with a flirtatious smile and a twinkle in his eye. "They had already been removed by the time I received Codex, and I believe The Heaven's Hounds have them. I was able to partially translate a few of the pages surrounding them."

"How did they get the pages?" I settled back into my seat.

"Have you heard of Matthew Hopkins?"

"He was an infamous witch hunter." I knew his name very well. A brutal man. He and his partner were responsible for about forty percent of the total of executions in the one hundred and sixty years of persecution in England. That many in only fourteen months.

"He was the one who tore the pages out. His 'cleansing' was a cover for the search for this book and others like it. He found the Codex."

The screams of men, women and children that he had tortured echoed in the room around me. I shivered and held myself tightly.

"After he found it, he 'retired.' The Chthonians had retrieved it, but the pages were already gone."

"Chthonians are the vampires and Shapeshifters..." I wanted to make sure I understood.

"And anyone or anything else that lives on the edge of the veil. Trust me when I say 'vampires' and 'werewolves' are by far the most mundane within the veil's borders." He sat back in his chair and watched me closely.

What the hell else is out there? Do I really want to know?

"I want you to study these pages, but I also want you to try to use your gifts. We need to know what the Hounds have and why. The Bahlael believe it is linked to Hekate's Crossing."

"Hekate's Crossing?" Hearing my goddess's name sent an urgency through my veins.

"It's a comet that passes every few thousand years. It's an omen of great change, a shift from light to dark and back again. I believe whatever the Hounds of Heaven have in store for you, it is linked to the Crossing."

"Do you mean the comet St. Nick?" A mosh pit of nervous butterflies hit my stomach. "The comet they spotted this month? That should be here around Yule? !"

"Yes. I believe so," he said in his usual matter of fact way.

That's so soon. "What do I need to do?" Uncertainty gripped me.

He open to the pages just before the tear gap. "This part here." He pointed to the bottom of the page with his long nail, to a sentence that had been cut off mid stride. "Do you see how it ends? And that the language used is a sampling of several?"

I had to take his word on that. It was jumbled mess of beautifully painted shapes to me. I recognized some of the shapes from the Roman, Greek and Arabic alphabets. Even hidden within the crease were runes, Oghams and Pictish swirls. The Oghams lined the crease mimicking tree trunks and the Pictish swirls acted like its leaves.

But then there were symbols I presumed to be letters, but they didn't look familiar. "I do not know these. Have you seen them before?" He asked.

"Yes, in my dream, but I don't remember what they meant."

"Tell me what you remember about the dream."

"I don't really remember anything... It's just a blur. It happened so many years ago. I remember waking up and sketching what I saw."

"Do you have the sketch or notes?"

"Not with me." I was a bit sarcastic. "I think my journal is somewhere in my house."

"We will make arrangements to get it. Till then, I want to help you remember that dream." he rested his hand on top of mine. "How do you feel about guided meditation?" His owl eyes peered into me.

"Uh..." I hesitated.

The migraine was a python that tried to squeeze my sanity from me. After hours in the library, I could go no further. I had reluctantly volunteered for his suggestion for a guided meditation. I wanted to try to crack the code of the mysterious Codex as much as anyone, maybe more. We succeeded only in giving me another nosebleed, now joined with a headache that could crack granite.

"This may hurt you, but I need to get you up those stairs." August picked me up easily with his thin frame. I wanted to go to my room for some blessed silence, but independent movement was beyond me.

We crested the foyer when Anna Belle hurriedly crossed towards us. "Is she okay?" Deep grooved panic held her face hostage.

"I am taking her to her room. She needs Sky." He answered, showing no signs of weakening as he held me like an infant.

"I'm here." Sky's soft raspy voice broke in. Through the blur and spots, a group of people came up behind Belle.

"Take her to my room." Anna Belle directed. Her usual silky tone was now sandpaper to my ears.

Joy's voice cut through my mind like jagged glass. "Are you okay? You want me to give it a try, August?"

"Go for it." My own sarcasm was a thunderhead against my eardrums.

"Not now, Joy. Grey, get my box." Sky hurriedly came to my side. Grey ran away on padded feet, barely louder than cotton hitting ground.

"August, what did you two do?" Belle softly questioned.

"I'm the one who insisted..." my shallow breath halted as the daggers went deeper in my head "that we keep trying."

"Any success?" Telal spoke.

"No, Vizier." August answered, "But I believe we came close."

"Can you people please save this conversation until after we get her to bed!?" Sky spoke through clenched large teeth.

"Of course."Telal acquiesced with cold calculation.

A surge of vomit hit the border of my throat as August made his way to Anna Belle's room.

My worn body was placed with care on her plush cool bed. My eyelids were rusty shutters. They quickly turned off all the lights save one candle that burned in a far corner. All blinds were locked down.

Telal and August left as Grey and Cerbina entered the room, letting in blades of light. Sky took her box and requested some hot water.

Only Sky and Anna Belle remained with me. I appreciated their silence and their love of darkness.

Cerbina's tap on the door was a like gunshot to my ears. She had brought a mug of hot water. Sky quickly steeped a mix of herbs. She spoke softly to me. "Honey, this will help."

"Thank you." I carefully took a sip. Mint and honey overpowered the scent of the other herbs but was welcomed.

"Mom, is she going to be okay?" Grey peeked into the room.

"Drink all of it. I'll be back later. Sleep if you can." Sky walked over to her son. "Yes, she just pushed herself too hard. Let's let her sleep." They left me in the soft care of Belle.

I was becoming drowsy as the pain began to wane. Anna Belle kissed me on the forehead as she laid down beside me and waited for sleep to release me.

A chaotic fury of thoughts raced through my mind, and a fierce sleep dragged me under.

A lucid dream was birthed in the darkness. I was still in Belle's bed, her body motionless next to mine. Whispers pulled from a distance.

I sat up, leaving my body behind. My ghost steps guided me through the mansion. No one knew that I was there. I was lured down into the house's depths.

From the ceiling, I watched as August sat next to me as we began the guided meditation.

"Lydia, listen to my voice." August's subdued timber.

The movie replayed the actions of my body relaxing and my breath becoming measured and smooth. His voice lost form and retained only tone, my body responded. My own purple aura spiked with yellow white fear. My body's heartbeat overpowered me. A jolt of electric energy popped and cracked. My past self jetted forward, breaking the meditation connection.

"Are you okay?" August asked.

"Yes, I don't know what happened." I answered in a surreal moment of listening from the outside.

August and my past self tried several times. Each time the lightning popped. It remained unseen to us in the past though it broke my meditation efforts. I watched as it spontaneously burst through the air and attacked my physical body. Its origin was slowly revealing itself. *If they did it once more, maybe I could find its start.*

"Maybe we should stop." He held my body's hand.

I was worn and my aura weak, but I needed to find the source of the attack. *Lydia, one more time.* I focused my will.

My body shook its head, "No, let's try again. I feel like I'm close to something." My voice was weakening.

August reluctantly began again. Once again my body went limp and my aura shifted and began the meditation path.

I made myself ignore my body's cries and focused on the hiss of the electrical force beginning to build. *Where are you coming from?*

    This time the lighting ball hit my body directly. My past self jerked forward and blood began to pour from my nose. *I taste pennies.*

I burst from my sleep with mad kicks and silent screams. A shadow form stood watch, and then he was no more. I caught my violent breath and stilled my limbs. My migraine was gone, but a fog took its place.

"Belle?" I heard no answer. Anna Belle was gone. The clocks cool blue light showed 3:23am.

Muffled laughing came from the corridor. I didn't want to be alone with the ghosts of my dream. I slid on my jeans and t-shirt and went to see what the good time was all about.

The house was oddly still. I made a lap around the bottom floor and ended in the kitchen. Still no one. "Hello?" I had a desperate need to see someone, anyone.

Click. The bookshelf door.

The hearth's eternal fire brewed softly in the ashes. A sharp cry escaped from behind the wall. I fumbled with my fingertips, looking for the release button.

Click. The bookshelf relented. There was something sticky on my fingers. *Blood?*

My body started to vibrate with anticipation and dread. *No, they're not like that. Belle isn't like that. What about Varrick?*

In the deep, music echoed. *Maybe I don't want to know.*

My feet hesitated, mocking my will. I heard a sharp laugh married with a cry of pain. I have to know.

I went down into the lonely stairwell. I thought it better to not turn on the lights. *They're my allies. Why, because they say so?* I argued with myself.

The door was slightly ajar and the yellow light faded into night air. I walked softly, easy to do in bare feet.

The warm crackle of a record playing gave way to the soulful voice of a singer long forgotten. A low rasping growl from the room made me suddenly aware of how bad an idea this was. The heavy smell of blood and bile wisped in the stale air.

My soul was scarred as deviant brutality and carnage revealed itself. The loveseat where I sat only hours ago now held the body of a naked dead woman. Her eyes were vacant, flesh pale gray, body ripped and throat open. She was being lovingly licked clean by Delphine as David absently fondled her lifeless breasts. Both of their naked bodies lingered over the broken doll, a guttural purr shared between them. My lip trembled in disgust and disbelief.

"No! Please no! I'm willing... you don't have to do this!" A hard thud came from the back of the room. "Please stop! Please! No!"

Growls penetrated the tinny music and I leaned further into the room. Delphine and David were blind in their ecstasy.

August, Telal and Anna Belle were arched and poised over a supine terrified woman. Belle turned to face August, and I saw that the beauty was gone and only a beast remained. *Anna Belle?*

Belle's left hand held their victim firmly by the throat against the hard wood table. The girl's legs kicked frantically, her hands scratched wildly at Belle's distorted face. Belle was unmoved.

August moved with a blur and held the twisting woman's legs spread exposing her already bruised and used inner thighs.

Telal stood like a demon sentinel at the head of the table, his already unnatural features exaggerated by blood hunger. He roared and stretched out his claws. His eyes burned with lustful fury. His jaw stretched, and his razor teeth unsheathed like a snake about to strike. Time stopped as my eyes were burned with the image of the three baptized in the woman's desperate blood. Belle bellowed, and August joined. They were demons in the flesh, no romance or nobility, only raw hunger and power.

"I'm sorry, please don't... I won't tell anyone..." The girl's screams were drowned and gurgling in her own blood. The creatures sliced slowly into her supple skin.

I was struck dumb by the horror of it all. August reached forward with his claws and hooked into the sweet spot between her inner thighs and cunt. With a rip and a horrid broken scream he lacerated her from thigh to calf. Belle and Telal displayed their sabers and reached frenzy. The demonic pride of lions enjoyed their kill.

Each was coming up for breath, staking their claim and drinking deep again from the fading girl.

I stepped back from the door gap and hit the wall behind me. The cold cement woke me to the reality. *I need to get the fuck out of here!*

I realized that the thrall of their feeding was uninterrupted by my spying. I ran as swiftly and quietly as I could. I stopped myself in the den and closed the passage with care. I nearly tripped over the coffee table as I made my way out towards freedom.

My trembling body, doped on adrenaline, tried for the front door, but it was locked with a bolt and there was no key in sight.

The back patio! My bare feet went cold against the marble floor. I heard then a different kind of laugh in the media room just off to the right of the ballroom. It was Joy.

I have to save her. I knew Bjorn wouldn't be far away from her. I tried to find my center before I went into the room.

Joy and Bjorn were snuggled on the couch wearing headphones, watching a B horror flick. I walked over and tapped her on the shoulder. She let out a squeal, and even

Bjorn was surprised. Bjorn's true form appeared for a brief instant till he recognized me. I was startled but did not react.

They took off their headphones, and I could hear the starlet's screams coming from the speakers. *She hadn't heard anything.*

"Sorry, did we wake you up? We used the headphones." Joy innocently smiled up at me. Bjorn knew something was wrong. "Liddy, are you okay? You look pale."

"I don't feel well." I stumbled over the words.

"The migraine? Another nightmare? Do you need me to get you something?" She asked as she stood up, leaving her snuggling behind.

I looked at Bjorn and concentrated on maintaining my control. I was sure he could sense something was wrong.

"Yeah, some food might help." I wanted to vomit.

"Okay. Babe, I'll be back in a minute. Could you pause it?" She followed me out of the room and once the door was shut I turned to her.

"Instead, can we get some fresh air?" I wanted to get outside.

"Sure."

Chapter 27

Tuesday morning
12 days until Solstice

"We got to go! We got to go now!" Panic pushed my voice
louder than I meant it to.

"What are you talking about?" She was confused and
worried.

"I saw them, the real them. They... aren't human..." Not the
words I wanted but they were all I had.

"Duh, they're vampires." She wasn't getting it in her silly
little bubble.

"No, I mean they're fucking demons! We have to go!" I
grabbed her arm and started pulling her away from the house.

"Okay? Where do you want to go?" She challenged me.

"My truck, is it still in the front of the house?"

"Anna Belle has the key. Do you want me to get it from
her?"

"No!" My forceful answer shocked her.

"We can cross the woods and hit a road in about an hour."
She was humoring me. "It's a full moon and I got my phone so
we will be able to see our way mostly. And it's a little too chilly
for snakes..."

"I don't give a fuck about snakes."

"You need shoes." She looked down at my feet.

"No, we got to go now. I'll be fine. Let's go."

She pressed the button on her phone and light ruptured
the dark. "No, not yet! They could see it from the house."

"I'm just checking if that's the way to the road. Thank the

gods for GPS, right? Yep that's the way, but it's a hell of a hike." She paused waiting for me to change my mind, but she soon realized I would not. "We go straight till we hit some railroad tracks, then we follow them to the right till we hit the road."

She turned it off, to my impatient relief. We walked across backyard acre, avoiding the guest houses and breaching the night woods.

The house lights and full moon disappeared behind the cover of old growth forest, some trees clinging to the last of their leaves, others stark naked against the star dusted sky.

"Can I use my phone now?"

"Fine." I'd always had pretty good night vision but lacked no depth perception. I was having to slowly feel my way with my feet for dips and crevices so not to break my ankle, but I needed to make better time.

What was I going to do when I got home? I can't think about that now. I just have to get me and Joy outta here.

The phone's sharp light burst on, and we began making better time. She tried to ask me to explain what I saw, but I couldn't speak the words. "They were just... ripping them apart. She was begging..."

"Are you sure you saw what you think you saw?" She didn't want to believe me. I'm not sure I would either. "Bjorn hasn't done anything like that. He's a big teddy bear. In fact, before you walked in..."

"I don't *care!* I'm telling you they are *fucking brutal killers!*" We both fell silent. *We must keep going.* We concentrated our efforts and strength on the hike instead of conversation.

My hair kept catching in the low branches, and the slide of cobwebs sent goosebumps across my skin. My feet fell on landmine pinecones and spiked shrubs. I pulled the thorns and hopped till I found the next booby trap with my other foot.

Silence. Nothing but a whisper of a breeze brushing against

the tops of branches. Soft mud squished in between by toes. A flash of my forest dream. *Déjà vu.* I was exposed and helpless.

"Hey, do you hear that?" Joy asked.

I took a few steps till my bare feet uncomfortably rested on some rocks. I listened to the silence. Any Southern girl knows where there is silence in the woods, there is danger. My eyes searched the blackness, but I saw nothing beyond the ground lighted by her phone. The constricted light made the surrounding darkness even deeper.

Snap! Crunch.

I turned my head sharply to find the source, but nothing.

Snap! Pop.

"Over there." I whispered. I held my breath.

She raised her phone and panned the area.

Another *pop* to our left.

"No, I think it's to the left." She turned and we saw four reflecting eyes, standing just as still as us.

"It's just deer." I almost cried with relief.

Snap. Crunch to our right.

This time the deer and we looked in the same direction. Everything went rigid.

The deer sniffed at the air, and I strained to see anything in the colorless night.

"I'm scared." Joy whispered.

"Shh," I commanded. I tried to silence my nerves so I could focus on seeing any auras, but I failed. My migraine began to threaten its return.

The breath of the forest was steady but shallow. Lightning brightened the sky between the long gnarled fingers of the trees. I heard only Joy's panting.

What was that? A large bulk of shadow weaved between the trees. My heart stuttered.

The deer sniffed the air again. I tried to pick up a scent futilely. There was only the smell of wet, burnt earth, it gave no hint of what was coming.

Another *crunch*. This time closer.

The deer burst into a run. They split. One banked left while the other charged forward in the brush. Bestial howls and tremendous trampling crashed through the woods. Joy and I both ran for our very lives through the labyrinth of wood and kudzu but were separated by the terrain. Her phone light strobed through black columns until it disappeared. I fled with clumsy steps, but I didn't stop, could not stop.

A huge thud hit the forest floor, and a deer cried out in the distance. Guttural growls and barking bathed the night. The sound of furious tearing and bone crunching rolled through the valley followed by fierce howls. *The Shifters. Joy knows where we're going, I'll meet her at the road.*

My feet caught on briars and were cut on rocks, but I was numb to everything but the paranoia only the hunted know. *I have to get to that road. Please be okay, Joy.* I said a quick prayer for us both.

I pushed on till I hit the edge of a kudzu snarl. It's tendrils snared and pulled as it tried to absorb me into its bedlam. I clawed my way through, feeling my adrenaline drop and my strength fade. I began to lose hope. I should have been there by now. *Where's Joy? Is she okay? I shouldn't have left her behind.*

Finally, after I had all but given up, I heard a train clattering relentlessly to its destination. *The road must be close.* Renewed strength of will powered through me as I tore through the snarl of vines.

The rhythmic clack and hum was my welcomed guide. The forest broke and finally gave way to the steel rails. The steady blinking of the crossing lights down the tracks beckoned me on. I 'm almost there. My feet, blue and bloody, pushed on till I made it to the train crossing on some back country road.

The bloodshot sunrise crested the horizon, giving me a pause of relief. *I need to turn south and follow the road. Where's Joy?*

"Joy!" I called out in a desperate foolish hope. "Joy! Where are you!" I waited warily on the edge of the woods at the iron crossroads.

Bang! A truck's backfire woke me from my exhausted daze. *This is my chance. I'm sorry Joy. I'll come back for you.*

I stood painfully up and rushed to the edge of the road. A 1950's Ford truck rocked steadily towards me. I waved my arms, no doubt looking like a mad woman. "Please stop!"

The truck pulled to the side of the forgotten road with ease. An older man and teenaged boy gave a welcoming wave.

"Gal, you okay?" The old man was a stern good ole' boy.

"I need to..." I had no idea where to begin. *Save my friend from the vampires and werewolves that could kill us all.* "Get a ride into town."

"Get in. Boy get out and let the young lady in." The preacher like old man playfully smacked the boy's arm. The boy looked like he could be a local hero quarterback, short cropped hair, chiseled jaw, long lashes and a broad smile.

"I'm Lydia."

"Justin." I looked up at the kid and saw a glimpse of the red cross shield tattoo on his neck. He slammed my head against the hood of the truck as the grandfather jumped out to help.

"Get her, boy! Quick!" The old man pressed a stone against my forehead that shot white-hot lightning through my mind's eye. I couldn't see or move, only hear the old man say, "Tie the bitch up. Hurry."

The sharp zip of plastic ties wrenched deep into my bruising ankles and wrists. "Open her mouth!"

The man placed a stone wrapped in a cotton handkerchief deep in my mouth, almost choking me, then sealed my lips with duct tape.

Weakness and swelling wounds overtook me. "Faerie stone. Let's see you try something now, whore."

Chapter 28

Tuesday
12 days until Solstice

I knew I was alive only by my pain and the soundtrack of
creaks and moans from the rough ride. I was tied like a trophy
deer carcass. Duct tape pulled at my eyes and mouth, my
head swelled and the truck bed bit my muscles hard. *I did this
wrong.*

A broken Morse code was tapped by tree limbs hitting the
side of the truck as we changed direction and headed down a
gravel road. Branches rained leaves and bugs down on me. A
sudden stop lurched me forward.

In the distance a neglected screen door opened, and a male
voice called out, "Got her?"

Justin yelled back, "Are we sure she is the right one? She
wasn't noth'n."

"Don't be deceived. She is the devil's priestess. She will
bring ruin to anything she touches," the truck driver warned
Justin as they cut the ropes that bound me to the truck.

Like a sack of grain, I was flung over the shoulders of
someone who was much larger than Justin or the old man.
"Take her to the basement. I have everything set up there,"
a masculine European voice commanded. The screen door
creaked open further and slammed abruptly shut as the heavy
steps of my carrier moved steadily forward. *I smell something
familiar.*

Bloodcurdling screams broke the silence within the bowels
of the house. The heavy weight of a dark presence pressed

down on me. The air was thick and unclean.

The clank of an old doorknob let loose a wall of musty decay. The giant who held me, skillfully made his way down creaking steps and dropped me abruptly on the dirt floor.

"Get the hook."

The hook?

I was roughly pulled to my feet, but I couldn't stand because of the angle my legs had been strapped together. Cold metal squeezed between the binds of my wrists.

"Pull."

I was lifted off the ground with a heft and groan of a pulley. My toes only teased the ground. Immediately my hands began to ache, followed with sharp pangs as my nerves were compressed and pulled. My shoulders throbbed, and my hips were heavy.

"Do it."

A searing rip and burn tore at my eyes as the tape was fiercely removed taking some of my eyebrows with it. The pain made me momentarily blind, but soon a blurry world became focused. Two raw hanging bulbs flanked me, ineptly lighting the dirt floor basement. My throat knotted when my eyes fell upon a wooden table sitting quietly in the corner with leather straps dangling.

I twisted around like a worm on a hook, and I saw a cage mounted to the ramshackle brick walls. I swung back to my far right to see a stoked and ready wood furnace.

The large man, who'd carried me, turned me back to center. The older man who had driven the truck stood ominously bathed in rough shadow. Each flushed with anticipation.

A handsome gentleman with disgust on his lips and hate in his eyes watched carefully. His full robes enveloped his frame, letting only his head and gloved hands be seen. His dark curly hair and blue eyes could have made him a classical model except for a small scar across his lips and chin.

"I want you to nod 'yes' or 'no' to my questions. Do you

understand?" He stepped closer and his tongue purred the syllables.

I nodded, but I barely heard him over the electric fire cutting into my wrists.

"Are you Lydia Keening?" The Italian asked. I didn't know what or if I should answer.

Slap! A violent sting burned my cheek. The old man delivered swift punishment with a calloused hand. The gorilla of a man caught me swinging in mid air and turned me back to center.

"Are you Lydia Keening?" He asked again in the exact same tone.

The shock of being hit in the face paused my answer too long. Another slap echoed off the walls. I feverishly nodded "yes" as hot tears of rage and despair bubbled.

"Good. We have a lot to discuss. I am Hopkins. My associates Young," he pointed to the large redneck who had carried me, "and Blackburne," he motioned to the old man who was clenching his jaw viciously. "But first we must examine your person."

Hopkins?

"Young." With his order, Young stepped over to me and pulled out a long hunting knife.

"Get away from me!" My voice was muffled by the rag and stone in my mouth.

I swung away, but he grabbed the rope over my head and halted me. I kicked but the pressure on my already cut wrists was too great. I pushed my energy but was met with a violent pain.

"Be still, witch. We don't want you to hurt yourself." Young grinned, his breath smelling like beef jerky. I met his narrow dull eyes and saw nothing of remorse or guilt. *You are enjoying this, you sick fuck.*

"Blackburne, help me with this." Young called to the older man. Blackburne came and held me still as the fat bastard leaned down and cut my legs free from their binds.

Crack! I landed one good kick across Young's fat greasy face. He was knocked off his heels, and Hopkins just glared at his incompetence. Young quickly grabbed my ankles with bruising force, pulling both his and my weight down against the thin plastic wrist cuffs. I cried out, but the stone gag began to choke me. The tears crept down my dirty face as anger was replaced by desperation for inspiration for freedom.

He locked a metal clamp around each ankle and strapped them to their own ground stake. I couldn't touch the ground, but the pain began to numb into pins and needles.

Young pushed the knife up the cuff of my blue jeans. The cold edge encouraged me to stay very still. A ripping sound filled the damp room as he sliced through my favorite jeans from ankle to hip on both sides.

He missed my boxers which he then twisted and ripped off my body. "Natural ginger. I shouldn't be surprised." Blackburne hissed and spat on the ground.

Young stuck the knife down my shirt, the hilt punched my chin, and with one quick movement split my shirt and bra in half. He ripped off the hanging cloth with a fury. My bra hooks snapped and clawed my flesh. I was naked and spread eagle on some S&M dreamcatcher.

"I think we might have something here, Sir." He brushed his hand across my strawberry birthmark on my right breast.

"Lower her." Hopkins ordered.

I was lowered slightly so that I was flat footed on the cold ground. Blood had begun dripping down my arms in thick warm streams. They tightened each leg to their posts.

"Begin the examination." Hopkins slight smile made my soul cringe.

Blackburne went over to the table and unrolled a leather tool holder. I couldn't make out much more than light reflecting off steel.

"We must make sure you are the one we are looking for after all. Don't want to waste either of our time." The robed man stepped out of the way handing Blackburne a brown vial.

"The tears of Saint Benedict."

Blackburne removed an eye dropper from the small bottle and walked slowly towards me. My chest was bursting as he lifted the dropper above my breast. My body tensed as the sharp frigid drop of liquid landed above the border of red skin. Their eyes bore into me. The off white oil slithered over the curve of my breast and began to heat up as it touched my birthmark.

Sizzling was audible and the heat began. A slow warmth grew into seething burn. I clenched my teeth and held my breath. I would not let them see. The oil reacted like wet lye against my purple red flesh. I could no longer hold myself still. It burned deeper still, and the smell of scorching filled my nostrils.

Hopkins nodded at Young. Young quickly threw cold water onto me. The burning ceased, but the look in their eyes, smug and righteous, gave me worry.

Blackburne held a single three inch needle in his hand. He softly brushed his hand across my tit then abruptly plunged the steel in deep.

"Fuck you!" My curse was muffled. I bit down on the stone in my mouth and tried to keep from closing my eyes.

Young enjoyed himself as Blackburne pulled the needle out and gave it to Hopkins.

Hopkins held up a stray piece of old paper against the awkward light and cleaned the bloody needle with it. The paper drank my blood till there was nothing left. "It is the mark."

He then pulled a leather collar, which had a faerie stone mounted into it, from his robe. He roughly locked the collar around my neck, and he then ripped the tape from my mouth, taking delicate skin with it. I had the urge to spew profanities, but my jaw ached too much.

"You are the one to help us." He was polite.

"Why would I help you?" I seethed.

"Because you have no choice."

"Go fuck yourself." My jaw cracked from a hard slap given by Young's thick callused hand.

"That is what I would expect filth like you to say. You are vile concubine of Satan, and you will do well to remember your place."

"And where's that?" I challenged.

"Under God's boot. Take her down. We will begin tomorrow."

I was suddenly dropped to the floor as the pulley let go. My legs were freed from the stakes, but the medal clamps remained tight as they dragged me into the 5 foot tall by 4 foot wide metal cage.

"Your hands." Young grabbed them through the bars, and Blackburne cut the biting plastic. They quickly clamped separate metal cuffs on my wrists, no doubt to be used tomorrow.

I desperately scanned the room for any way out. *Damn, no windows.* The cage was bolted to the wall, and the dirt floor was too hard to dig.

Young picked up my shredded clothes and threw them directly into the furnace. Blackburne was the last to leave. Following the others up and out, he turned off the lights. *I'm not leaving here.*

Droplets of blood welled up from my punctured skin like liquid garnets. The only light came from an antique coal furnace, its asbestos insulation falling away like shedding skin.

Along the walls were paintings of Jesus on his cross, bloodied and raw. A crucifix hung from each wall with the crumpled weak silver man drooping from nails on lacquered pine.

A chair loomed in the darkness; steel spikes stood in ranks on its surface from inch to inch.

What are they planning? My limbs went weak, my mouth dry.

I clawed at my padlocked collar. The stone was suspended

in a decorative hole that made sure it was always touching my skin. *What is this thing? What the fuck is a "faerie stone?"* Whatever it was it took my ability to see with my third eye and to feel or work with energy.

I sat bare-assed in the corner of my cage looking at the camper's toilet, locked down against the cage, that had been provided for me. *No one is coming for me... I will have to save myself.*

A squeak and a blinding light from the top of the stairs cut into my cage. A woman's silhouette breached the basement's threshold, mad screams followed her down from the house above.

She flipped a switch, and the two naked bulbs turned on with a buzz. Justin was following dutifully behind her.

She was a woman around my age with country features, thin lips and sunken eyes. Her blonde hair was tied tightly in a bun and her face was drab. She was wearing a long blue jean skirt and a loose long-sleeved blouse.

Justin handed her a Styrofoam bowl as she opened a can of cream of mushroom soup. She filled the bowl with a sticky plop and handed it back to him. Justin stuck a plastic spoon into the thick goop like a flag. She then pulled out a can of soda that was unopened, popped the top and poured it into a paper cup.

"This is all you get. Don't waste it." Her gray eyes scanned my nakedness with disinterest.

"Why are you feeding me?" I asked with impunity.

"Unclean things don't get to ask questions of the faithful." She spat on the floor beside her.

"What if I don't eat it?" I pushed.

"You eat it this way or we will make you eat it off the ground like the dog bitch you are." Her sour voice corrupted her virtuous face.

I met her eyes with fearlessness, a sharp pain pierced my mind's eye as I instinctively tried to read her. My hand raised to cover my forehead as I recoiled. "Don't try to cast your dark will upon me. I am protected in God." She reached not to her gold cross around her neck, but to a pouch which hung above her heart.

"Dark will? Who has who in a fucking cage!?" I snarled.

"Enjoy." She placed the food on the ground just within my reach. "Make it last." She smirked.

My eyes fell closed to a scattered sleep. Time passed with no definition, marked only by my stomach's increased demands. I couldn't resist the soup goop or flat soda any longer. The blob slipped down my throat and I quickly tried to wash it down with warm Coke. I gagged, but my stomach was silenced.

I was alone with only the company of the implements that impatiently awaited their master's return. They would not be waiting long.

Heated voices drifted down from above and then suddenly stopped. Loud footfalls echoed in the dim space. Justin flipped the light switch and hurriedly shoved some coal into the furnace with a quick smile.

He began to lay out the tools methodically. The smell of rubbing alcohol cut through the room as he cleaned them with a lover's touch.

"Why bother? Afraid I might get an infection and die?" I smarted off. *If I could only do what I did to the boy at the club... If I could just touch him.* But I knew the stone around my neck prevented me from using any of my talents.

I never realized how blind mundanes were. I'd been spoiled by my gifts of insight and energy manipulation. Everything was so empty, gray and lifeless.

"We don't want you dy'n on us... too soon." He chuckled.

"Why am I here?" I ignored his innuendo.

"Because you're a filthy whore of Satan, witch." He said
with detached serenity. He dipped his rag-covered fingers
deep inside the crevices of a medieval speculum. Its screw
key spread slowly with his fingers' girth. My hands began to
shake, but I would not let him see. *Stay on point.*

"Satan? I don't believe in Satan. I'm pagan." I tried to
argue reason. I knew it was a waste of time, but time was all I
had for now.

"What do you think those other 'gods' are? Satan has lied
to you, and you chose to fornicate with him like the whore
that you are." He walked up to the cage and leered at my
uncovered body with the speculum still in hand.

"Stop calling me a whore." Anger began to burn inside me,
but my power hit hard against the stone on my neck.

"That is what you are... whore, slut, harlot..." He got up
close to the bars of the cage.

I had the sudden urge to grab him and smash his head
against the bars, but the keys were hanging on the wall across
the room.

"Get away from her, you stupid boy!" Hopkins voice
bellowed. He grabbed Justin by his hair and thrust him to the
floor.

"She can't do noth'n." He dared me to try.

"Never underestimate the power of the witch. Even with
the faerie stone, she is dangerous." Hopkins looked into my
eyes and I did not look away. *I will find a way out and when
I do...*

Blackburne and Young came down the stairs and paid no
mind to the boy brushing dirt off himself.

"Young, put her in the Judas chair." Hopkins had a box
about the same size as August's in his gloved hand.

They looped a dog catcher pole around my throat and
forced me into the spiked chair. Its points dared my flesh to
split.

Blackburne tightened the straps across my wrist, chest
and legs. No punctures, but my skin grew taut over metal

pyramids.

They pushed the Judas chair in front of the table as Hopkins unlocked the box and revealed nine loose pages. They were from the Codex. The same ancient herb smell invaded my senses as it had at Belle's. I saw a sudden flash of my nightmare in the woods, the lights hunting me.

"Do you know what these are?" Hopkins asked.

"No." I answered, maybe too quickly.

He nodded, and Young tightened the straps on my legs. The sharp points pressed into my calves. I clenched my muscles, but soon realized if I relaxed, the spikes didn't hurt as much. *Deep calming breaths. Breathe in, breathe out.*

"Come, now. I know you have been working with that creature August."

I tried not to show my surprise at August's name.

"Do you know what these pages are?" He knew the answer. He was just trying to gauge me.

"No. Your kid's art project?" I prepared for a slap on my already aching face, but it did not come.

He only nodded again and Young pulled the straps tighter. The points began to pop my flesh.

I sucked air and felt pain but did not say a word.

"Do you know...?" He nodded at Young again and began to tighten the strap across my chest. *Pop!* Skin gave way to metal.

"Fuck you." I bit my bottom lip and concentrated to relax my body further. *Deeper breaths. Breathe in, breathe out. Breathe in, breathe out.* Unwanted tears began to roll down my face as the triangles bore into my back. *Pain is in the mind.* I wept to myself. I would not fail.

Hopkins was reading me closely but for what I didn't know. His expression shifted, and I knew a decision had been made.

"Get the thumbscrews." Justin was disappointed as he reluctantly put down the metal pear and retrieved them from the table. He quickly regained his perverse grin. "Wipe that smile from your face, boy. We are doing God's work!" Justin's face grew somber but his eyes couldn't hide his pleasure. A small vice like thing with a huge ornately designed screw was handed to Young.

"Do you know what this does? This is a thumbscrew. We place your finger in it and slowly tighten it to our liking. You ever smash you finger with a hammer?" Young grinned with sweaty teeth.

I instinctively curled my fingers in, but Young forced them straight, breaking my skin with his dirty, ragged fingernails. Blackburne mounted the screw on my right thumb.

"Why do you care if you tell us? They are vampires and lycanthropes. They are demons, not me and not you. You could save yourself. Be forgiven and accepted by God." Hopkins' accent curled through his words with compassion.

I remembered the demon lioness that Belle was just the morning before. Blackburne reached for the screw. I heard Wicked Wendy's voice in my frantic mind, "Those of us who have to fight for so much tend to make battles where there is no need for one. Save your energy for the real battles to come." I knew they already had the answer - *so why am I fighting?*

"It's the Codex." I gave up the answer and instantly regretted it as Hopkins smiled with self-satisfaction

"Yes it is. Do you know what the Codex is?" He already knew these answers. He wanted to show he had power over me, and for now he did.

"It's a Book of Shadows." My calves were twitching from the metal invading my skin.

"Justin, that is the devil's book of spells. This one has a very important spell. In particular, these pages." Hopkins turned to Justin.

I studied the pages silently. It had the same rudimentary drawings as the mother book, and the same mix of languages. I saw notes that were not much different than August's merged into the pages.

"Solomon' s Gate." His voice suddenly directed itself to me "and you, my 'good' woman, are going to help us decipher what has remained a mystery." Hopkins loomed over me, close enough for me to smell fresh frankincense and myrhh smothering his robes.

"And how am I supposed to do that?" I gritted my teeth.

"Bleed." His tone dropped, and sadism smeared across his face. "Your blood is the key."

"How?" I sneered.

"As I have the blood of Matthew Hopkins pumping through me, you have the blood of the Codex authors."

I had no witty quip or venom to share. *Authors? More than one?*

"Don't worry. We don't need much, for now."

My lips stayed sealed as Hopkins face glowed and turned hot with pleasure. Young and Blackburne stood aside with arms crossed waiting for their next order. Justin could barely contain his glee.

"We have the key to the Codex: you. We have been able, over several hundred years, generation by generation, to figure out some of its mysteries, but the true details lay hidden. I don't think even your 'friends' had a clue. Ironic, since their trade is blood. But we had a breakthrough with a witch who lived in the colonies a few hundred years back. Such a shame she died before we could get all the answers, but never mind that. We have you now, blood kin to the rogue monk who wrote it."

"How do you know that?" I challenged him.

"We were pointed to your book. Very interesting but a little juvenile, with exception of the protection ward, the exact same symbols, down to the last line." He glared down at me. "We had to run a little test to confirm what was told to us. You passed. God's grace was watching over us. He has guided us every step of the way. So God has sent you to us so we may save you and humanity."

He pulled from the depths of his robes, a long intricate

braid made out of human hair. It was raven black with complex beading and had been wax sealed at its ends.

"Your ancient grandmother's lock of hair was used as the bookmark for the Codex, her flesh for the pages. Your lineage was born of deviant devil worshipers who thought they could fool the Church. They were wrong, and they paid for their sins. Save yourself." His face grew dark.

I looked at the lock of hair and the pages and was overwhelmed by the knowledge that this was the flesh of my family. The dream dog's barking haunted me.

"Do you see the blood on the corners of the pages, Lydia?"

"Yes." I was half dazed.

"We just prick your finger, you place it on the page, and the secrets are revealed."

"What if I don't want to help you?"

"This spell is for the good of mankind. They have lost their way, and this is for them to find their way back. Solomon's Gate is the key to humanity's salvation."

"And who are you to know that? !" A sharp slap hit my cheek, but it was from Hopkins himself. His cool exterior faded, and red heat burned through him.

"I know better than some whore who sleeps with demon sluts," he snarled. "You will help us. And once the gate is open you will see. I am doing this to save you and all people." He believed it.

"Young." With Hopkins' orders, he came over to me and began to undo my collar.

"Don't get any ideas," Young said as he tapped the pouch around his neck. It was what all of them wore over their hearts, a charm bag.

The instant the stone detached from my neck a wave of intense frantic energy and blinding colors hit me overwhelming all of my senses. All my hair raised on end. *Pop! Pop!* The lightbulbs shattered, and darkness fell upon us.

I was disoriented but soon found my equilibrium and my inner powers centered. No one made a sound for a second or two, but I could feel their panic, even from Hopkins himself. Energy hummed in the air. Two flicks from a lighter produced a flame that barely lit more than the rough hand of Young.

A terrible squalling came from upstairs, the same person I had heard before. "See what is wrong with It."

Young made his way up the stairs. He left the door open which disjointed the darkness. I sat there feeling the blood from my calves pool around my feet. A shadow danced in the corner of my eye. We were not alone.

Justin's breathing began to hasten. I tried to feed on his surplus of energy but was blocked by whatever was around his neck. He started to run to the door. "Stop right there, boy!" Hopkins had heard him move.

Young came back downstairs with frantic fat steps and bright lanterns and chased the shadows away.

"It's freaking out!" Young yelled.

"Get her back in the cage now!" Hopkins flew up the stairs. I was hastily unstrapped, peeled off the spikes, and shoved back into my cage. I landed hard on my back against the steel bars, and they stomped their way up to the surface.

Howling continued joined by more yelling from my captors. Their voices were carried by a vent.

"We cannot afford these delays! The Crossing is in less than two weeks. And you! Acting like child afraid of parlor tricks! Was I wrong to think you were ready for this? Someone shut that thing up." The howls transformed to lunatic laughter.

Justin's voice was a strained pitch, and I couldn't understand his words.

"Stop picking on the boy!" The woman's voice demanded.

"You said she was weak and had no idea what she was doing." Young was no longer like an obedient crony.

"She is." Hopkins held his authority.

"It was a reflex from removing the stone." The woman answered his question.

"And you didn't tell us! She could have killed us like she

killed Stephen." Young was shocked.

"With the St. Benedict pouches you are perfectly safe. Now pull yourselves together." Hopkins demanded.

"What do you want me to do about Alex?" Blackburne finally spoke.

Who is that poor soul, Alex? What have they done to him? I had to find out.

"Don't say Its name." She warned.

"Feed it." Hopkins was done.

Hope was my only company in my little cage in the flickering darkness. That hope was born of their fear, their fear of me. It wasn't born of moral prejudice but of the reality of me. Their biting conversations dissolved into the cool air around me, and their dull steps gave me a sense of calm as I began to tell which steps belonged to whom.

My punctured calves had scabbed and bruised. My matted hair stuck to the wounds on my back and opened as I reluctantly pulled my hair away and up. *Wish I had Sky's elixir.*

A quick flit of a shadow in the corner of my eye. I reached out my mind into the blackness and felt a presence, a presence of curiosity, not of malice.

"Hello?" I tried to make contact. "Show yourself." I paused, still reaching in the depths of the room. Its energy was strong and focused.

Something hit the floor on the other side of the room. The room grew colder, but the furnace fire had not dimmed. My breath began to fog.

"I won't hurt you." I carefully drew a crude protection circle around me in the dirt. *Just in case...*

"My name is Lydia. What's yours?" I kept my energies calm and centered. A quiet washed over my senses and spirit. There was a shift in the atmosphere as the presence moved closer and quietly around the outside of my cage.

"What's your name?" With that I pushed a ball of energy into the room so it could be used by the spirit to manifest.

The usual tickle of my right inner ear began, as when something from the veil tried to speak to me. A rasping unearthly breath hit my ear, "Walker." My body shivered flesh to bone.

"Can you help me?" I couldn't give any more energy, I was still too weak.

I heard no answer. "Can you help me escape?" Silence except for the people above. "Please, can you help me escape?" A flicker in the room as something walked in front of the furnace's light.

"Please." I stood up and stepped out of the safety of my circle, and I pushed what energy I could into the room.

Chink! The cell key fell off the wall by the stairs. They were out of my reach. I didn't know if the spirit was trying to help me or mock me.

The door opened, and Blackburne came down with a stepladder. Justin walked behind with a flashlight. The intrusive light made my eyes ache.

My feet gently erased the circle before they took notice of it. I grasped the steel bars and watched them at work. They took great care to avoid my gaze.

"You know Hopkins is crazy. Casting that spell is not very Christian, if you ask me," I taunted.

"Shut up, witch, or you'll get no food. Justin, hold the ladder still." Blackburne threatened.

"Damn, and mushroom gloop is my favorite." I heard an ethereal giggle. Justin reacted as if he heard something, but quickly put it out of his mind.

Blackburne huffed as the last lightbulb was replaced. He began to situate himself to make his way down the couple of steps when the ladder was pushed abruptly over. He collided hard into Justin, both crashing the ground. "Boy, I told you to hold the damn ladder!" A childlike giggle filled my ears. I had an ally.

My body ached, and I smelled like sweat and dirt. The lump on my head had gone down but was still tender. The pockmark punctures were closed but inflamed. My blood had vulgarly solidified on the Judas chair's points.

I had been ignored except for food and soda. That was brought to me by only the woman. She did not acknowledge me no matter how I baited her. *It's been two days, maybe?*

Walker, the spirit, had not shown itself since it pushed over the ladder. I thought I could still feel its presence but wasn't sure of anything anymore. I continued to speak to the emptiness, but loneliness and worry infected me because I had only the night and the twisted depictions of the Hounds martyr Christ to keep me company. *All they know is suffering.* "Walker, are you there?"

Finally, Hopkins and his men visited me with grave intent. I sat curled in my corner and watched as they went about their plans. They placed candles strategically, then precisely displayed the pages across the table.

They had brought down two kitchen chairs and a light cotton gown. I was tossed the hand-me-down gown and told to put it on.

Blackburne opened the cage as Hopkins motioned to one of the chairs in front of the table. I suspiciously sat in the chair offered. *A new approach. Why?*

"Does the gown make you feel more comfortable?"

Hopkins sat next to me and gave a friendly expression that was unnatural to his features.

"Does it you?" I steeled myself for whatever was to come.

Young rolled out the tools and chose a three-inch blade. My eyes cut to the blade, and my heart began to quicken.

"We are just going to make a little cut, then you are going to touch the pages and you are going to tell us what you see."

"May I ask you a question first?" I remained still but could feel the buzzing of raw nerves from the two cronies.

"If I answer, will you do this without a fight?" Hopkins was calm and certain of himself.

"Yes." I knew I had no choice. I was going to have to do it either way.

"Okay. What is your question?"

"Who are you? Really."

His aura flashed bright yellow, then went back to its usual dark red core.

"I am Matthew Hopkins, The Witch-Finder General of the Hounds of Heaven. Those of my family have been hunters in the service to God almighty for hundreds of years, and the Church needs our help more than ever." His Italian accent became thick and sentimental.

"What help? Are you going to kill me? What are you...?" The questions fell out of my mouth.

He raised his gloved hand, "You have had your question answered. Now it is your turn to give me answers."

Six pages were laid in formation in front me. Four sheets were in the middle making a square, another was placed at the top, and the last one at bottom, the pattern making the shape of a crude diamond.

In the center of the Codex page diamond lay a complicated diagram with spiraling texts and a sketch of the six pages laid out in the same pattern. The other three papers were set off to one the side. Old blood stained the edges of the pages like rusted petals.

I turned quickly as I heard Justin and the woman come

down the steps. He had a small video camera and table tripod in his hands.

"What should I expect?" I watched the young man set up.

"It's a surprise." Hopkins said, but I could tell he didn't know exactly was what coming either. Worry threaded his aura, the same as the others.

The now-gloved woman came over to me nervously and vigorously washed my hands clean of dirt.

She quickly stepped to the side and gripped her pouch.

"Ready?" Hopkins asked everyone. Justin turned on the camera and nodded.

I hovered my hands over the pages and I could feel the same hum as I did with the book. The same pull called my flesh to come down.

I swallowed hard. "Yes." I was afraid, but I admit I wanted to do this. I wanted to know if this was real. I wanted to explore this connection to a book that has interrupted my life.

"Your hands?" Young politely asked. The nervousness of all those in the basement was palpable.

My heart pounded in my ears as I offered my shaking hands palm up. A flit crossed the walls. *Walker?*

"I will make it quick." Young's dark eyes focused on his goal. Walker's energy became frantic.

With a quick slice across my four fingertips, the blood fell to the sheets below. I watched for a forever second as my blood melted into the pages and diffused into the leathery flesh.

"Careful." Walker's cold breath slipped over my shoulder. My little hairs raised across my body.

I centered and grounded myself. *There is no going back. I must move forward.* I placed my tips onto the center page like a pianist about to play the concert of her life.

It started with a tug on the blood, then flesh, my energy and my very essence. I was being pulled down into the page itself. The spiral words dragged me deeper and deeper...

The room began to fall away, and I sunk into the pigments

and ancient flesh. I was beyond fear of death, and tried to fight it. I tried to pull myself out of the tunnel, but the more I struggled and fought, the more ferociously I was carried down into the swirl.

Violent flashes assaulted my eyes, faces I did not recognize, places I had never seen. My body was gone. I was floating in nothingness.

Whispers grew around me, not Walker's. The whispers turned into the screams of a woman. The shade parted, and she was naked on the rack. Her white flesh exposed, her belly revealing an angry scar. The wheels were turned by faceless men, one last scream and one last loud *POP!*

The flicker of torchlight quickly demurred into candlelight. Twin wax pillars sat on a plank wood table. Heavy smells of hay and animal feces befouled the air. A man, skinny and tall, hunched over an inkwell and parchment. Dark things danced around him, his bane. His orange-red hair was turning white and his skin was gray. He was lost in obsession. His fingers were bleeding, and his eyes were swollen.

I moved towards his works. Old notes, scrolls and several clay tablets with cuneiform were gathered with care. He was a man working out of madness. This was Thomas Chandler, my blood.

The room began to spin once again, and I was the axis. I was somewhere in the time I knew. I was on a bridge, and five creatures stood in its center. Red-cloaked figures marked a perimeter for a ritual.

Overhead the constant glow of a bold comet, followed by a meek sister, crossed the sky.

A portal opened, Solomon's Gate. It grew fierce and strong.

A horrid thing stood at the center. It came from the blackest pit beyond nightmares. The gatekeeper had a great ring on its bone claw. The ring fell with a loud clank, marked with Solomon's sigil. I saw a flash, Cerbina's stonelike face.

A dagger was hilt deep in monstrous muscle. Its great howl turned the winds into flame. The blade emerged weeping with black orchid tears.

My hands held rivers of its blood. My knuckles turned white against the grip of an ancient dagger, Solomon's seal etched deep into the bone handle.

Spinning. Pulling. Sinking.

I was sitting in a swing in a small park I knew from my teenage years, hidden on the side of Red Mountain in Birmingham.

The area was beautifully still like it used to be when I went to be alone. The cold nipped at my skin, biting hard on my ears and nose. The same steel gate I remembered stood ominously alone in the dark locked by Alabama Water and Power, daring access to the depths under the city.

It had always called to me, but now I could almost see the faces in the dark exhaling my name. I walked closer and saw what I had seen a hundred times in my youth, the huge pipes and valves of the utility companies. The same free water ran in its depths. A glint of steel seen in the nothingness.

Bam! My head hit hard on the basement floor. I had fallen and taken the chair with me. My body felt as if I had been beaten from the inside out. My head ached and my ears throbbed.

Young and Justin stood over me with a look of horror and disbelief. The middle-aged woman ran over to me, and Blackburne lifted me up while still in the chair.

The woman began to wash my face and hands. She dipped her shaking rag into her bucket, and I saw the familiar pink. I felt wrong, so very wrong, wrong on the inside, to my core.

Justin stopped recording. He looked too afraid to breathe, move, or think. Blackburne smacked him on the shoulder. Justin quickly ran upstairs.

My blurred vision found focus slowly. I had almost forgotten where I was. I sat there for a few minutes as the woman gave me water. I didn't care if it was opened then or an hour ago, poisoned or not. I already felt like poison was drifting through my veins, like cold acid.

Justin had returned with a laptop. He tried to insert the USB into the laptop, but the video was refusing to play. *Error message. Loading. Spinning hourglass. Error. Loading. Frozen.* Justin scratched his head absently. The elders were beginning to lose their patience.

"Matthew, we have an issue!" A man I had not seen slammed the door open.

"They're coming! They're coming!" The mysterious Alex shrieked...

Hopkins went up the stairs with a flurry of his robe. Moments later he called down into the basement. "Everyone get up here now. Make sure she is locked up." Young picked me up and hurriedly put me in the cell.

Blackburne locked the door and put the key in its place. Justin half-assed closed the laptop and ran up the stairs.

Many heavily hurried footsteps rushed overhead amid yelling and doors slamming. As quickly as the commotion started, it stopped.

I was weak and sore, unable to really move, but I tried to find a comfortable spot on the dirt floor. I was being watched. "Walker?"

A loud clack called my attention. The laptop had fallen to the floor landing on its side opening a little wider. The error message remained. A strange humming noise began, and my face jerked to life on the monitor. It seized and lurched.

I didn't recognize the person sitting in the chair. Yes, she had my red hair and my face, but that was only a mask. Her eyes were solid white with bloody webs stretched across the void. I had a squatter in my body in that moment. My stomach revolted at the image, I threw up suddenly and violently, clotted blood spattered on the ground. I wiped my mouth with the back of my hand.

"Blood, bone, flesh, will, spirit." Her voice was contorted, and her lips curled unnaturally. It repeated these words with twisted repetition. Hopkins had asked it something, but I couldn't make it out. The video was corrupted. Its stolen face began to bleed, first from its nose, followed by its dreadful eyes, blood finally escaping from its ears.

"The Crossing, the vessel, the ring... She knows the ring keeper."

Battery Low flashed on the screen, and the laptop turned off.

???

??? days until Solstice

I leaned my used body against the cool steel bars. The crackle of the furnace fire and its golden glow were the only beauty I could find in the gloom and filth. A prickly numbness touched my brain, like the pins and needles of a coma limb waking.

Optical fireworks exploded in my vision, ushering in a blinding migraine. Hot wet fell from my nose as I tasted metal.

Voices beyond my self echoed off the walls, voices I knew.

"David, to the right!"

"Hello! I'm down here!" I screamed out.

"Wait! No!" The same voice called out. *Delphine?*

"Anyone!" I tried to answer.

"Go!" Another voice. *Varrick?*

They were not in the house. These voices weren't material, they were riding the ether.

Faces burned into my mind like an atomic flash. A world covered in a Vaseline haze choked my thoughts.

A shotgun roared. Blood erupted. Teeth bared. Bodies fell, crumpling. David snatched the throat of young Justin. David's head exploded, his corpse still twitching.

"Stop!" But the vision didn't stop. I heard the dry laughter of Alex cracking through the walls of my dungeon, where my body stayed.

Devils in their true form, human and vampire alike, tore into one another with gruesome precision and pleasure. My mind stuck in an eternal loop of gruesome images of a grim battle.

The door crashed open, and my mind came back to my limp body. *How long was I gone?* I wiped the drool and blood from my face. My body and mind greeted each other unsteadily.

Young and Blackburne carried someone down the creaking stairs. It was a stout bald man with duct tape across his mouth. *Varrick.*

They hung him with the shackles mounted into the basement walls and tightened them till there was no movement possible. I stood cautiously and watched quietly as they hastily made sure everything was in its place.

"You have company." Young latched a bronze mask over Varrick's face. I could see only his closed eyes.

"What about the others?" The woman appeared and quickly made her way down. She picked up the laptop and placed it back on the table.

"The others are dead, and you see him here." Blackburne was holding a gaping wound on his forearm. "They took eight of us."

"We need to get you upstairs," she said.

"I'll meet you there in a minute, Mary." He waved her on.

"And the boy?" she asked,

"He didn't..." His face clenched so tight his jaw looked ready to shatter. Mary turned her hateful glare towards me.

"Woman, get going. I know there are others who need you upstairs."

"What happened?" I didn't let on that I knew Varrick.

"What do you think happened! Your devils sought you out!" Young slammed a crowbar against the cage, nearly hitting my fingers. I backed deeper into my box.

There was the pull of someone watching me, and I glanced over to meet Varrick's silver eyes glowing behind the medieval mask. I didn't want them to know Varrick was watching so I was sure not to let my gaze linger.

"And don't you worry about your friend here. The faerie stone works on all of Satan's abominations." Young headed up stairs and Blackburne followed.

"Abominations? That's a big word for you." I quipped. "Can you spell that?"

Young started to turn around and come after me. Blackburne caught his arm. "You make it too easy for her. We will have our time." They slammed the door shut and bolted it.

I turned my attention to Varrick. None of his wounds were healing. He did not stir, nor did he seem to have the will to move.

"Is there anybody else?" I asked.

He shook his head "no" weakly.

I heard the Hounds of Heaven gathering their remaining numbers in their meeting room over my vent.

"It's that bitch's fault! She needs to pay." Young was overrun with emotion.

"We need her." Hopkins maintained his calm cool demeanor.

"We can get another witch." Young challenged their leader.

"She is the only one who knows where the ring is." Hopkins was losing patience with his insolence. "The book will speak to her alone."

"Can we even trust what we saw?" Young pushed on.

"Yes, we will get our answers tomorrow. Tonight we need to fortify and rest." Hopkins asserted his leadership.

A crash was heard on the opposite wall. Broken glass rained down on the floor as heavy steps disappeared across the house. *The ring? Solomon's ring. Cerbina.*

Another night of stressful sleep was interrupted by Young banging on the cage door. Young's purple maddened face dripped contaminated sweat. Blackburne stood at the base of the steps watching Varrick hang like art on the wall imitating their eternally suffering martyr.

I knew what they wanted. I hoped to dissolve in the dark corners of my jail, but I knew I wouldn't be able to avoid what was to come. If I told them what they wanted to know, they would most likely kill me. It would be better than torture, but if I told them, goddess knows what they would bring into this world. I can't let something like that be set loose. Not when Ember, my daughter, could suffer a worse fate than mine if she lived through it. *I must fight. I must hold on.*

Young dragged me out by my hair. *If I could just touch him...*

Varrick began to struggle against his chains, but he couldn't break them. His mercury eyes burned as Young and Blackburne tied me in the middle of the room again, arms over my head, my legs spread. With great violence Young ripped my sliver of a gown off.

Blackburne shoved some metal rods into the furnace as Young rolled out the leather pouch and tools. I prepared myself. *Breathe in, breathe out.* I tried to find my center.

"Tell us where the ring is." Blackburne demanded grimly.

"I don't know what you're talking about." Young slapped

me hard, harder than before. He was angry, so very angry. Heat pulsed from him.

"Solomon's ring. Where is it, Ms. Keening?" Blackburne drew close, only inches from my face. The odor of iodine reeked from his fresh wounds and bad breath invaded my nose.

"How would I know?" I braced for another slap.

"Because the Codex told you. We know it did." Young growled while he stoked the flames.

"No, it didn't. It just showed me the monster you would be calling."

"Monster? The only monsters here are this thing," Young spit and slammed Varrick's head hard back into the wall, "and you."

"Vampires and werewolves are worshiped as idols of lust in movies and TV. The demons who lurk in men's hearts are welcomed and encouraged. We have fallen away from God, and we are here to help people see their wayward path."

"By bringing a demon into this world?"

Blackburne chuckled. "You think small."

"You're all fucked in the head."

"*Enough!*" I received another hard slap across from Young, and my jaw popped out of place. "Tell us what your vision was."

"No," I growled, my head ringing.

"Fine, I like the hard way." Young unhooked a knotted flogger from his belt.

A hard hit went across my back. A thud followed by a harsh sting. Its raw tendrils wrapped and bit into my stomach and ribs.

I grunted loudly with the punch of the weight of leather. I bit down on my tongue to give me a focus. Tears welled as another brutal hit crossed my back. The heat from the first strike added to the next.

"Tell us where the ring is, Ms. Keening"

I refused and only grunted with the pain. Another hit

clawed into my breasts. I screamed out and tears gathered but did not fall.

"Where is the ring, Ms. Keening?" Blackburne stood caught Young's hand. "I'm sure you can feel a renewed passion in Young's throws. It's only going to get worse."

"I don't know where the ring is," I cried, my tongue bleeding. "I don't even know what the ring is!"

"Tell us what you do know."

I dropped my head and heavily shook "no."

The flogger lacerated my flesh again and again, and I couldn't help but scream with every blow. They were steady and unrelenting. My entire body was a raw nerve.

"I don't know!" I lied. *I must hold on to the lie.* It was my only anchor of sanity.

"*Tell us, witch!*" Young screamed. He was losing himself. Another string of wild uncontrolled hits. Stray straps ripped my face.

"Fuck you!" I growled. I channeled the pain into barbed hatred. I focused on Varrick. His eyes burned with the same power and pain.

Young threw down his flogger and punched me in the stomach. I lost my breath. I hacked and coughed, trying to find air again. Blackburne stepped in and pushed Young back, silently scolding him for losing control.

"Where's Hopkins?" I snarled. The lights began to flicker, and the air began to turn electric.

"Not here. He had more pressing matters. Why?" Blackburne asked.

"I think he would be disappointed in his minions losing to a woman, a heathen woman no less. Pathetic." I spit watery blood on the floor. *Hit me again Young! Do it!*

Young began to run at me, but Blackburne barely caught him. "Sit down!" Blackburne ordered.

"So you think your tough kicking my ass? I had harder hits when I was in middle school." My lips swelled and tore.

Young broke through and punched me in my face.

Everything went bright white then black for a split second. My eye socket and cheek throbbed.

"Pussy," I taunted again. I coughed up some more blood. *Knock me out, you son of a bitch!*

Young caught himself from coming at me again. He and Blackburne knew what I was trying to do. He was furious at Young; only his reddened eyes gave it away.

"I will never tell you sick bastards." My ears rang, my eye swelled shut.

"Fine. Let's try something new." Blackburne's calmness scared me more than Young's rage. He went to the furnace and pulled out a red poker.

"Tell me about the vision. Anything to do with the ring would be helpful, Ms. Keening."

I was shaking scared, but I centered my stare to the far wall and prepared myself. *Breathe in, breathe out.*

I didn't feel it at first, only heard the sizzle. Then the burning smell and searing pain came. "Fuck you! You sons o' bitches!" The lights flickered.

Young got the other poker. I heard the sizzle, then felt the pain. I choked more garbled profanities.

Young came only inches from my face, I could taste his foul breath. He pressed the iron to my breast. I let out a guttural howl.

"Let's clean the filthy whore!" He put the iron to my cunt. I cried out till my voice was broken glass. The light shuttered again.

I focused all my rage on him and willed him pain that Hell would envy, but the pouch around his neck spared him. My will crashed against its shield.

"Walker, help me!" I begged and pleaded. I pushed out any energy I could and gave it to Walker.

"Walker?" Young looked and Blackburne. "How does she know where we are?"

I was spent on the ropes; I had nothing left in me.

"Never mind that. She's a witch. That is what they do,

speak to devils." Blackburne walked over to the bag of tricks and brought out the needle he had used before.

He leaned down to my foot and looked up at me. "One last time before we get nasty. Where is the ring?"

"Eat. My. Fuck." I answered him.

"Such a lady." Blackburne thrust the needle under my big toenail. It was as if I had never had pain in my life till that moment, words fell short. It ripped through me, and I cried out louder and farther through this world and the next. I burst into tears and sobs.

"Again?" He asked. Young even cringed.

I sobbed and shook my head "no." Again the indescribable pain pierced through the other corner of my toenail. "Stop! *Stop!*" I cried, my body shaking uncontrollably.

"Ms. Keening, where is the ring?"

"I don't know." *Must hold on to the lie for Ember.*

Another needle slid under my toenail, and I screamed out, "*Cerbina!!*" Before I could stop myself, my voice betrayed my mind. The horror of what I had just done washed over me. *What have I done! Please, Hekate, no!*

"Cerbina?" Blackburne looked confused.

"The maid?" Young asked.

How do they know who she is? Please don't ask me... please just kill me. I'm so sorry. I was sick with guilt.

"It's the blood demon's servant." Blackburne and Young confirmed with each other. They had been keeping tabs on all of us. *How? They must have someone on the inside.*

I started to go cold though my body dripped with sweat. He withdrew the needle invaders and placed them on the leather pouch. I started crying uncontrollably.

Both men headed upstairs, Young took one last lingering look. I dared not look up at Varrick. I was too ashamed. I was not strong enough.

I just hung there and silently wept, each salty tear stung my wounds. My body was beaten and burned. I had nothing left. I deserved this. I loathed myself.

I heard a thud of something falling on the floor above me. Young came swaggering down the stairs.

"We aren't done."

I looked for Blackburne to follow behind him. "He ain't coming to save you. Hopkins has the information he wanted. Now you're mine. I can't just kill you." his yellow teeth snarled.

"Why are you...?" I was too weak to continue, my spirit broken.

"Why? Because your friends..." he slammed his fist into Varrick's stomach. Varrick groaned. "killed my nephew to save a worthless piece of flesh like you, Lydia. A whore. A filthy dirty whore."

He had gone mad, his eyes wild and soulless. Foam gathered at the corners of his lips as they twitched with every word.

"I told you all I know," I weakly lied.

"I don't care," he menaced. "After I deal with you. I will be serving some punishment on your friend here." He gave another blow to Varrick's ribs. "Think he can help you? He is as helpless as a kitten." With that, he sunk a large blade into Varrick's chest.

"Don't worry, he won't die. It's really not that easy to kill vermin like vampires, but the faerie stones makes sure he feels everything nice and proper." He started chuckling to himself. He had lost it.

"I'm sorry Justin died." I tried.

"Don't!" He had tears bubbling. He smelled of old sweat and drink. Tremors violently rocked through me.

He slowly danced the knife against my face as he held my head in place. He kissed me. His rough beard scratched off layers of skin, and my broken lip began to bleed again. My damaged jaw popped and cracked.

"Maybe you just don't know what it is to be a good woman. A good woman serves her man. A good woman doesn't fornicate with she-devils." His spittle hit my face. "You need to know your place, witch, servicing a man's needs. If you had been on your knees to God and a husband... you wouldn't be here."

A hard swell of dread smothered my chest. He licked his lips, he cut my binds, and I collapsed on the floor. My body and my sex were still wounded. He lifted me up, and I seethed. The lights began to flicker furiously.

He threw me hard, stomach first, onto the table. I could not find air, but I found his St. Benedict's pouch in my hands. I smiled.

He rushed in behind me, crushing my hips against the table. I managed to turn around as he struggled to pull down his pants. Fueled on fury and will, my auric shield claimed brute force and shoved him across the room. He crashed into Varrick. Varrick tried to grab him but failed.

A new power surged through me, a dark stillness. "You want to know what a witch can do? Let me show you." The bulbs popped; shards rained down to the floor.

I raked my fingers across the air in front of me and his stomach flesh tore open. He started to run upstairs. I closed the door and locked it with one clear thought.

"No running. Show me what kind of man you are. Put me in my place." I growled. A hot and icy wind swirled in the basement.

"Thank you. I had never believed this power existed, but

you have proved me wrong. And now I am going to use it, on you." My voice was cold. Pain shot up through my body with every step, but it only fueled me more. He backed away.

"Don't you want me anymore?" I could see the visible shaking of his hands.

He ran towards me and grabbed my neck. He crushed me against the cage bars with a loud slam. The lock bit into my raw flesh. I dug my thumbs into his eyes. He slammed me again and again against the cage.

I tapped into his aura and I began to purposely pull all that I could. The lights flickered. I felt his rage, his fear, his pain. His massive hands crushed my throat. My face became tight, I couldn't breathe, but I didn't care. I stole his energy, more and more. His grip weakened, and still I took more.

He pulled out his knife, and I flung it away with a thought. I pushed off the cage with my feet, and we slammed into Varrick. Varrick let out a groan. His eyes had transformed to their demonic state.

I looked into Varrick's face, and I called the knife to my waiting hands. I punctured Young's flesh and slit his belly wide.

Varrick and I shared in the intimacy of Young's death, connected by something truly primal. I stepped away, and Young collapsed to the ground.

His life force pumped through me. I was charged to the point of overload. The material world lost definition, and I found myself in a world of only energy once again.

Metal keys dropped to the floor. I grabbed them like a drunk and stumbled over to the chained vampire. "Thank you," I whispered to Walker.

"Be good," I warned Varrick. I still vividly remembered the speakeasy. My horror of what he was still lingered.

I reached behind him and unscrewed the bronze mask. It hit the floor with a hard clank. I ripped the duct tape from his mouth; he spit the stone out and let out a fierce growl. His eyes were bright and heated as his wounds began to heal slowly. I unlocked his ankles and then used Young's oozing corpse as a stepstool to unlock Varrick's wrist chains.

I stepped down from Young, picked up the forgotten laptop, and went up the to the top of the stairs with a very weak Varrick.

I tried the door, but it was still locked. I tried the other keys, but they did not work. "I think I broke the lock." Varrick tried to break the door down but was too wounded. "Walker, can you help us?"

Click. The door unlocked. "Thank you."

"Walker?" Varrick whispered.

"I'll tell you later."

He and I cursed the sunlight as we made our way into the overexposed world above. The musty smell of the basement gave way to the pungent aroma of chemical flowers. My senses were peeled, wounds gaping and raw. Auric colors were the only hint at boundaries to the forgotten world. Varrick, still weak, began to heal as only a vampire could. Curdled metallic slurry wept from his wounds. My wounds would need time and treatment.

Blackburne was laid out on the kitchen floor with his cell phone next to him. Young had knocked him out cold. Apparently, Young had planned not to be interrupted.

"I'll get the phone. You take his clothes." Varrick hobbled over to him.

Luckily, Blackburne was a thin man, and I was able to strip him down to his boxers. His shoes were a little big, but that was all the better for my swollen bloody toes.

"Blackburne's last text." Varrick held the prepaid phone so I could read, "Ring. Cerbina the servant, Belle Mansion." My shame drowned me.

He immediately made a call. "August? Varrick. The Hounds might be coming for Cerbina. I'm not sure. Something to do with a ring. Meet you at the spot."

11:20AM glowed from the microwave. *Funny the simple things you miss.* Varrick's body shifted to feed, but then he stopped very suddenly. "There is something in his blood.

Foul," he grimaced.

"I think I know what it is." My body vibrated from Young's energy, but something was growing dim inside me.

On the kitchen table were the usual trappings of an herbalist, but a line had been crossed from naturalist to witchcraft. Colloidal silver was being used as a base mix in an herbal concoction. There was a mystery mineral in one of the stone mortars. It smelled slightly like a penny with a strange heavy after scent of something else. My head began to spin and my power began to get smothered. "I think they were dosing themselves with the "faerie stones." Or should I say 'dust'?"

He took a sniff and turned green. "Yes, I would agree. We should take this back with us. August might have something in his books."

"Way ahead of you." I wrapped the herbs and stones in a leather satchel that lay idle on the kitchen table.

The screen door opened, and a key scraped into the back door lock. It was the blonde woman, Mary. She jiggled the old lock with some frustration.

Varrick disappeared. My broken body was barely able to hide behind the dividing wall.

Mary walked in juggling grocery bags and bumped the back door closed with her hip. A crunching thud sounded as she dropped everything and ran to Blackburne's side. She began to reach for her cell phone with shaking hand, but was met with the swift blur of Varrick holding her in his claws. Her sobs became silent, but the tears still fell.

I limped out of hiding. "How dare you wear his clothes!" She hissed. Varrick tightened his grip.

"Do we have any questions?" He rubbed his face against her veined neck. "You haven't dosed today, have you?" His fangs extended from their gum sheaths. His silvery eyes melted into blood and mercury.

I felt a flicker of fear at his shift, but it soon gave way to the growing numbness within me. I found my heart beating cold for her.

"Where is Hopkins?" I leaned in close.

"Never." she fought back.

"I said that once, too." I flatly told her.

He inhaled her. He slowly scraped his teeth against her flesh. "I am so very hungry." A horrid snarl displayed his weapons.

"Kill me, then!" she defied. Bright strips of red angry energy sliced and swirled around her body. She would die before giving her people up. I gave a shake of my head, and Varrick knew what he had to do to get our answers.

"I will feed, but you will not die. No, I will make you into a vampire, and you will serve The Bahlael." He seethed. I knew he was lying, but she didn't. Her aura turned a bright sickly yellow white.

"You wouldn't let him do that!!" She pleaded. She went pale, and her breath labored.

I chuckled to myself. "You said you had God to protect you. Why don't you try praying?" I ripped off her St. Benedict's pouch and put it with our collection. He sank his teeth very slowly into her flesh. I was about to give up my bluff.

"He is at the bridge!" Her voice cracked. Varrick withdrew, but he held her firmly. I could see him straining not to kill her. He wanted her. Her wanted her blood. He needed it.

"What bridge?" I asked curtly.

"Hell's Gate Bridge in Oxford." She began to cry with shame. I knew her pain. She betrayed herself as I had.

"Why?" He saw that my resolve turning to ash.

"It's a portal spot for the ritual. That's all I know."

"And the faerie stone?" I regained myself. She started to fight again. *We are running out of time. Others will show up soon.* "Varrick is feeling very peckish."

"It's a special kind of hematite known to keep tween and Cthonic creatures at bay." Her energy was a vivid yellow with absolute desperation. Varrick was turning. He couldn't hold back much longer.

"How many men does Hopkins have?"

Varrick's features contorted into the primal devil I had seen before. He dug deep into her flesh and began drinking her in.

"No!" I helplessly called out. She didn't even get to scream.

The brutality of his thirst was not romantic or sensual; it was raw dark hunger. His eyes never left mine. He shared his kill as I had shared mine. I was locked in that moment with him as her life energy dimmed into obscurity. I envied her release from her betrayal.

A jolt of warning went through me. *Walker?* "We have to go," I told Varrick, breaking his spell. He dropped her without remorse or care.

"Help me! *Help me!* Don't *leave!*" A broken child's voice yelled from the back of the house.

Alex? I had forgotten about the poor kid who I had heard screaming throughout the days in my hurry to leave it all behind.

"What is that?" Varrick asked suspiciously.

"Another victim of the Hounds of Heaven. We have to save her." I was worried that time was running out. Blackburne was going to wake up and others will surely be coming home soon.

"Her? Are you sure?" Varrick was right. The voice was not clear. There was something off about it, yet it was familiar.

"We have to go get her... him... Does it matter? Let's go."

"There is something not right about this. *Its* voice does not sound..." He held my arm in a weak gesture of protest.

"*Please don't leave me!*" The voice was now clearer and more feminine.

I grabbed Mary's truck keys, which had never left her hand, I shoved them and her supplies from the table into a grocery bag. I headed towards the back of the house with burning focus.

Varrick silently followed me as I went down a small paneled hallway. He was not alone in his uneasiness. The splinters of unease dug into me as well, but I was compelled to ignore them.

"Please! I'm back here!" The voice tapped into my maternal need to find and protect the child.

The *wrongness* sat in the air. The colors of the world began to decay and tinge black. *What have The Hounds done to her?*

"Help me! I'm scared."

"We're coming. Where are you?" I called out against Varrick's quiet warning.

"Something doesn't smell right. You see it? Don't you?" Varrick challenged my conviction.

"We have to help her. She is just a kid."

"Is she? Because I smell no child." He answered gravely.

"Mommy?"

"Ember?" *Was that my daughter's voice?* My heart jumped and sank. "I'm coming! Mommy's coming!" I ran forward, ignoring the darkness enveloping the hall.

I stopped suddenly in front of a room with six padlocks lining the doorframe. I raised my hand to the door, which had the protection seal of Solomon etched into its wood, a close variant from the one in my book. My fingers hovered inches away. I felt the wall of the seal, but there was something behind it. Something I had never experienced before. *What...?*

"Mommy? Are you there? I need you. I'm hurt." A tearful sob. The icy chill of nightmares passed through me.

"Mommy? !"

"I'm coming! Varrick , I need your help. Rip these off."

"No. That is not your daughter." He tried to reason with me. "What do you feel behind that door?" I was distracted by Ember's sobbing. "Lydia! Look at me. What do you feel behind the door?"

"Help me!"

"Lydia, what do you feel? What are the odds your daughter is behind that door?"

"*I have to try!*"

"Run. Run *now!*" Walker's astral airy voice found us in the depths of the hallway. The walls began to vibrate. Pictures began to fly off the walls, and bulbs exploded.

The voice behind the door began to crack and howl. "Save me! *Save me now, you stupid bitch! This is your fault!*"

"Listen to the goddamn ghost! Let's get the fuck out of here!" He threw me over his shoulder.

"You're weak! Pathetic whore! You deserve to die! Your daughter hates you! You left her! You abandoned her! *You are NO mother!*"

I began to cry uncontrollably as utter despair opened an abyss in my heart. Varrick crashed through the house and was about to go out the front door when Walker screamed "Back!"

"You are a *monster!* A whore and a killer! *Witch! Burn the Witch!*" the voice cackled.

Varrick, without hesitation, followed the ghost's orders and went for the back door. He found the same truck in the yard that had brought us both there. He took the keys I had found and began to head to "the spot."

My shattered heart watched the side mirrors as the dilapidated farm house disappeared in the distance. A faded sign was its last goodbye, "Walker Farm Est. 1884".

Fall was turning into winter. A blur of barren trees passed as Varrick weaved in and out at a steady pace on the interstate. The smell of musk and Blackburne from my borrowed clothes filled my nostrils . The voice from behind the door echoed in my mind, slowly driving me mad.

"I let everyone down. I wasn't strong enough." I was barely audible to human ears.

"Pathetic!" it accused.

"You withstood more than most. The woman, she broke with a threat of an idea. Everyone has their breaking point." His gravel voice was miles away. A cold numbness made its home within me. "What does Cerbina have to do with the ring?" He tried to reach me.

"Lydia? What does Cerbina have to do with the ring?" He asked more forcefully.

"I don't know. I had, I guess, a vision of the ritual and the ring." I shuttered at the fiend I saw. The emptiness. "There was the ring, and then I saw Cerbina. I just know they're linked somehow." I didn't have the will to talk.

"You're weak! Pathetic whore! You deserve to die! Your daughter hates you! You left her! You abandoned her! You are NO mother!"

The familiar pins and needles crawled across my skin, and I found myself standing outside The Belle Mansion. Those who had taken shelter there were making their way to their cars for a quick departure. Rummer and Delphine guarded Cerbina on the way to a champagne colored SUV.

Hopkins' men were on their way and not far. I called out to Rummer and Delphine to hurry, but they couldn't hear me. They split to different roads across the countryside, all planning to meet at the "spot."

In the distance over the winding hills, the Hounds of Heaven closed in. I tried to warn them. There was a loud crash as an old rust bucket of a truck collided with the champagne SUV.

"Lydia!" Varrick grabbed my arm as I was slammed back into my body, my heart beating out of my chest and white-knuckled grip on the dash.

Where am I?

"Are you okay? We're here."

"They got Cerbina." I tried to take deep breaths and to find my center once again.

"Are you sure?"

"Yes. I saw it." He watched me intently, and he knew I was telling the truth.

"Welcome to The Den of the Black Paws. We'll see what the others have to say." We were parked in a clearing amongst four cabins in the middle of thick Southern wood.

"Where are the others?" There was no movement or sound. I was too spent to see with my third eye. The dark whispers were still with me, but I focused on what was before us.

"Stay here." He got out of the car and transformed into his dark self as he searched the dying light of the forest.

A low bestial growl vibrated through the car windows. Six pairs of hot glowing eyes peered from the darkness. Something large moved from behind, and another seven pairs of eyes appeared.

One of the beasts stepped into the dappled light with heavy steps. It was the largest wolf I had ever seen. It must have weighed easily a hundred and fifty pounds. With hackles raised, it directed its attention toward Varrick.

Varrick held his arms out wide, teeth snarled just like the wolves. I could do nothing but watch these fierce creatures.

"Monsters! Abominations!" The little girl's voice would not be silenced.

The black wolf sniffed the air and then changed its posture immediately. Its stiff bristled tail dropped and it covered its teeth. Varrick responded by retracting his posture as well.

The great wolf shook its body as if it was covered with water, and the sound of vertebrae popping like a firecracker revealed Sky naked, her tribal tattoos fresh and beautiful, her long hair barely covering her small breasts.

The others began to step out of the woods. They weren't just wolves. Some stood on two legs with dark skin and coarse sparse fur, an infernal hybrid of human and beast. None changed to their human form. Sky silently motioned toward the largest silver-back, and they all melted silently back into the pine and oak.

I got out of the truck with a whimper — my wounds had begun to stick to my clothes. My face was tender with every unconscious expression shown. The pain made the dark whispers fade, if only temporarily. Sky came up to me with worry and a gentle hand.

"Where are the others? Cerbina?" Varrick asked as he looked for his people among the Black Paws.

"They haven't shown up. I happened to be here checking on the kids when I got the news. They should have been here by now." She frowned.

"When were they due?" He and Sky started to help me into the house.

"About an hour ago. I thought it best to hold down the camp than to go looking. I sent the young ones to stay with family. The rest are keeping watch." Sky placed her hands on my broken body and exchanged a charged look with Varrick. I missed a step and cried out in pain. "Let's get you washed up and fed."

The magick of her transformation barely registered with

me as I was still lost in my eternal loop. *"Pathetic whore! You are weak!"* I secretly pressed on my wounds. The pain helped me focus on the external world and not the void trying to consume me.

We went to the largest of the cabins. They peeled off my shirt, and it opened my wounds afresh. My toes were infected and swollen.

Sky looked on the verge of tears from rage. I stood naked in front of them and the mirror with no shame, tired and detached. My body was knotted and angry, my face misshapen and purple. Old brown blood stained my pale skin. My back was covered in wide open wounds. The scratch I had gotten from the house cleansing was no more than a small white scar. *What happened? How long has it been?*

"You got what you deserved."

I took a long, hot shower and let my blood dissolve into the clear water. I closed my eyes, pushing my head under the faucet and drowning out all noise within and throughout. My mind was closing down. I lost myself to the emptiness and welcomed the unnatural calm inside me. I was thankful the whisper had faded.

I was allowed to stay in the master bedroom as Sky meticulously cleaned and treated my wounds. I remained quiet, barely even there, staring at the walls. Pictures of the family and pack were displayed proudly. A particular picture held my mild interest. It was Grey, no more than five, sitting on his mother's back in her wolf form, a beautiful picture of love and subtle magick.

"How are you doing, Lydia? You're safe." She tried to reach me. I could smell wet earth on her. Skinwalkers have such a distinct smell, something purely of the elements.

"You're one of us, family." Sky added. I looked into her dark eyes but felt nothing, emotionless.

"I know that you saw the vampires feeding." She adjusted her robe as she second-guessed herself in continuing the conversation.

"I failed. I was weak. I told them what they wanted to know. Stop taking care of me. I deserve this." I pushed her away and curled in a ball on the bed.

"Will she be okay?" Varrick wasn't cold or distant like he usually was. Sky nodded.

Varrick sat down on the bed. "Lydia, you are a fighter, a warrior. I am glad you are on our side."

"Am I?"

"If you are not on theirs, you are on ours. You don't have a choice. I have decided I like you and you are not allowed to go." He had a very dry smile.

"I'm just a human," I imitated his disgust from back at Belle's home.

"You are a witch," he said proudly. "Pretty bad ass one at that."

A great number of howls bellowed through the air, and Sky stood up saying, "They're here." I reluctantly threw on one of Sky's sundresses and made my way slowly out to the cabin's porch.

Some of vehicles from my vision slammed and skidded to a stop as a demon wolf form of a lycan chased behind. The champagne SUV wasn't among them.

"August, where is everybody else?" Sky asked.

"Grey's with Joy. They should be here shortly. Bill is missing," August, his clothes covered in blood and gore, answered her as he opened the door to his car and started to help people out. Sky didn't let the others see her concern, but it screamed at me.

Delphine looked immobile, she had burn holes all over her body. Otto and Laughing Dog were clumsily pulling Rummer out of the little sports car. His wounds were similar to Delphine's. A fierce battle had been fought, but I could not name the winners.

"What happened?" Sky tied her hair back.

"A shotgun." Laughing Dog was bewildered.

"How is that even possible?"

August looked furious. His eyes, shifted to his shadow side, sent a chill through me.

Sky started barking orders, getting everyone organized and telling her people to continue guarding the perimeter.

Bjorn and Anna Belle stepped out of his red Corvette. Their eyes shifted, teeth free and bodies moving with predatory purpose. My guts twisted into knots, a reminder of why I tried to run.

Everyone was heated from the battle, but when Anna Belle saw me her features found their beauty. She put her hand on my face like she had when I first saw her, but this time her hands were hot to the touch. I pulled away in distaste.

"They did this to you?" She growled.

"I'm fine. Take care of your people." My lip split open again.

"Lydia!" Varrick called for me to come back into the house. Delphine and Rummer were laid out in a child's bedroom on twin beds. Rummer's body was barely able to fit. "Is this...?" He lifted up a cloth covered in a mix of blood and something like metallic shavings.

"Demons and devils! Hopkins is right!" The child's voice broke its silence.

I took the rag and knew at once it was crushed faerie stone. "Yes." I forced myself to wake up and function. I refused to hear the voice again and willed the fog of hopeless numbness to clear. *I will have time to be broken tomorrow.* A new surge of focus charged through me. "Make sure people wear gloves. August, I need to know anything and everything about faerie stones. I think it's some kind of alchemic bastardization of hematite."

"It sounds familiar. Let me get my books from the car." August moved too quickly for me to see.

"We have stuff in the truck that could help." Varrick followed him out.

Howling began again. I looked for Sky's reaction. "It's Grey." Her face softened into some relief, but she continued her work with the wounded. I heard the motorcycle pull up a good minute later. I went outside to meet them. Grey was driving, and Joy was riding bitch, holding Grey tightly.

"What happened?" Sky appeared on the porch behind me.

"We had some trouble shaking them." Grey answered his mother while grabbing the saddlebags off his bike. "Is dad or Rummer here?" His was more like a man than a boy at that moment.

"Rummer's inside." Her face was grim. "We don't know where your father is."

Joy came up to me and grimaced in thinly veiled disgust. "What happened to you? Sorry about the woods. I got lost and went back to Anna Belle's." she answered. "Everyone was really worried about you. So what happened?"

"I was kidnapped and then tortured," I answered flatly.

"Are you okay?" Grey asked. I didn't know the answer to that question. Grey leaned over and gently hugged me. "I'm so glad you came back to us."

"Are you good with computers?" I asked avoiding any sticky feelings.

"I do okay." He was worried about me like everyone else.

"Good. I need you to get into a computer. I think you will able to read the memory card on your own system."

"Meeting in ten." Varrick announced.

"Okay. Let's begin with who's missing." Sky was taking the lead, and Anna Belle stood silently beside her. The light smell of the cabin wood and stew cooking made welcome to the unusual collection of the worn and frustrated beings who gathered. The silhouettes of our protectors weaved throughout the forest in the dying light of the day beyond the framed windows.

We all had looked better what seemed forever ago. Anna Belle was not sparkling but held a somber tone. No longer wearing gowns and heels, she wore blue jeans and boots, ready for a fight like most who gathered here. She was still beautiful despite my misgivings.

Only Joy maintained her fashion forward priorities. Her hair was only slightly disheveled, and her glittery bow had begun to sag. She still wore her Lolita punk style with impunity. She was a cotton candy jewel in a room full of sobriety.

"Telal, Cerbina, and Bill." August raked his hand through his hair. "We know that they took Telal and Cerbina. We are not sure where Bill is."

Sky steeled herself. "What about the wounds of Delphine and Rummer?"

"They're caused by something called a faerie stone. I think they crushed it up and used it like rock salt. It is very strong and keeps people like us from using our... advantages." *Like us.* I fondled the smooth hematite like rock within the leather pouch. "I think their bodies are rejecting it, pushing it out, but it is going to be slow."

"David got shot with the same stuff, but point blank. He didn't make it." Varrick spoke as a general. Belle held August in silent comfort. All I could clearly remember of David beyond his orange hair was his lust for a dead girl in his arms.

"If it's not a head shot it only hurts like hell and paralyzes. With time and care they should be fine." Varrick raised his shirt, revealing his chiseled ivory abs with bright red scars that were severe wounds less than a twelve hours ago. "Although I am not sure how it reacts to shifters."

"Do you think they're keeping hostages at the farm?" Bjorn asked.

"We should send someone out there," Otto interjected.

"No. They seem to know what we are doing before we do. Besides, we have some information about a bridge in Oxford." Varrick was working something over in his mind.

"There was a girl..." I started to say, but I lost my will.

"A girl?"

"I'm not so sure it was girl or even human." Varrick warned. "Let's get our information together, rest and make a plan. We took a collection of notes and journals from the farmhouse that we need to start sifting through. If they wanted them dead, they would be or are. Either way we cannot afford to go in blind again. They have a time table and goals bigger than just picking a fight."

"Agreed." Sky ground her teeth. "Grey will be working on the computer that Lydia and Varrick brought."

"Why, Cerbina?" Laughing Dog finally spoke.

"I had vision of a ring, and then I saw her face... and they made me tell them." A hard knot swelled in my throat. *"Weak and pathetic!"* The unwordly voice from my captivity screamed inside my head.

Varrick placed his hand on my shoulder to show his support. This did not go unnoticed by the others. They had never seen him ever give sympathy. They witnessed the Hounds of Heaven's persuasion on my flesh. The room stayed quiet for a moment.

"Cerbina is just the help," Joy finally found something to say. Her perfect makeup and cute outfit made a seed of resentment grow inside me as my pulsing pain remained strong and steady. "Belle, how long has she served you?" Laughing Dog asked.

Anna Belle searched her memories. "She had been passed down to me by my sire and his before him. She had been a part of our house through generations of vampires, but I am ashamed to say I do not know her origins."

Generations of Vampires? What is a generation to them? I couldn't guess as to the amount of time we were talking about.

"We need to find out." Laughing Dog's enlarged hickory brown eyes moved across the room.

"What I didn't tell them is that in the same vision I saw a dagger that could kill the thing that they are trying to bring over."

"What thing? What are they trying to do?" Sky didn't hide her urgency.

"They want to open Solomon's Gate," I answered. The elders lost all of their hard edges as the recognition of true horror washed over them.

"What's that?" Joy spoke up.

"A door to the underworld," August said, searching his mind for answers.

"Are you sure?" Anna Belle gasped.

"Yes, but I know how we can stop it, a special athame."

"Where can we find it?"

"I don't know. Maybe it's in the Codex. When is the Crossing, August?" I asked.

"It's supposed to be here December twenty first or twenty second."

"Yule." I had the hard reality check that I had no idea what day it was. "Wh... what day is it?" I stuttered.

"December twelfth."

"I was there less than a week?" I mumbled. My mind began spinning down into the darkness.

"Anything else, Lydia? Anything at all." Laughing Dog wasn't the only one desperate for more information, but I was gone, falling ever deeper into my mind. I barely was aware of the room anymore. I was back at the door at the farm. *You stupid bitch.*

"She needs her rest. We will wait till Grey gets the computer thing working." Anna Belle and Sky took me back to the bedroom for some rest.

Chapter 38

"Do you need anything else?" Belle placed a cold drink on the nightstand.

"No. I just want to be alone." I wanted the dark. I wanted the silence. I wanted the loneliness.

"Be sure to drink the juice. Its Sky's mix, so you will be well on your way to recovery."

"Tell her thank you, but I don't want it." I turned away from Anna Belle and wrapped myself up tightly in the soft covers that smelled slightly of dog and campfire.

"What do you mean you don't want it?" Belle scowled, but I didn't care.

"You heard me. I just want to lay here."

"So why not heal while you lie there?" She tried a sweeter approach.

"Leave me alone, Anna Belle. Just leave me alone." I wanted to feel the pain. I wanted to suffer in silent solitude. I deserved it.

"Fine. Maybe tomorrow you will feel better." She started to go to the door. "If you need…"

"No." Doubt and ache gnawed at me. "Wait, I want to ask you something." My spirit wounded, I turned so I could see her face, her beautiful face.

"Anything."

"Why? Why did you fuck me? Was it to prove something? Was it to have power over me? What? What was it like to fuck cattle?"

"Yes" the voice answered. I squeezed my wounds with raw hands. The pain was my only connection to what was real.

I wanted to inflict pain on her, but maybe more it was the hope I could poke the viper so it would bite. *Distract me from my mind, that is more insidious than any snake could hope to be.*

She was silent for moment. "I will not engage or encourage whatever this is."

"See? She did it to use you. You're just another whore to the succubus."

"You just wanted to use me. Did you want the gate yourselves? You *are* monsters! Real fucking demons. I saw what you did to that girl. You did more than take her life, you tortured her, and you *got off on it!* Maybe Hopkins is right. We are what's wrong with this world. Corruption. Death."

Damn it, hurt me! I thought of the people I had killed. I thought about the horrible voice behind the door. I wanted to be the girl in the depths of the speakeasy. I thought of all the voices and people in my life who knew I was different and abused me for it. Maybe they were right, and I was so very wrong.

Her glowing eyes searched my spirit and sadness welled. "You are right. We are death, but from death comes life. We are the only protection from the actual demons beyond Solomon's Gate. We go where angels dare not tread. I cannot walk you through the haunted halls of you soul, but I will be here waiting on the other side because I care about you."

"As a witch or a lover?"

"As both, and more." A sad smile touched her face. "I will be here when you need or want me." She closed the door behind her and left me alone in the night.

I regretted my words. I didn't understand why I said those things, but I couldn't stop myself. But even in the confusion of my reasons, I was still disappointed that I could not scream and fight. She would not allow it. I needed to explode, but I would find no such release. Something ate at me like battery acid. I needed to get the poison out, spit it at the world with venom and hate. She didn't let me, and I hated her for it.

I was boiling on the inside. I tried to still myself, but the irrational emotions were choking me. I pressed more into my wounds, but the distraction was only temporary.

I tried to ground myself. *Breathe in, breathe out. Breathe in, breathe out.* But there was no air.

"Stupid bitch." I jerked my eyes to the dark corner from which the voice had come. This was not the child's voice but more real and familiar.

"Hello?" I was a cliché greeting the darkness, but what else was there to do, put my head under the covers?

"Fucking whore. You deserved all you got and everything you will get."

A chill streaked up my back and down my limbs followed by an unnatural heavy stillness. I was not alone in the room, and I knew that voice. *Young.*

I narrowed my eyes and saw his bulky silhouette watching from behind the door. I began to fight a growing tremble.

"What are you doing here, Young?" I tried to find my strength and focus, but my sadness and guilt siphoned it all away.

"You're not to forget the evil you are. You killed me, and you liked it."

"You were the asshole first," I quipped tiredly.

"How about me?" Another thinner, smaller shadow shifted across the walls. A sharp memory broke out of the night, a young man's face being drained of all life.

"The boy from the club?" Malignant shame grew.

"The boy? *The boy!* You don't even know my name, do you?" He was growing enraged. The room became heavy and grew crowded with unseen beings. Claustrophobia gripped me as I was getting lost in a rising sea of people.

"My name is Stephen, you stupid cow."

The shadows began to whip into a slow storm. I wrapped

my hand around my purple black toes and squeezed for every ounce of delicious hurt. It pushed away the mounting voices for only a second.

"Get out. You're not wanted here."

"Liar. You called us here," Young answered.

"Leave now!" I tried to force my will as I had in the house cleansing, but my will was cracked and thin.

"You deserve this." A profane voice brought the feeling of uncleanliness to my soul. The voice from beyond the farmhouse door.

"I demand you leave. I call upon..."

"You call upon no one. You are nothing. I was wrong about you. You're no witch. You are a girl playing pretend. You have no power here. No Gods hear your voice because there are no gods. You are all alone here," it hissed. "Alone with us." It's voice shifted from a childlike innocence to a perverse snarl.

"Goddess He–" I began to cry out. I was forced back down on the bed with hundreds of invisible hands. Some shoved themselves down my gullet as an immense hand squeezed my throat shut from the outside. I was paralyzed against the bed by an unseen force. My chest was being crushed by a tremendous weight. I tried to scream and fight, but I was powerless.

"You deserve to die."

"Slut!"

"Whore!"

"You're no witch!"

"You're a little girl playing pretend."

"You're just another special fucking snowflake like everyone else!"

"There are no gods, only monsters waiting in the dark."

Images of my sins sent earthquakes through me. Ice filled my veins where my flesh met with phantoms' clammy touch.

"None of this is real."

"They were right to take your daughter from you."

"You're not fit, living in your fantasies of gods and magick."

"You're nothing."

"Hopkins is right about you."

"The Hounds of Heaven will save us all from things like you."

I struggled for my freedom but was pulled down deeper into the ethereal quicksand of shame, doubt and sin.

Above me, a form began to flesh out of the shadow and mist. Dead white eyes looked down upon me as it continued to crush my windpipe. Its decayed breath invaded my nose and lungs. The voices raged against me. My wounds festered as crawling things dove under my skin and began to nest.

I tried to scream, but my voice was stolen. Its gaping mouth opened and presented Hell. Its childlike laugh could be heard as its form became more solid, more real. I was going to suffer, and I deserved it, forever.

"Lydia, can you hear me?" This was not the phantom.

"Lydia, answer me." She was so far away.

"They are not your friends." The white faced ghoul clung to my body.

"What's wrong with her!?" Another distant voice.

"You deserve this." Its waxy face began to melt slowly. Its blank dead eyes never left mine.

"I deserve this." I answered.

"You are no witch." It pressed in with its will, its mouth ever gaping. Rows of hooked teeth pulled me in.

"I'm no witch."

"You're nothing"

"Find her and bring her here! Now!" A command rang out. *Varrick?*

"I'm nothing," I repeated after the fiend. My will faded, and my strength became a memory.

"You have nothing to fight for." It assured me.

"Nothing to fight for."

"You're no mother. You abandoned your child for fantasies."

"Come into me. You deserve this."

"I deserve this."

I burst into hot tears. My spirit rose from my paralyzed body, and its gaping mouth widened, welcoming me. I began to climb into the gash, the slice of canines scraped deep across my soul.

Its teeth began to rotate like a corkscrew down into its gullet as I crawled deeper in.

"In the name of Hekate, be gone!" A woman's voice crashed and burst the beast's eyes as it vomited me up from its gut.

"Be gone now. She is a daughter of Hekate!" The voice was strength and certainty, will and spirit unshaken.

I gulped air as my spirit melted back into my body. I reached up, clawing my way to freedom or to Hell, I wasn't sure.

Wise green-brown eyes looked down on me as Wicked Wendy pressed a cold compress against my clammy skin.

"You'll be okay. I'm here." Wendy rinsed the rag and methodically began to clean my body. I still stood between this world and next. This world was more like a dream and the other the reality. The room smelled of sage and sacred herbs. Black candles, eggs, salt and a broken mirror littered the table. *Exorcism.*

The rocker squeaked on the rough wooden porch with my gentle push. The cold winter rain fell lazily as the sun flirted through the passive clouds. I held myself tightly in an old red flannel blanket. I wasn't quite my old self. I held no foolish hope that I would ever be again.

Wendy and Sky gave me no choice but to drink their concoctions, but the nightmares still found me in my medicated sleep.

Belle was never too far away, but Wendy made it clear I was not to be bothered. But I longed for Belle's touch. Her scent found me in the dark places in my mind. I wanted to hold her. I wanted to smell her jasmine perfume. I watched from the corner of my eye as she played with her necklace out of frustration and boredom.

I had always seen Wicked Wendy as a friend and mentor, but I had never appreciated her as the powerful earthen witch she truly was. I don't think I would have understood what I saw only a few months ago.

The others, werewolf, skinwalkers and vampire alike, held a stiff respect and, I dare say, fear of Wendy. She wasn't the soft smile and welcoming arms I had taken for granted over the years I had known her. She had a laser like focus, and she didn't tolerate someone questioning her orders concerning me. She was polite but with a straight edge that was not to be crossed.

I had kept to myself but still remained friendly. I had no desire to play the "I'm okay" bluff or call poker. I had to find my balance between the truth of me and what happened. Even that luxury, I could ill afford and neither could the Bahlael. Time was running out. Yule and the Crossing fast approached. The pressure bore down on me. I found myself holding my necklace, much like Belle but so tightly it was leaving impressions on my fingertips. I opened my locket and said a silent prayer for Ember, her face in my mind years younger than her age now. *I miss you. I love you. I think about you all the time. Can you feel my thoughts and love for you?* The torturous words from my enemy a few nights before rattled in my hollow heart.

I could not utter words about what I saw and what I would have done if Wendy had not pulled me, against my will, back to earth. Thank the Goddess no one forced the issue. I was thankful but afraid. *Can I trust myself?*

I needed to think. I needed to find peace within with what choice I had made. For now my only choice I could make is to live or not live, to have life merely happen to me or to move forward with deliberate purpose. "I choose to live deliberately." My promise melted into the stippling rain. *I choose to live deliberately for you, Ember, and myself.*

"You feel like joining us in the kitchen?" Wendy peeked from behind the screen door.

Chapter 40

Saturday
8 days until Solstice

I gradually made my way to the crowded kitchen table and pulled up a side chair. The table held cold cups of coffee and tidy piles of research materials. As usual there was food cooking, wafting the soft scent of rosemary and garlic throughout the open cabin. Some soft mumblings of plans and findings went around the room but nothing really tangible.

Belle thumbed through one of the journals from the farmhouse at a very brisk pace as did Varrick. The weakened Delphine slowly worked through her own pile, giving a pained expression crossed her perfect ebony face every so often as her body was still rejecting the Faerie Stone inside her.

Laughing Dog hung up his phone with a deep scowl on his bronze features. "Nothing in Oxford. Our people can't find one sign of Hounds of Heaven. How is that even possible? Are you sure that is where they're going?"

"That is where the woman said. Hell's Gate Bridge." Varrick confirmed, not looking up from his studies. "Oxford is mentioned in this notebook as well. They had scouts down there back in April."

"Nothing on my end." Otto sighed. His thin mouth in a permanent frown, so different from when I had first met him.

"Same," Bjorn told the room, with Joy perched at his side on her phone playing a game.

Rummer could be heard yelling on his phone as he stood outside by the kitchen window. "I don't give a shit. They can't just fucking disappear. Do I have to come down there? Sniff them the fuck out. Get in touch with the skinwalkers and vamps." He limped his way through the back door, his woolly hair frizzing with frustration. "I know it's fucking Oxford. The Dark Spiral already has a few people down there and the mosquitoes..."

I saw the vampires cast annoyed glances at his name calling, but they weren't surprised. "I'll text you with a meet-up point." He looked around the room and realized he might've been talking a bit too loudly. "Be nice," he sarcastically growled as he hung up the phone. He sat heavily on the couch next to Grey who was still working on the computer. Bill had been the one who worked between the groups, but now Rummer was thrown into a position that he detested and didn't have the temperament for.

August remained quiet and was intently trying to decipher the Codex. His fine raven hair fell in front of his face, barely hiding his amber eyes that noticed nothing but the Codex, not even Rummer thundering through the house.

"Any luck?" I asked August. He ignored me. "August?"

"Oh my apologies, I think I found something on the dagger. Is this it?" August turned the human leather book my way, revealing a sketch of the very same dagger I had in my vision.

"Yeah."

"That's Solomon's Athame." Wendy's voice trembled ever so slightly.

"Yes it is." August confirmed. "Solomon's ritual dagger. It says roughly here 'that it casts fear into the heart of Hell's angels. It is kept in "The Pit." He strained to decipher the old language. "A place in between this world and "Hell." He created an artificial pocket specifically to hold his Athame. Solomon deemed in too dangerous to be used and too powerful to be destroyed."

"It's kept in the tween. In my vision I saw a park in Birmingham. Shouldn't it be in the Middle East or something?"

"The thing about places like 'The Pit' is you reach them by walking through the veil." Wicked Wendy offered her wisdom.

"Like a portal?"

"Yes, and there are portals all over the place. The question is do you know the combination to unlock the right destination, and what could be waiting for you there?" Wendy searched her thoughts. "But that is something a witch is good for." Her crone features had a youthful twinkle.

"There is an iron gate that's locked. It leads to utility tunnels, but I have heard rumors of it leading to an old mine..." I had lived in the Magic City for twenty years before moving to Huntsville. "Birmingham is riddled with old mines and caves."

"So you think there is a portal in the utility tunnels?" Sky pulled the obscenely large roast from the oven and leaned against the counter. I was growing hungry for the first time in days.

"How will we find the portal once we get in there?" Anna Belle asked.

"I know of a spell that might work." I was happy to finally be able to contribute something of my skills.

Wendy gave me a wide smile. "I'll need to look through my journals. There is a potion that is used for portals, but it is very tricky. August, I'll need your help with the Codex to get the right location. Only an anointed witch can walk through, though." Wendy was back to her focused intensity.

"I'll go." Joy interjected gleefully.

"There's no doubt that there will be something guarding the Athame, something big and nasty." Varrick enjoyed watching Joy go pale. My resolve began to weaken.

"There will be a 'test' given by The Keeper. I will try find more information." August scribbled some notes down. I didn't have time to worry about it, so I would leave it to August.

"Lydia, maybe you can make sense of these notes of

Mary's?" Varrick purposely distracted me with a beaten up notebook.

Barely readable handwritten notes about the Walker farm were scratched deep in the yellowed pages. Random symbols and doodles touched every page. "It's something to do with Walker."

"About the farm or the ghost?" Varrick made a bitter face as he drank a sip of his cold coffee.

"Ghost?" Laughing Dog asked, surprised.

"There was a ghost at the farmhouse." The ghost was the most normal thing I've had to deal with these many weeks. The journal contained crude sketches and occult symbols from many different paths. "According to this, that's why they chose to stay there." The handwriting was barely legible, and I couldn't make out most of it. "But I'm not sure why."

Otto interrupted my straining eyes, "I've heard from New York. They say they cannot find records of Cerbina before her service to the Houses of Lilitu."

I stole the Codex from August to take a closer look at the Athame. I studied the faded ink. I then noticed something familiar, a purple red spot on the edge of the back of the book. I closed the Codex, marking a page with the same feather that August had been using. I flipped the book over and saw large raised red wine colored scars. I placed my left hand over my right breast. *Is that a birthmark like mine? But it looks like an old wound.* My marks were not raised but matched in color and intensity.

"Hey, I think I got it working!" Grey stood up triumphantly.

"I haven't seen much, just Miss Lydia sitting in a chair. The drive is a little touchy." Grey ever so gently used his unusually long finger and tilted the thumb drive into place.

I saw myself, dirty, tired and small, back in the dingy dark of the basement. Hopkins was off camera. Blackburne was motionless, streaked in shade.

Young stood, popping his knuckles. A flash of him in the bedroom, his cold dead hands on my body. Panic broke my mental wounds wide open. *No, I choose to be here. Now. Breathe in. Breathe out.* I grasped my locket.

Everyone watched as my hand was sliced and placed on ancient flesh. My video skin went pale blue, and my body began to twitch and jerk as if jolts of electricity ripped through my nervous system.

My digital eyes thrust open and exposed weeping, blood-filled scleras. My mouth moved unnaturally, pushing out guttural tones that barely mimicked a language.

"Does any one know what I'm saying?" I asked the room.

"No." Wendy and August answered in unison.

"In the Lord Almighty's Name, I command you to speak English." Hopkins leaned into the shot. I continued to speak in words barely more than growls and hisses.

"By The Lord Jesus Christ, I command you." He placed his Bible on my head.

The stranger on the screen went suddenly silent and

still. Its strange eyes looked up at Hopkins from under a sweaty furrowed brow. "Are you He?" A voice clawed out of a strangled throat. Something deep and dark squirmed inside.

"I am not The Lord but I will be the bringer of salvation. I will bring back the true faith. Back to Mother Church." Hopkins answered.

"Faith by way of fear." My shadow self gave a brutal smile. Even the killers who sat next to me were put at unease.

"The fear of the Lord is the beginning of knowledge, but fools despise wisdom and instruction. Proverbs." Hopkins' pride swelled.

"Then all the peoples on Earth will see that you are called by the name of the Lord, and they will fear you." My voice strained and twisted. "Deuteronomy."

"I didn't expect a witch to know scripture." Hopkins was pleasantly surprised.

Again the strange me just stared at Hopkins with a cold smile.

In the distance of the video, strange howling grew. The door.

"What do you want?" The video me sneered. "Savior?"

"Solomon's Gate."

The strange redhead with wild matted hair started to laugh. It was a woman's laugh, my laugh, but it soon turned loathsome. For a split second, a face not my own looked into the camera. *Did anyone else see that?* Blood slithered from my digital nose then soon turned into rivers.

"Blood, bone, flesh, will, spirit." It answered.

"Cthonic elementals. Yes." Hopkins was becoming impatient. The screaming in the background became more deranged.

"The Eternal, The Changing, The Beast, The Corruption..." the video began to stutter. "The Cthonic Towers..." another jump of the video. "The Crossing, the vessel, the ring..." the video began to lock up.

The images jumped and my stolen body flailed, and the

217

screams from the behind the door wouldn't be ignored. The flame-haired thing thrashed back, my body fell out of frame, and we could hear the hard hit to the ground. The video stopped.

"Sorry about the freezing and stuff. Best I could do."
He closed the program and then another program opened automatically.

It was an instant messenger chat box. Grey suddenly went white. "Son?" Sky was concerned.

"I...I know how they found you, Miss Lydia." He grimaced.
"How?" My nails dug into my hands soft flesh.
"She told him where to find you when you took off."
"Who?" My mind raced.
"Who?" Belle growled.
"VampireKitten69."

I turned towards Joy with white hot shock. That was Joy's handle. Bjorn snatched her up by her throat and stood in the middle of the room. His body instantly changed to his shadow self. She dangled helplessly two feet off the ground. He also knew the screen name was hers.

"How could you?" I was in disbelief.
"What's happening?" Sky asked confused.
"That is the name she uses online," Bjorn answered as he tightened his grip.

Grey leaned out of my way while I began to scroll back through their conversations.

There has to be some mistake. I read the back and forth between VampireKitten69 and JB1542. She had told JB1542 about Belle's home, the people there and even the Codex. She was bragging. "You told them everything. You... *everything!*"

"He was just a friend I chatted with. I didn't know." She was beginning to tear up. Her face inflamed and swelling. "I didn't know! How was I supposed to know he was with the Hounds of whatever?"

"The Hounds Of Heaven, you stupid bitch!" Fury raced up and down my body. "Do you know what they did to me!?" I screamed. The lights in the cabin began to flicker.

A prickling of energy crawled across my skin. She was my friend, and she betrayed me.

Snap! She hit the floor like wet sticks. Bjorn had twisted her neck without remorse or thought.

"No!" I screamed with guttural rage. I shot my will out with a blinding light. Bjorn slammed against the back wall. I felt the familiar silence within me. I stepped toward the very pissed off vampire intending to continue my purge of pain.

"Lydia, stop. No." Varrick stepped between Bjorn and me. The onlookers' faces were both impressed and concerned. The shock of their witness broke the silence, and my hate drained from me as I crumpled on the floor. "Why!? Why did you kill her!?"

"She betrayed you to those men." Bjorn snarled, his flesh already healing. "She could not be trusted. You put down the dog that you cannot trust."

I looked into Joy's dead open eyes, her blue glitter and pressed jewels unmoved on her face. Her glittery bow lay on the floor next to her awkward limbs.

"Shouldn't you kill *me?* I told them about Cerbina!" I spoke with tremors in my voice.

"You did not just give up the information for ego, and she was not one of us." Varrick answered.

"Pack before all others." Sky added. "Even in this menagerie."

"Is *this* what it means to be one of you? No mercy?" I asked.

"Mercy is for those who can afford it, and we cannot. We are the Bahlael," Varrick answered as he picked up Joy's burned phone and tossed it aside.

I looked at Wendy for help, for something, anything. She had known Joy for longer than I had and had seen her face almost every day for years, but there was no sign of shock or remorse.

"The Gods do not suffer fools and neither should we." She

was dark and furious. Tears glistened but not freed.

"We have a job we must do." Otto tried to reassure me.

"Job?" My tears flowed unhindered.

"Lydia, why do you think we exist?" Wendy stepped between me and the others.

"We are the dark guardians of this world. We are the devils it takes to keep this world safe from the real evil beyond the veil." Belle's jet eyes reflected images of a life long lived and wisdom earned.

Wendy took my head into her hands. "This is not the time for tears. We have to prepare for what is to come. She put you, us, and our mission in grave danger. We don't have the luxury of mercy or humanity."

Night followed behind us in quiet steps. The creatures of the forest, day and night, traded their shifts. Our bags crunched down into the winter blanket of frosted leaves at the edge of the glade. The light scent of damp earth and pine welcomed Wendy and me.

"This is perfect," she said. The spot chosen had been about an hour deep in the woods, but Sky assured us it would be worth it. She was right. It was a little meadow surrounded by old growth trees. It even had a sleeping fire pit. We inhaled the twilight and approved with a shared smile.

We had a lot to do before day break. I had to push away what had happened with Joy. I had to push away anything that wasn't for the good for our purpose. The swell of mourning ebbed and flowed. *Not now.*

We worked in silence as we prepared our sacred space. She gathered kindling and stone and brought the hearth back to life. I created the outside border with log, rock and quartz. We both found a large, flat field stone and maneuvered it into place as our earthen workspace altar. We placed our candles and incense at the ready, and our tools were cleaned and charged.

"Are we ready to close the circle?" I asked as the biting wind chewed on my fingers and nose. It was time for me to do what I did best, spellcraft.

"Yes, I think so." Wendy walked the perimeter one more

time. Her colorful skirts were the only bright spot in the dull winter.

She and I stood in the center across the fire. A small well-used cauldron hung above the sputtering flames. We took our pause as the clouds began to crowd the sky, overtaking the shy moon.

We centered our minds, bodies, hearts and spirits with three cleansing breaths.

Breathe in, breathe out.
Breathe in, breathe out.
Breathe in, breathe out.

We started from the center and spiraled out to the edge of the outside boundary as we began our chant.

"This place between places,
this time between time,
this sacred space,
be yours and mine.
Light and shade, you are welcome here,
without doubt, without fear.
From above to below,
we welcome the ebb and flow.
Love and trust is the key.
So it is, so mote it be."

We envisioned a crystalline bubble growing from the center. As it did, it pushed any malign forces from the marked circle. Its shell enveloped us in its protection. We raised our bundle of smoldering herbs and smudged our sacred space to gather productive energy.

The frosty wind bit no longer. The clouds parted above, surrounding a coy moon. "Do you see it, Lydia?" Wendy pointed to the sky with one knotted finger.

My eyes raised, and for the first time I saw the comet. It was a large bright pinhole in the night. It was twice the size of any star or planet that I had ever seen.

Lady Hekate, I welcome you. Please guide me with your light in the darkness, wisdom in the silence, and courage in my fearful heart. So mote it be.

"It's time." She said. We both removed our clothes and neatly piled them as a place to sit. She brought our her djembe, a sacred African drum, and I put on my bells and charms. I laid a gentle kiss on my locket and let the stillness of the night hold me.

Her finger tapped and stroked her drumhead near the fire, coaxing it awake. The three-foot drum was remarkable, goat skin, handmade, well worn and cared for. A heartbeat slowly rose from the newly born night as she skillfully wooed her drum, softly and steadily.

I let my breath make pace, and my own heartbeat fall in line with her percussion pulse. I rubbed warm ash on my body and squeezed my toes deep in the earth. I began to stomp my bells to the beat.

We began a guttural hum and let out a soul breath, a breath from deep within, imbued with our life force and will to charge the sacred space.

In a clear and commanding voice I called out into the beautiful darkness. "Circle, set and bound, I call to the corner of the East. Air, mind and intellect. Join us." I repeated this two more times to honor the power of three. The wind, as if waiting for its cue, began to gust in the trees, and the clouds began to swirl. "We welcome you."

Wendy's beats began to pick up volume and speed. My heart and body kept pace as the power began to rise.

"I call to the corner of the South. Flame, will and creation, join us." I followed the rule of three again. The fire began to grow bolder and silent lightning began to flash across the sky. "We welcome you."

Wendy fell in a trance of her own rhythm, her dreads falling forward as her hands moved with the magick only a musician can weave. My body began vibrating and curving as I swam in the energy evoked.

"I call to the corner of the West. Water, heart and mystery, join us." Twice more said. Wendy's beats quaked, my body hummed.

"I call to the corner of the North. Earth, body and the material, join us." My feet met the clay with the pounding djembe. Nature herself danced with us. "We welcome you. So mote it be."

"Air, fire, water, earth." I chanted and twirled in the mist, my copper hair curling and whipping like a mane. The lightening flashed, and the animals called.

I found my place in the center of the circle and began to call to my goddess.

"My Lady Hekate,
I call upon you this night,
so you may join us in our fight.
Please join us. Join us. Join us. So mote it be."

The energy level was overwhelming, my entire being vibrated to the edge of oblivion. The world fell still and silent. The lightning crashed, and dogs began to bark in the unseen distance. A large black dog with mirrored eyes stepped to the edge of the tree line and sat stoically. The elements suddenly spun back to life, finding their place in our magickal dance without stumbling. I steeled my nerves, nodded my respect and continued.

"My Lord, Horned One,
I call upon you this night,
so you may join us in our fight.
Please join us. Join us. Join us. So Mote it be."

A great bleat was heard, and a great white tailed buck with massive antlers worn as a crown walked a the edge of fire light. It stood noble and courageous. He held his court and watched us play in the mist and flame.

An explosion of drumming took over the circle. Wendy's head bobbed, but her face was unseen and her hands a blur. The fever of the music overtook me in celebration of the Hekate's and The Horned One's arrival.

For us witches, time held no meaning in our sacred circles. I danced till my body collapsed and Wendy's fingers bled, and we both dripped with enraptured sweat and laughter. All worries, doubts and mourning cleansed from our hearts for now, we made our offering of wine and bread. Then we began our work in earnest.

Wendy set her will on making the potion, The Key, to unlock the portal to the correct destination, The Pit.

I was tasked to find a way to maneuver in the utility cave to find our way deeper into the belly of Red Mountain on which Birmingham city sat. The Codex offered a spell that could help us, The Lantern of Daedalus. August was kind enough to translate the ancient Greek for me.

It taxed my limits of skill and knowledge of oils and spellcraft to recreate the magickally infused oil. I readied and charged the old lantern that Sky had given us to us. I merged the two carefully. It would be our light and guide in the darkness to the portal. It was set aside to patiently wait for its destiny down in the depths.

"I think we are done here." I announced as I carefully packed away the lantern oil and while Wendy bottled our brew. We were to the point of absolute exhaustion.

Chapter 43

Monday
6 days until Solstice

"We're in a sacred place away from distractions and listeners. I need for you tell me more about this park." Wendy sat comfortably down on her piled clothes.

"It was a park I used to hang out at, was drawn to. It was a place I could recharge. I would sometimes think I would see things there, but they were more like mirages. I would see something standing in the shadow, and then it was just a rock."

"Describe the creatures you think you saw."

"They were... I don't know, there but not there. They were definitely not phantoms like a lot of people think. I don't think they've ever been human. I've always had the feeling they were guarding something. I guess I was right."

"We'll need to know how to deal with them. If the portal is their charge they will not let us pass easily."

"They can shift from a tree to a solid being. They weren't in a physical form, they existed only in my third eye. They didn't like the streetlights. Definitely creatures of the tween, between this world and the next. Pale shadow is the only description that come to mind."

"Did they look like this?" Wendy sketched a creature that appeared almost like a stereotypical alien, with overly large eyes, no nose and long thin body and limbs.

"Yes..."

"They're Changelings. They're known all over the world.

They're drawn to the energy of portals. They're used by powerful practitioners to be guardians. They're beyond our skill."

"Will they take an offering?"

"I believe it is customary to give them raw pig and alcohol, but that's if we get that far." Wendy gazed up at the still swirling sky and the comet. "There will also be things in the tunnels, no doubt. The energy calls a lot of attention. Whether they are there by choice or placed by someone, friend or foe..." She wandered in thought.

"You'll have to go alone," she said as I swallowed hard against a knot in my throat. "Vampires can't leave this plane in the bodies they are locked in. A lycan's being is too unstable. Skinwalkers, their magick conflicts with that kind of high magick. I'll have to be outside to maintain the barrier and glamour. Even if we're able to strike a deal with the Changelings, they can't be entirely trusted."

"You seem to like the skinwalkers," I changed the subject as my nerves began to quake in my stomach. My thoughts jumped from the portal to Joy and back again.

"I trust where they come from; they're from the energies of the earth. The lycans and vampires were created with unnatural energies by practitioners who were desperate to win battles not too unlike the one we are about to fight."

"Which people? Which battle?"

"That tale is too long to share tonight." She patted me on my leg. "I see you have a soft spot for Grey."

"He's a cool kid. I think he's Sky's and Bill's only kid."

"I'm surprised the Dark Spiral people let him live."

"Why?" I was horrified.

"It's complicated. Very complicated. Skinwalkers and lycans are not the same but similar. They have a fragile truce but... it's complicated. A mixed child is rare and usually not tolerated. He has a hard road in front of him, but don't we all?"

"Joy's road ended in death," I blurted.

"So does ours." She brought an intricately carved box from the bottom of her bag. "Lydia, I mourn for her too, but you cannot let them see it. Our feelings for her will be seen as weakness. Don't let their pretty faces distract you from the fact they are not human. They are predators, and we must be seen as their equals." She opened the box, carefully showing many compartments filled with oils, herbs and other items. "If you have to run with the lions you must not be afraid to bare your teeth and earn your place in the pride."

My sadness knotted and choked me, and guilt ate at my insides. "I don't know what to feel. She gave me over to them... but she didn't do on purpose. She was... my friend."

"We will honor her journey when this over. I promise." She held my hand and we reigned our sadness into place. "But for now, I would like to help you with the journey to come." She presented an amber bottle that was no bigger than a pinky finger. "Tell me about this second 'awakening' you've been experiencing."

I locked my pain away and pushed forward. "You mean the complete lack of control over my abilities?" *Over anything.*

"Yeah, but can you be more specific?"

"Well my dreams are what they have always been but more... just more. I touch things or people, and I lose myself or blurt out what I feel or read off them. My third eye has always been better than most, but it feels like it did when I was a kid, walking into the sunlight after being stuck in the house for weeks. I'm fine with hues of color, then I am blasted and overwhelmed." I began to feel the frustration with my loss of control and comfort with my gifts. "The most terrifying..."

"Is?" She already knew the answer, like always.

"You saw what I did to Bjorn, and then there is what happened back at the farmhouse. With Bjorn, I was overcome with rage, just like I was at the farmhouse." I was piecing things together. But I held back. The silence I felt scared me.

"Tell me what you felt at the moment at the farmhouse."

"I was so angry, then I looked up at the basement door. I

wanted it closed, and it closed."

"What did you think? Did you tell the door to close?"

I sat there for a minute and ran my memories through my head. *Why am I hiding anything from her? She is all I have.* "Actually, at that moment, I felt still inside. Beyond anger, numb. Beyond feeling. I was completely still. Even beyond that. I wanted the door closed, and it closed. I've felt nothing like it. Like the eye of a hurricane. Silence."

"Remember that silence. If you can hold on to it, you can learn to control it..."

"I don't like the way it feels; it feels like nothingness. Well, the way it feels afterward... I can't explain it."

"Make a separate place for the 'feeling' inside you and learn to tap into it."

"I'm afraid of it because, in the moment of stillness, I don't care about anything or anyone. I am not distracted by anything like morality or emotion."

"With time you will be able to control and use it. Just take it slow. Now back to The Pit. You are going to be tested. How, the Codex doesn't say, but I want to help you as best I can. Close your eyes." I did as I was told. With the tip of her finger she skillfully marked my forehead with warm oil.

She spoke words that I didn't understand, but I experienced spiritual warmth flowing within me and through me.

"May Hekate and The Horned One protect you.

May the raging river be calmed and guided.

May your heart be open and mind be wise.

May your spirit be brave, and body be strong.

Blessed be, my Sister."

"Thank you." The confusion and nerves melted away, and a certainty found me.

I opened my eyes and saw Wicked Wendy smiling at me with a grandmotherly love. "This will help with the new awakening, the loss of control. Now let's get back to the cabin."

"How long have we been out here?" I was tired but content, expecting to see the sun peeking through the trees.

She glanced outside the circle at her watch, careful not to break the boundary. "Only three hours."

"What?"

"Vampires hide from time, but witches mold it." Wendy gave me a wink.

"Still nothing!" Sky's veneer of stoic strength was beginning to crack. She was starting to snap at people and retreat into herself, but she didn't stop trying. I don't think she could've if she wanted to. She barely slept, barely ate. Good sleep was a false hope for all of us.

We all had spent days pulling together the details of Solomon's Gate. We watched the video too many times to count. We read and reread the Hound's notes and The Codex, but without those free pages we had all that we were going to get. Our combined efforts and skills had reached a dead end, and we had no more time.

My wounds had healed but left their scars. Delphine and Rummer were both improving, but only Rummer would be joining us in Birmingham.

I refused to find time to think about Joy. *I will mourn for her later.* I avoided being around Bjorn for any length of time, as he did me. I was so utterly confused about what I should do or even feel. *Not now. Think about it later.*

"Tomorrow we go to the park." Varrick confirmed as I watched the mixture that Wendy and I had made the night before spin slowly of its own accord sitting innocently on the kitchen table.

"Yes." August had packed the Codex with care, he would be sending it with Delphine and Otto to a safe place. His sharp features and deep-set eyes looked worn and frustrated. "Let us go over everything one more time."

"The Lantern of Daedalus will show us the way once it's lit. It doesn't give off much light, but it should be fine." I placed the lamp on the table next to the living potion.

"The Key is ready." Wendy was pleased with our success as I marveled at its perpetual motion.

"Lydia, are you well enough?" Belle sat next to me.

"I'm okay, but it doesn't really matter does it? I need to go."

"We need to organize the groups, the ones in and out of the tunnels. I wouldn't think any more than four or five in each." Varrick was deep in his element.

Sky scratched at the table with her claws, "I need to burn some energy. I'm definitely going in." A low growl rumbled in her slender throat.

Belle played with one of my stray curls, "You are not leaving my side again."

August playfully sneered, "You know I will be there."

"Me too." Laughing Dog sat down at the table and started eating some left over pot roast. He was always the protective older brother, his little sister was always in his sight. To be honest we were all worried about her. Her features took the shape of the primal more and more with each passing day, and her heart was in pain.

"You ain't leaving me out." Rummer was ready to tear someone apart for his humiliation and the loss of his best friend. "For Billy," he said while raising his wolf's head flask.

"For Billy." Sky raised her drink with a warrior's fervor.

"Bill." Laughing Dog held Sky's hand.

"Bill! And for Telal and Cerbina." Anna Belle added respectfully.

"For all of us." I raised my rum and Coke. We needed this.

"May the night protect us all, as we protect the night." Otto found his absent cheer.

Clank. Robustly tapping the varied cups, glasses and flasks, we drank in their honor and the honor of our allies who were still with us. Great howls were set loose by the Black Paws and Laughing Dog. The vampires joined their allies. Wendy and I added our voices to their warrior song. The power of the primal shook the walls and crashed through our bodies. Laughter found the room as Rummer grabbed for a bottle of rum only to have it crumble in his hands. "Rummer and his damn puppy paws." Sky slapped Rummer on his back as he struggled to find breath from laughing too hard. The huge mountain of man began to snort, which sent the rest of us over. It was the most human experience I had in months.

Belle took her chance and grabbed my hand to lead me into the chilly night.

"Where are you two off to?" Wendy coolly stood in front of us.

"I was going to show Lydia the night sky." Belle smiled widely, her eyes sparkling. I went hot and red. I wasn't sure I wanted this, but I wanted her.

"Don't stay out too late, ladies." Wendy's pine colored eyes glanced at Belle with warning as she handed us a picnic basket that Belle had been reaching for from behind the front door.

"Yes, ma'am." Belle eyebrows arched with mischief.

We passed the lycans who stood guard. Their hot, fogging breath and gurgling growls made them seem almost dragon-like in the dark. We floated through the shadowed forest as Belle's vision led us through without fault to a small clearing with a round boulder jutting through the clay and overhanging a small but fierce creek.

She quickly unfurled two blankets like a matador and spread them out on the rock. She then unpacked a thermos of hot cocoa and poured me a cup. "With marshmallows." *She is so fucking beautiful.*

I took a sip and licked my chocolate mustache away. "I wanted to tell you I'm sorry..."

"Hush. I am not worried about that." She touched my lips with her slender feminine finger. She and I sat down on the round boulder. "I wanted to know how you are dealing with

Joy."

"I don't know. It seems so far away." I replayed the image of her body hitting the floor, but it was more like a movie than truth.

"We value loyalty above all things. Our ways may seem extreme, but we have not survived this long by being forgiving."

"Especially forgiving a human, even for a mistake?" I didn't shy away from her obsidian gaze.

"Yes." She didn't hold back. She was going to offer me blunt honesty as recompense. "I am sorry that you had to see us like that." She motioned with her hand across her face. "We are killers. We kill to eat and for pleasure, as deviant as it may seem to you."

"What does that make me?"

"I do not understand the question."

"I've killed. I've been a witness to death, a death of a friend, yet I didn't do a damn thing."

"You are in a different world with different rules than the one in which you once lived. Time is the currency of your old realm, death the coin in this one."

I sat holding my warm cup of cocoa and looked up to the stars, the comet had shifted slightly in the sky, the beginnings of its tail emerging. *So bright, but what follows? Darkness.*

"I have a gift for you." She pulled something from behind her back. "This is yours, I wanted to give it back to you." She held in her hands my dagger.

"I thought I had lost it at the club." I was happy to see it. How many times I'd needed it. "Thank you, Belle." I was falling for her. I wanted to tell her, but the words caught in the web of my doubts and fears. I pulled out the blade, sharp and a little worn like me. It was a part of my old self I thought I had lost. It was my protection, it was my tool, and it was my friend.

"Lydia, my witch," A curse from any other mouth but hymn from hers. "I do not know what will be in the coming nights, but the thought of never tasting your lips again is unacceptable. You may think me a devil, but you are my dark angel."

Her eyes glowed with her true nature. Her teeth unsheathed slowly. "This is what I am, and I am not ashamed or apologetic. I chose this. I love the taste of blood and fear. I also love the taste of you."

I was afraid of the power that smoldered within her. She held my face in her soft hands with gentle claws and kissed my lips with a velvet touch. I missed her. I wanted to taste her and feel her again. I wanted her despite my anxiety, my knowledge of what she was capable of, what she made me capable of. She was my guide in this new Cthonic world, be she my devil, my savior or both.

"Your eyes glow green when passion finds you, my witch." She smiled and kissed me again, forcing my mouth to open, to take her in as she stole my tongue into her.

My own power began to rise. I wasn't the girl she'd first seduced. I was no longer a child of the human world. I had found my power, as clumsy as it might be. I grabbed the nape of her neck as her onyx silken hair feathered against my flesh.

I met her passion with the same fierce force. She tried to top me, but I refused and swung myself over her perfect body. I straddled over her full hips and held her hands over her head.

The anointing was helping me regain my control, my magick rushed through me, and she felt it too. I saw a faint glint of surprise cross her onyx eyes that turned quickly to hungry lust.

My lips found hers once again, and I bit down on her bottom lip as I slowly pulled away. I could feel what she wanted. I was happy to take her there.

I lifted her shirt off as our kisses turned feral and passionate purrs turned to growls. She lifted my shirt off revealing my wine stained skin and fresh scars. I was not ashamed. I was set free. I let go of her wrists and traced her curves with my fingers, from the contour of her pert small breasts down to her bronze belly. Golden peach fuzz shimmered like amber dewdrops.

I bit down on her chocolate nipple and she cried out in pleasure. She tried to get up, but my magick will held her down with just a thought. Silence in the storm.

"You're mine tonight, Belle, my sweet devil."

We drove through the tight, twisting neighborhood that climbed the side of Red Mountain, winding our way to the small children's park, Valley View. My attention was held by the comet that had grown longer and leaner in the night sky. *Time is running out.*

Wendy, Rummer and I were the first to get out of the three cars as they parked in the small dead end parking lot. I wrapped my favorite leather coat tightly around me, fending off the random gusts of winter wind on an otherwise mild night. Wicked Wendy scanned the hillside as stray dreads rode the breeze.

Rummer's heavy boots echoed off the sharp hillside to the road above us. The park wasn't very big at all, maybe two acres. A steep climb of zig zag stairs led to the road above where we saw three large men, lycans, standing at the lookout point where they were able to see most of Birmingham and us.

A gazebo, freshly painted, sat on the edge of wood warmed by a lone streetlight. Most of the people of the neighborhood were finding their way to sleep. Only a few stray tv-lights flickered behind closed curtains.

A young woman in her twenties walked out from the gazebo. Her short blue-green spiked hair and big boots made her look to be your average South Side street kid. A large toothy smile, her overly large irises, and her auric burn gave her away as the powerful lycan she was. Hers was not the only aura I saw in the shadows. Seven-foot humanoid colored blurs haunted the tiny patch of forest to the right. Submerged in darkness, forms wandered its worn paths etched between the trees.

"Rummer." She moved like an alpha predator.

"Moss." Rummer stepped away from Wendy, and I move towards his contact. They both knew their parts. Rummer pointed his nose into the air and bared his throat. Moss came only inches from his neck flesh and took in his scent. She was satisfied.

She stepped back and bared her throat by turning her head. He did as she had done and sampled her scent with approval.

"Thank you for meeting us and letting us into your territory."

"We're pack." Her voice was low and gravely. "We do for family. You're keeping interesting company." Her dual colored eyes, one green and the other bright blue, scanned over Wendy and me and landed harshly on the well tinted cars.

"These are interesting times," Rummer strained to sound civilized. "With your permission..."

"Yeah, of course," she answered grudgingly as she chewed her gum loudly.

Rummer motioned with his large hand, and the vampires exited their cars along with Laughing Dog and Sky.

"Laughing Dog, Sky, nice to see you both again. It's been a minute." Moss held out her hand and was met with respectful handshakes. "Your wedding, right?"

"Yes," Sky held herself in great reserve.

"Don't you have a kid, a boy?" Moss asked as she scanned the stiff group of vampires.

"Grey. He's still a bit young to have this kind of fun." Sky had a note of protection in her voice.

"I get it." Moss took a deep breath and put on a fake smile as she turned toward the vampires that had gathered behind us.

I stood quietly as I watched an undercurrent of apprehensive energy weaved through the group. Bjorn tightly tied his blonde locks back and took his place beside his friend. August, raven-like features keen and alert, was no longer playing the part of bookworm but killer lying in wait. They were growing as impatient as I was. My nerves began to gather in my gut. I'm gonna be sick. Let's get moving already.

"Moss, let me introduce you to Anna Belle, the Ambassador of the Holy House of Lilitu." Rummer gave a clumsy introduction.

Belle met Moss' gaze with a shared polite nod. She walked slowly by me and her sweet jasmine perfume gave me a sense of peace and encouragement. "Thank you for your help, The House of Markus will not be joining us tonight, as per your request." Anna Belle reassured her. Belle was a skilled diplomat, sharp, focused and empathetic. Belle's determined gaze met Moss' with respect and equality.

"Thank you, it's appreciated, but let me remind you I have let you come into our territory only because Rummer vouched for you. Please don't let me regret this." Moss no longer spoke like a street kid but as someone with education and training.

"We'll do what we must and leave." Wendy respectfully answered her.

"I know you..." Moss hinted at her darker nature.

"This is not the time." Varrick was becoming restless. "How many of your people are in the woods?" His muscular bulk tensed, eager as he held a large duffle bag at his side.

"Enough." She answered, finding her street kid persona once again.

"Eight," I answered for her. I watched the burning auras hold steady in the trees beyond Moss. "Not including the three above us on the lookout platform. Of those men, seven are shifted lycan and the other four are still in their human form, and let's not forget the one unchanged above us to the right in the large tree."

"Yes, the tree hugger is ex-Special Forces, good with a scope. Rummer, you know Jeri. I'm guessing you're the witch who is going in, Lydia?" She bore into me.

"Yes," I didn't cower under her intense scrutiny. I had bigger things than her to worry about.

"We can protect you from unwanted visitors, but we've got no pull with the creatures who live here." Her nervousness floated to the surface. I suddenly noticed that none of the lycans crossed the shadow line that marked the territory of the Changelings around the tunnel entrance. *Can they see it or only subconsciously feel it?*

"That's fine. That's our job." Wendy grabbed the duffle from Varrick. She led us all to the picnic table that was on the border of the playground and the dimple in the mountainside that cupped the black iron gate. She and I unpacked our works, letting the scent of oil and herb escape into the cool air.

I began to feel the presence of the Changelings. A tickle in my ear began as their voices mingled in the gusty breeze. Wendy smiled at me in reassurance as she saw the same forms taking shape. The others were unaware of the Changlings except for the feeling of being watched.

"We'll first create the glamour and protection around the park borders so people won't stumble in on us." Wendy's full lips scrunched as she gathered her thoughts. "But no one can break the circle. If anyone steps outside its borders, it will be undone."

"Understood." Moss nodded. "Not our first rodeo." Everyone took a few steps away from us. Belle looked on with pride as she rubbed her necklace between delicate fingers, and Varrick clenched his jaw and watched closely.

We set our canvas cloth down, revealing the black pentacle that had been drawn in sacred ink on it to mark the placement of our candles. Wendy and I held hands, hers were rough and dry, mine cold and shaking. Without one word uttered she and I met eyes and began to fall into each other's rhythm.

Breathe in, breathe out.
Breathe in, breathe out.
Breathe in, breathe out.

The energy began to pull towards us. We continued to pull the energy to the center of the cloth over the five candles that sat on the corners of a pentacle star. We parted hands and used them to cup the ball of white light. It had the same feeling as the push and pull of magnets. Pins and needles crawled under my skin.

Wendy had coached me on what to envision in my mind's eye. I imagined the park empty of all beings. Lonely swings lazily swayed. The trees stood like morose statues. The thought became more and more real.

I would hear no sounds but the stray cat and night birds. I smelled nothing but the metallic scent of Birmingham. I imagined a feeling of foreboding and warning surrounding the park so that no one would dare come in. *There is something not right here. You don't want to be here.*

I let this image, this embodiment of the park, grow in my mind and become solid and real. Wendy focused on the same goal.

The glowing orb of protection and glamour hovered over our candles and floated between our fingers. It swelled as we gave it more and more energy. It enveloped us extending to the borders of the park.

We both jerked forward as if we had been pulled on a fishing line. The line snapped as she and I both felt the release of energy and will.

I needed a minute to recover, but Wendy didn't. Her experience and power were evident. She stood up, and she flicked her hand with a sharp jangle of her bracelets, making the three streetlights blink and fade out.

"You ready, Lydia?" Wendy was concerned but confidant.

"Yes." My heart was trying to break free from my chest. My hands began to grow colder and shakier. *Sweet jasmine.* I wanted to hold Belle close to find my courage, but I had a job to do.

"You got this!" Varrick encouraged me.

I kissed my locket with Ember inside and began to walk towards the strange door embedded into the rock. Cast off signs of warning scattered the ground. An obnoxiously large padlock held the rusted door firmly shut. It wasn't just dark inside, but bottomless. Something hummed within the endless empty like it always had, but now I knew what it was. The portal called. Water ran freely deeper into the mountain, daring me to follow.

Abruptly, a pale creature appeared on my left that had looked like a boulder the moment before. It looked at me with its red glowing eyes with dangerous curiosity. Another changed from the silhouette of a tree to something vaguely humanoid.

My company couldn't see them as Wendy and I could. I was now in their territory around the mouth of the cave; they were not happy.

"I ask your permission, Guardians, to enter the cave." I spoke with purpose and will.

The hair on the back of my neck slowly began to rise, spreading down my limbs. The vampires' eyes began to glow as the shifters began to bristle. I held my hand up to signal my friends to be still. *I can do this. I must keep moving forward. Breathe in, breathe out.*

"I ask your permission, Guardians, to enter the cave." I swallowed hard.

A small army took form, encircling and separating me from the others. Eight stood on the edge of the hill above the iron door. They peered down on me with malice in their black eyes. The others followed the edge of the small cliff till they found even ground, enclosing me within their circle. *Breathe in, breathe out.*

"I ask your permission, Changeling Guardians, to enter the cave." This time I spoke with authority.

"Why?" was whispered on the wind.

"I must find the portal so I may to stop The Hounds of Heaven from flooding our world with demons," my words were swept up into the night sky.

"What do we care of demons?" The large pale shadow that was the boulder stood tall and slim with no features. No mouth or nose could be seen.

"Because someone is going to open Solomon's Gate."

A rush of whispers turned into a whirlwind and suddenly halted. Again no mouths could be seen to move. "We do not care."

"We have offerings of pork and mead." Desperation threaten to crack my voice. We had no way to get past them if they didn't agree.

"Still we do not care. Go away."

Only Wendy and I were able to hear them, so with frustration I told those beyond the Changelings' curtain their answer. "They don't care and won't take the offering."

Bjorn crashed through the invisible shades and tried to rip the gate off its hinges. A huge, vulgar face with six-inch teeth lunged itself at Bjorn, passing through the gate like mist. Bjorn flew through the air and fell hard on the rocks marking the Changelings border around the mouth of the cave. He held his side and lifted his shirt, revealing a bloody twelve-inch bite mark in his porcelain flesh. August and Belle quickly helped Bjorn up and out of the way.

"Our teeth are bigger than yours, vampire." They hissed as they made their voices able to be heard by all.

"Please let us through. The world..."

"We still do not care." The chorus was growing inpatient. The air around me began to grow stale.

Belle called out to the Changelings. "Do you like being at the top of the food chain? We do. Help us help you to keep your place at the top. If those foul things cross over we all lose."

The wind was crowded with whispers. Static energy began to build. I was afraid of the answer to come. I prepared myself for pain.

"You make sense, vampire." They agreed. "We promise entrance but not protection."

"Thank you," Belle and I answered relieved.

"But the offering must be made, swine and mead."

I placed the uncooked ham on a large flat stone protruding from the Alabama red clay. I poured the mead into the largest divot in the rock. I jerked back as the ham was pulled apart and dissolved and the honey mead was slurped into the stone. They made no move to stop my group from walking forward.

"Be safe, sister." Laughing Dog hugged Sky.

"You, too." She gave him a kiss on his cheek.

The shifters stripped off their clothes. The skinwalkers neatly folded their clothing and placed them on the picnic seating. Laughing Dog and Sky seamlessly morphed into giant wolves, their auras moving like water. The crack of joints popping sounded like river stones crashing into each other. Their eerie intelligence glowed behind their golden eyes. Laughing Dog was only set apart from his little sister by his larger size and darker coat.

The lycans threw their piles of clothing to the side and quickly began to burn hot. Their auras were blinding and painful. Cracks, pops and sizzles echoed off the rock walls. I watched in awe as Rummer flexed and stretched while his body burned into the werewolf form with brutal beauty and terrible speed. His muzzle broadened and his height grew by two feet. He was terrifying, even though I knew he was a friend. Moss shifted into her beast form with the same speed and blinding auric shift. She gained height but was nowhere near the size of Rummer, who dwarfed even the Viking Bjorn.

The vampires looked on with guarded hesitation but soon let their shadow side surface completely, shedding their civilized masks. Darkness swallowed their eyes and glowing orbs pierced through. Their claws and teeth unsheathed, and their skin grew cold, hard and pale.

The energy around me was making me feel punch drunk.

Wendy lit the antique lantern as I focused all the extra energy I had into the spell work of the Daedalus oil for an extra boost. The flame burst and crackled with new life. Wicked Wendy stuffed a flashlight into my jacket pocket. "Just in case."

I went to the duffle and pulled out my secret weapon, a small bag of faerie dust, and placed it into my other pocket. "Just in case." I smirked at Wendy.

"I wish I had something that wasn't so close up and personal," I placed my dagger on my belt, "but I think the sound of gunshots would be a bit much down in the tunnel."

"I don't think guns would help against what is waiting for us." Varrick encouraged me in his own way as he gave me a terrifying yet friendly smile.

Bjorn held back to keep guard as August made his way to the tunnel entrance. They nodded their understanding. Laughing Dog and Moss headed to the top of wooden stairs free of worry that a mundane may see them, hidden by our glamour.

The Alabama Water and Power padlock on the gate was our last obstacle. Rummer grabbed the steel lock in his large hands and twisted it off like it was tin.

"Safe journey and quick return." Wendy placed a necklace from which The Key hung around my neck.

"Be safe yourself." I took in one last deep breath of fresh air, kissed my locket and followed Rummer's huge form into the tunnel.

Chapter 46

Thursday
3 days until Solstice

The Lantern's flame flitted and furled until it found its
bearings. I tasted wet decay in the air as rushing water
tumbled into the void. We were surrounded by manmade
things, pipes and wires, falling into slow disrepair. Dirty signs
were screwed to the blackened cement walls. There were piles
of old worn clothes of fools and the foolhardy, homeless and
druggy alike. All were unlucky enough to have picked this as
their sanctuary.

We came upon another steel mesh gate, this one even more
rust encrusted. Rummer flexed his large claws and plucked
the gate from the wall, tossing it to one side. He ducked down
uncomfortably to fit through the shrinking channel.

The lantern light caught the rogue, still forms of
Changeling Guardians, there, then not there. The promised
"safe" passage did not lessen my unease of the stony, lurking
Changelings with their alien eyes and formless faces. The
others didn't see them and had no issue with the blinding
depths.

A wisp of firefly-like embers drifted to the right. "Turn
here." My voice tripped over my own heartbeat as I expected a
Guardian to lurch out and drag me into the chasm.

The labyrinth aged with each step. Cement turned to hand
placed brick and mortar. The shallow stream of rainwater
turned to a small river eagerly pushing under foot. A small
waterfall seemed not too far away, but with the echoes, it

was impossible to tell. I was limited to my patch of light, the others stepped into the abyss without hesitation.

We went deeper into the mountain, and the energy of the blackness became thicker and heavier with the Changelings becoming fewer until there were none. The sparks fluttered, and the flame pointed left. The lycan stepped through the boundary of the human made path into the raw cave, finally able to stand at his full impressive height.

There was a distinct presence. "Something's here," I announced. My aura felt the pressure of a new auric field.

"I don't see anything." Belle's shadow self looked as at home here as in her own estate.

"Sky, Rummer, do you smell or see anything?" Varrick rubbed his hands over his shaved head.

Sky's wolf form snorted and shook her head "no." Rummer peered over his tufted shoulders with gleaming eyes and confirmed Sky's assessment with his own gestured "no."

The feeling wouldn't leave me; it hung heavy in my mind. We nevertheless moved forward cautiously. Rummer's back bristled. Sky held her tail high with her teeth bared. Belle's black eyes blazed with Varrick's silver ones glowing beside her. August's thin frame moved cautiously and purposely, quick and nimble. My lantern released more glowing ash that spiraled deeper still. The portal wasn't that far away. It hummed a melody that only I could hear.

Rummer stopped abruptly and made the exaggerated motion of sniffing air.

"I smell it too," August confirmed.

"Blood." Varrick's accent flirted through. "Old blood, sick blood."

"And something else," Belle reached out, "but I can't see."

"Dim the light." Varrick pointed at the Daedalus lamp.

I turned the tiny metal knob on the lantern till there was only a whisper of flame. I was swallowed by the darkness, but as my eyes adjusted, I could see something in front of us: energy fields. I could see the swirl of the portal deep into the cave hall but there was something else. I could barely see beyond Rummer's aura. "Do y'all see that?"

"No, where is it?" August stepped forward, his trench coat floating free against his lithe frame.

"There is something up there. I see the portal, but..." I walked under the great beast of Rummer, who smelled like burned earth, and went a few steps ahead. A blue-black flame-like auric field took an ominous shape as it silently gripped the ceiling and wall.

Everyone began to move forward. "Stop!" I let out a harsh whisper. The thing twitched. It heard me. "There is something waiting for us."

"Where? I do not..." I barely heard Belle's voice.

"I can only see its aura. I don't think it knows I can see it." I watched as the dark blue entity readjusted its many long legs quietly only a hundred yards away.

"We must keep moving," Varrick answered. "Prepare yourselves."

"I can't see where to step; someone's going to have to walk me." The creature held its hunter's patience. Another quickly and quietly joined it.

"There's two, now."

Varrick and Belle separated and moved to the opposite outer walls. With no energy to see, I lost most of their body in the pitch. They did what vampires do and melted into the darkness. Sky stayed close to my side and acted like a guide dog, lending her tail for direction. August and Rummer quickly took their positions.

I had a gut feeling, and I glanced behind me. There was another creature coming up from behind, clinging to the walls and ceiling making its way closer. "There's one behind us."

"Where?" Varrick asked.

"Seven o'clock, ceiling," I told him. August and Anna Belle fell behind me as we walked toward the heartbeat of the swirling portal.

Find the silence. But I couldn't. The expectation of the fight to come was overwhelming my thoughts. *Breathe in, breathe out. Breathe in, oh shit!*

A high screech assaulted our ears. The many-armed creatures clawed their way towards us, their talons making the horrendous sound of hundreds of rats skittering against stone. They swooped down upon us like banshees. Their features glowed with the excitement of the hunt.

I was pushed into the icy water as Sky jumped my attacker and was thrown hard into the jagged tunnel wall. Varrick yelled out as I heard another deafening screech crack against the stone sides. I could see the creatures' energy clearly, but could make out only the absent outline of the vampires attacking with unbelievable speed and precision.

A tremendous roar from Rummer equaled the Screechers' in power. The largest creature spread its arms wide; a membrane flexed between its limbs. It let out a dreadful scream through a ghastly mouth. Its own body acted like an amplifier. I was stunned, and my Lantern shattered.

I struggled to pull my flashlight from my jacket pocket as I crawled to find the wall in the dark. I flipped the switch to meet a gruesome feminine face with no eyes and leech like mouth only inches away. At the same moment, Rummer's huge gnarled claws grabbed it from behind, tearing open the Screecher's webbed flesh. As she was pulled away, her numerous arms with talon-like hands tried to catch the sides of the tunnel, setting sparks free.

Another Screecher knocked the flashlight out of my hand. The light spun through the air, creating an epileptic strobe. Its serrated tongue flicked out and slid across my skin like razor grass.

Belle ricocheted off the wall by pushing off with her legs, grabbing the screecher by the throat as Varrick joined her in the struggle to pull it down.

The vampires were holding their own with the larger of the she beasts. As Rummer was going one on one with another, Sky and August were pulling theirs apart at the limbs.

The flashlight gave me enough light to see another smaller Screecher begin to skitter towards me. I grabbed my knife with surprising agility and sliced into its wet gooey flesh. It let out a squeal of surprise. I tried to hold it off me, but my grip slipped off its slug like skin. We were dealing damage but not enough to stop them. They kept calling out, and more were coming.

"Get them all together!" I yelled over the Screechers. I reached into my pocket for my last resort.

Everyone herded their opponent to the center. Varrick pushed one into the group like a linebacker. Rummer picked the largest off the ground and threw it into the others like a caber.

I grabbed the leather pouch out of my pocket and stood upwind. "Get behind me and hold your breath!" Everyone did so while the beasts struggled to get on their feet.

I loosened the leather pouch just enough and threw it into the pile of Screechers. The flashlight beam reflected off the faerie dust plume like silver snow. The creatures inhaled deeply to defend themselves with their bellows but began to choke violently as burning flesh was joined by burning lungs. They lost their voices but not their fury.

The pile of Screechers plugged the tunnel. Beyond them swirled the purple and gold vortex of the portal.

"It's just behind them. I've got to get past." My nerves were pushed aside by a new found bravery.

"Okay, Let's make way for her." Varrick nodded at Rummer, who became berserk with a hellhound howl.

"Good luck, my witch." Anna Belle gave me a quick kiss, her eyes momentarily blinked to their human form. She followed Varrick into the battle like a Valkyrie. August, with the deadly grace and speed of a rogue, leapt into battle. Sky held the line around me. The thud of flesh meeting bone and grunts turning into battle screams drove me on.

I quickly took the glowing potion from around my neck and drank it down like a shot of Jack. The taste of metal and bitter herb filled my nostrils and mouth. The liquid hit my stomach with a slow burn and shooting ice.

Everything began to swirl, but I held my eyes on the portal, its song growing louder. I barely missed being crushed by Rummer as he was slammed against the wall just beside me. I squeezed through the slimy remains of a disemboweled creature at threshold of the ancient door.

Find the silence.

Breathe in, breathe out.

Breathe in, breathe out.

Find the silence.

Anarchy is behind me but I must find the silence.

Breathe in, breathe out.

Breathe in, breathe out.

A peace, a separation, a silence sat with in me as the storm raged dangerously all around me. I had to trust my friends to keep me safe.

I raised my right hand and focused all my will on my destination. I pressed my fingers forward, hitting the barrier that cracked like thin ice under my touch. I was pulled in and a hot static electric charge consumed my body. *Breathe in, breathe out.*

Chapter 47

Thursday
3 days until Solstice

Silence.

Behind me through the arch, the titans had exploded into violence but were suspended in time.

It could have been a gruesome work of art hung for show, a beautiful atrocity, monsters killing monsters.

I had no light to hold, but it was unneeded. The smooth carved walls were covered in bioluminescent stars, quiet creatures living quiet lives on the black and glittering stone. Symbols and spells were scratched on the walls, some in haste, others in prudence.

A light drip of water began, ringing like an ominous child's bell. It came from a glow that was to be my destination. Strange music whispered from behind the rock walls, played by the elements themselves. A roar of a fire over took the musical mystery and began to grow.

My breath became shallow, as did my sore steps. My eyes grew wide and my mouth became dry as a great altar and throne room emerged. The throne was large enough to fit ten men and was gilded, with gems and stones I'd never seen before. Books and more books and scrolls upon scrolls were stacked upon the walls. There were so many that I wouldn't have been able to read them all in a hundred lifetimes. The ambient energy was blinding, and I couldn't distinguish one object from another with my third eye. I looked above to the top of the carved dome where the great Solomon's Seal was embedded into the rock ceiling.

The roar of flame swelled, I couldn't find its source, but the heat continued to rise. I took off my jacket and carefully went deeper into the strange room. I didn't know where to begin or what I expected to find. *A test?*

A simple stone box laid centered on an opulent table. That's about the size of the Athame. Salty sweat swam and pooled down my body. I was about to put my hand on the box, but it felt wrong to be a petty thief. *I can't.*

"What do you want, little one?" A voice like a great furnace spoke to me.

I turned quickly and was faced with a tornado of blaze. I fell back into the table, nearly knocking it over. My skin began to redden and grow hot. The blaze began to solidify into a humanoid giant, sixty feet tall. His crown was blue and white flame trimmed in liquid gold. It melted into his lava-like flesh.

My eyes began to burn as I rained sweat. My long hair suffocating me like wet rope. My lips began to crack, and the great heat stole my strength.

He cooled his being, and his surface became blackened with gold inscriptions glowing through. Only his eyes remained flame.

The room itself began to cool and I was able to once again breathe, but not deeply. My clothes were drenched and sticky. All I tasted were salty lips.

He took steps forward, and sheets of black cooled lava fell to the ground hard, revealing an average-sized man within. He was completely hairless, his burning eyes and the swimming glowing texts across his black body remained. His earlobes pointed and reached his shoulders. He had a long thin nose and jewels embedded in his flesh. Only a golden loincloth covered the perfectly carved dark-skinned man.

"I'm sorry." I was in awe and terrified. I had never seen such magick. I'd never thought it possible. This is my life now.

"What are you looking for?" His voice not as grand but still raw.

"I'm looking for an athame," I spoke timidly, and at that moment I realized the floor was made from human bone. *Breathe in, breathe out.*

"There are athames in your world. Why come here to mine?"

"I'm looking for King Solomon's."

He bellowed a great laugh. "Oh little one, I think you're lost."

"It's not here?" A mash of anger and defeat squeezed down hard on my chest.

"Maybe but that is not what I meant." He held a latched golden book in his left hand close to his body, as the Pope would hold a bible.

"I didn't want to steal it."

"I know, or you would be dead already."

"Are you the 'Keeper'?"

"How bold." He sat back into his black stone throne, his mere presence filling the space completely. "You are the trespasser in my chamber, and you ask me questions. Who I am is not important, little one."

"I'm..."

"You're Lydia Keening of Alabama." The mundane sounded strange coming from this being's large full lips.

"You know me?"

"Yes," he chuckled, "but you don't know whom you talk to."

"No."

"Yet you come here," he smirked to himself.

"I had no choice. I have to get the Athame."

"Don't be simple. We all have a choice. That's the fun. What do you need it for?" I got the distinct impression he already knew the answer.

"I need to get the Athame so I might stop Solomon's Gate from opening."

"I see. It can do that? Why would you think I would let you? Where do you think you are? And how did you think you would leave?" He was distracting, charming and sinister.

"I...I don't know." *I came here on faith, in my allies and in myself, was I a fool?*

"Simple girl, or are you? You did make it through the door, and you stand before me frightened but strong."

"I need to do something..." Frustration frayed my nerves.

"Again, how bold of you. But at what cost?" He stopped for a moment, and he turned to face me directly. "You have The Codex."

"Yes." I hesitated.

He grew straight and tall and came towards me. "You've been touched."

"Excuse me?"

"You have been touched. Show me."

"Show you what?"

"Where is your mark, fine witch?"

"You mean my birthmark?" I asked and he nodded. I lifted my sticking shirt to reveal my side.

"You have been touched by a true demon, something not of your world, an Other, or you wouldn't have been able to enter my world." He traced my mark with a long golden fingernail. "Well, at least one of your ancestors was... Did you know King Solomon had a similar birthmark? Not that you're related, but it does infer your fate."

"Does that mean I can get the Athame?"

"I love the red of your hair and its chaos." He touched a loose strand of my soaked hair and gained a playful demeanor. "Reminds me of home. Would you like to be my lover?"

"No! I want the damn Athame!" I smacked his hand away without thinking.

"And fire of the spirit. I like you. I won't kill you, for I admire your boldness, though short-sighted it was. I'll even reward you. I am Hagenty, the Keeper, the wish granter, the wisdom seeker. I will grant you three choices."

"Not wishes?" I arched a skeptical eyebrow. *The test.*

"Simple choices for a simple witch." His diamond teeth

were in stunning contrast to his midnight skin and burning eyes.

"I grant you choices three, freedom, power or destiny." With a wave of his extraordinarily long, broad hands a white stone cup appeared and filled with a clear bubbling liquid, a large emerald glimmered, and finally the box in the middle opened revealing the Athame.

"The first, freedom. Take it in and drink it down." The cup had the scent of my childhood, that safe place where no one could find me. It was the back of my mother's closet. The smell of her perfume, fabric softener, leather purses and shoes. "It will let you have all that you want but can't have. You will no longer be a witch. You will be the mundane mother. You and your daughter will be together. You will live out your life being on the other side of normal. The judge, the town, the world would embrace and accept you."

I looked into the glass and watched it reveal a story of Ember and me. I was the taking Ember to her first day of school, not her stepmother. A few years pass, and Ember and I are eating a lunch of mac and cheese after painting her bedroom pixie purple. Another couple of years and she is in the school play...

"You could have all of it. Just drink. You'll not remember any of this. You'll live the life of the mother you wished you could be." Hot, painful tears rolled down my face.

"How about power?" He motioned to the emerald. "You could just take her back and punish the judge, the town, and the world for their insolence and cruelty. You could take her and do anything you want. Not like now. Your talents are sporadic, inconsistent. With power, it would be as you will."

I peered into the sparkling stone and saw myself calling a storm of lightning and fire. My face was enraged but joyous. I had my daughter. I had the power. I could do and have everything I desired, but I did not recognize myself. She lacked patience, empathy and wisdom to wield such a responsibility.

"You could win the battle that is to come."

"Which one, should I choose to prevent it?"

"Silly witch, that is the world's fate, not your own. Your choice is where you will stand."

"The world's fate... and the Athame?" I looked deep into the blade, but it showed me nothing.

"It is simply a tool used by a great man who lost his way." He gave a cruel smile.

"As great people do."

"But you could be better than them."

"I would become them."

"Maybe not a simple witch after all. Are you sure you don't want to feel me inside you?" A debonair smirk crossed his cunning face.

"How about you bend over first?" I snarled.

"I do like you. If you choose the chalice, you'll feel relief and the joy of ignorance and the freedom of being normal. Choose the jewel, you would be a force of nature, a witch like the world has not seen in a millennium. You would have the power to make the world as you want it. Finally, choose the Athame. It is a simple tool for a simple witch. Because I like you, I will warn you. It will inflict great pain like you've never had before."

To be "normal," a mundane, would be a lie, and I knew deep inside I would always know it was lie. Power, that kind of power, without skill, compassion and hard earned wisdom was too dangerous, for the world, my daughter and even myself. *I'm not afraid of the unknown, I 'm not afraid to choose my own destiny.* "I choose the Athame."

He motioned for me to pick it up. I hesitated for the pain that was to be inflicted. *Breathe in, breathe out.* I placed my hand onto the hilt. Nothing. I looked at him confused yet relieved.

"It is yours till it's not."

"That's it?" I asked.

"Yes, that's it." He walked around the altar. "Now you may

leave, unless you want to ride me like an Athenian bull." His breath was hot against my skin, and prickled my flesh.

"No, thank you." This seemed too easy.

"I so like you. Before you leave my chamber, I want to give you a gift."

A warning went off deep inside me. He placed his palm on the front of my left shoulder above my breast, and I felt a sharp piercing pain.

"The world's path, with or with out you."

The vision hit me hard. I fell to my knees, the splintering pain was nothing compared to the stripping of my nerves up and down my body from his touch.

Lines of burning pyres, like forest fires, surrounded the Washington, DC reflecting pool. Hundreds of witches were burning, screaming and dying. Crowds of people gathered in victory and shame. A madman spewed forth fevered words of Biblical justice.

"This is the world's fate and now your destiny."

I fell back into the world of cracking bone and blood spray. The deep was a blur. A Screecher was on top of me. I jerked my dagger and the Athame up to defend myself, and the creature was thrown back by a powerful energy pulse. *How?* My only answer was the glow of indigo coming from the Athame.

I took a grounding breath and found my quiet place inside. I put my daggers up again in defense. *It is a tool, it is an athame.* I focused my will and desire. I brought the daggers to my lips, and with a soul breath of will and spirit I pushed my energy out, creating a wall of warding.

An electric web pushed past and through my friends but snared and forced the hideous creatures back. Their claws dug deep, setting brilliant sparks flying along the way. I walked forward with purpose and focus, pushing them deeper into the mountain. I raised my arm and drew a clockwise circle in the air from the ceiling to floor and to the ceiling again.

I lowered the Athame to point directly at the monsters in front of me as they retreated. "I cast this circle of protection and power. None shall pass with harm in their heart, all evil depart. So mote it be." My voice was spoken from the silence within, pure focus and will. There was a tax on my energy, but I would be okay with some rest.

"Lydia, you got it." Belle was relieved to see me. Her face was torn and weary from the battle.

"He liked me," was all I could say.

"You just left." August shook the goo off his trench coat.

"And you know how to use it." Varrick scrutinized me closely.

"It's an athame; it's just a tool. Besides, it's what witches do." Admittedly, I had impressed myself. Solomon's Athame amplified my skills but at a high energy cost. I wasn't as strong or skilled as its previous owner.

It also helped with my passive skills. I could even see the faint outline of garnet energy hugging the vampires and details in Rummer's and Sky's auras like I had never seen before. I wasn't sure how to begin to interpret it.

We slowly made our way out of the catacombs, but something didn't feel right. As we made our way closer to the surface, I soon understood why, there were no sign of any Changelings.

"Hurry!" Varrick yelled as the group began to rush forward. I trusted their instincts. The flashlight was little more than a security blanket. I made my way through seeing and feeling the energy of the cave walls and floor.

A calamity from the outside world crashed through the tunnels, nearly bursting my eardrums. Varrick and Rummer broke through the entrance with Sky following quickly behind. August and Belle stopped at the mouth and held their hands up to catch me.

All hell had broken loose. Wendy stood her ground at the gate to give us protection, holding up her crone hands and creating an energy bubble around her and the opening. She was growing tired, but with her last ounce of strength she forced her will into the bubble and pulsed it out. The Changelings, Bjorn and lycans alike were thrown out. Wendy was pushed back with equal force with a crack against the rock.

Sky jumped for the Changeling that was about to tear into Wicked Wendy. Wendy helped Sky twist to miss an incoming blow and let her bury her canine teeth in its pale jelly flesh.

Other Changelings came forward to the mouth of the cave, and Rummer sprawled out his large monstrous arms, scooping seven of the creatures up. They morphed while in his arms and dug claws and fangs into his fresh wounds. He let out a great howl.

Belle and August pushed forward as the Changelings tried to enter the cave. They used the bottleneck to force the Changelings to come at them only one or two at a time.

Varrick was wrapping his thick arms around a cave guardian's throat as it tried to bite into Bjorn's skull.

I looked across the park to the borders of our glamour and there Hopkins stood next to Blackburne, holding a little girl at the end of a dog loop pole, her hands tied in front of her.

Ember?! It was my daughter, but something was wrong. My mind arrested, and my heart tripped. I pushed my way through the fight blocking the cave opening. I held the Athame in front of me and willed a ward shield as I pushed, with arduous steps, the Changelings away from the cave and my friends. Ember's dark, sullen eyes met mine. She can see me through the glamour.

Sky was about to be attacked by three Guardians when Laughing Dog jumped from the platform above, landing hard on their backs. Sharp yelps and deep growls escaped from the ferocious giant wolves. Laughing Dog's huge form moved swiftly and with deadly accuracy, defending his sister.

"Fall back to the cave!" Wendy yelled out. Moss' crew were scattered, her sniper a ragdoll at Hopkins' feet just outside the ward. Neither Hopkins nor Blackburne seemed to be able to see anything beyond the glamour. Hopkins hovered his hand just outside the border, jerking it away when he got too close, but Ember was following all the action within.

My daughter was weak, wounded, thin and pale. The silence found me. *I will kill you all. Breathe in, breathe out. Let the Silence embrace you.* The Athame glowed with power.

"No! Lydia!" Wendy grabbed me. "We need to protect our people."

"That's my daughter!"

"What?!"

I started to the edge, and Wendy grabbed my arm again, her grounded energy stilling my feet.

"Not yet!" For the briefest moment, it crossed my mind to will her away. *No, she's right.*

My shield failed as my focus was lost, and I weakened. A Guardian came at me, and Belle came crashing forward. She began ripping through bodies only to have them morph, free and healed. The same happened with August, who sliced the pale shadow's flesh as he moved quicker than an arrow.

Abruptly, three of the Changelings stopped mid-attack, looked towards those standing outside our protection, and then brutally mobbed Bjorn. They threw him across the circle threshold. A bright burst of light and thunderclap stunned us all as the glamour and protection ruptured.

"Be still!" Hopkins yelled across the park. Bjorn was crumpled into a windshield of a rusted Buick, not moving.

"Give me the Athame," Hopkins demanded. Blackburne pointed a Glock at Ember's head.

"You do, and you die." The silence with in me was beginning to crack with uncertainty.

"Is you magick quicker than a bullet?" Blackburne cocked the gun.

"Give me the Athame, Miss Keening." Hopkins stood, so sure of himself. Sirens began to scream in the distance. Laughing Dog, who had lost his wolf form, laid limp and blooded. His sister stood over him, her paws dug deep and her powerful teeth bared. Moss, in her awesome form, limped quickly over to the fallen Laughing Dog and began to help drag him back to the cave.

"Mommy, is that you?" Ember's big green eyes swelled with falling tears.

"Ember, everything is going to be okay. I love you."

Laughing Dog's battered body was behind the gate along with Moss and Sky. There was still no sign if Bjorn had survived; his body had been torn to shreds. The unnamed lycans were scattered like dolls after a tantrum, some having returned to their human skin.

"Mommy, he just wants the knife." She had an odd tone in her voice. Her aura was so sick and black.

She wore thick shackles and a collar that hummed with dominating power. *She is just a child, why?*

"You son of a bitch!" I snarled.

"Better to be a son of a bitch than a child of a devil's whore." He cut his eyes to Ember. "You are going to give us the Athame, and you will be coming with us."

"Never. If you hurt her in any way..." A stream of Laughing Dog's blood passed quietly by me.

"What? The Changelings will kill you." Hopkins black robes caught a light breeze, his hawk-like eyes locked onto his prize.

"We will not allow it." Wendy held on to the stone wall, she was unsteady.

"At the cost of your daughter's life, Lydia? You may taste the lips of heartless devils, but are you one?"

I watched Ember in my peripheral vision, and she wasn't herself. She didn't seem afraid despite the monsters in front of her and holding her. She was... *amused.*

I was freaking out on the inside, I didn't know what to do. *What are my options?* I looked around. Half of my crew was severely injured, some unconscious and a few dead.

Breathe in, breathe out.

Breathe in, breathe out.

I focused my attention on Hopkins and Blackburne. Their auras were calm but heightened. They had no intention of killing Ember. Both of their energies were terrified and protective over her.

"You won't kill her." I nearly choked on the words in the fear I was wrong. "You want the Athame? Come get it yourself, you *fucking* coward, hiding behind a *child.*"

Hopkins chuckled to himself and lifted a small black book

with his gloved hands. He started to read an ancient language, and Ember let out an unnatural scream.

"What are you doing, stop it!" I held up the Athame and tried to focus my will but my heart was breaking. *No, Lydia! Focus on that bastard!*

As he continued, Ember began to levitate, her eyes consumed by blackness, her flesh turning gray and blue as unclean energy spewed forth. She was possessed.

Ember began to laugh that haunting laugh that set my very soul on edge, that same chilling cackle that had come from behind the farmhouse door. Her shackles and collar began to glow red hot. She raised her arms in front of her, and I was raised off the ground.

There was a pressure in the center of my chest where gravity still held firm. My limbs went numb, and I grew drunk.

"Make her drop the Athame." Hopkins ordered Ember. The police sirens drew closer.

From my left, Varrick and Rummer bounded towards Hopkins and Blackburne. August and Belle joined them from my right and Moss and Sky from behind me. A scream emanated from a bystander watching from her bedroom window.

A twisted and demented smile spread across on my daughter's ripped face. She pushed with her right hand. Sky and Moss were sucked back into the cave and met with an explosion. Rocks collapsed and closed the entrance. Ember's left hand lifted Varrick and Rummer, her right, August and Belle.

Her black and bloodied eyes bore into me, and electric needles pierced and wedged between the joints of my hand. My hand flung open as a scream broke free. Ember enjoyed the pain she inflicted.

"We don't need any of them but her." Hopkins raised his Bible, and two men got out of the Sunday school minivan.

Her death stare focused on Varrick. She wrung her hands

in front of her like a rag. Varrick twisted in the middle like a twig. *Crack!* His back was snapped, and he hit the ground with a sickening thump. He was still.

Her attention glided over us with a sick joy. My little girl was corrupted. She twisted her face toward Rummer, malignancy grew. Her left hand made a fist, and Rummer cried out as his limbs were crushed into his body and as he was thrown to the side like a used tissue.

Her dark will fell upon August. My little girl threw him into the top of the tree, piercing him through the chest with a large branch. He began choking on his own blood.

She hesitated on Wendy and Belle. She watched me suspended in the air and then glanced at Hopkins.

"Keep the whores alive, but you men hang the old woman." Hopkins was impatient.

Ember dropped Wendy, and her ankle broke with a chilling snap. Wendy refused to yell out. She held up her hands and started to chant for protection. I tried to join her, but we began choking and foaming. Ember took our voices but not our will, we fought on. Wendy was close to being spent when she sent the men flying back twenty feet.

They recovered quickly and charged her. A slim heavy knuckled man-boy shoved a noose around her neck. She began to kick and claw with all she had left. They dragged her through the dirt, her skirts tearing, as did her exposed skin. The men rushed between bodies and threw the rope over a heavy tree branch which overhung the dimple in the mountain where the gate sat in pieces.

I wanted to close my eyes, to scream, to fight, but I was powerless in this demonic suspension. They began to pull her up, Wendy's eyes widened as she spat profanities. Her face swelled and her eyes bulged as she suffocated under her own weight.

"God is truly watching over us." Hopkins turned to back to the van. "Put them out." The sirens were almost on top of us.

There was a sharp pop in my ear, a bright light and then darkness.

Chapter 49

Saturday
1 day until Solstice

Fuck! I found myself once again in a cage, mouth gagged and hands tied. I was greeted by a tall patch of cheery yellow dandelions peeking through the bars. A canvas tarp lay over the top. Sunlight cast a shadow of a drawn magick seal on the coarse cloth. I could still taste the fresh paint in the air.

The hard knot of a rag-wrapped fairie stone wrestled my tongue, while a leather flat gag pressed hard against my pained lips. I fought quietly with my shackles even as my blood oozed.

Breathe in, breathe out. What can I do but wait? I will take this time to find my strength.

I found my most comfortable position and centered myself. The day passed as shadows crossed, and the sun began to set. I listened to the nervous chatter of Hopkins' people talk of the "new vampire." Belle was okay for now. Ember was only spoken of once. The speaker was chastised deeply for it.

My daughter, what has happened to you? What have they done? How can I undo this? I have to help myself before I can help you.

Breathe in, breathe out.

Calming my mind.
Calming my body.
Calming my spirit.
Calming my heart.

I am here in this moment, and I am okay.

Air, give me clarity and sharp thought.
Earth, give me strength and stability.
Fire, give me courage and inner power.
Water, give me peace and wisdom.
Lord and Lady, bless me and keep through these
dangerous times.

So mote it be.

I repeated my prayer over and over till there was nothing but my will and thoughts.

Night slipped silently into place, and time went on. The Hounds of Heaven had been busy and were soon to their beds. Only the lonely footsteps of a night guard rambled by occasionally. After a while, even he found sleep and his snores marked the minutes.

Arctic gusts of wind flirted under the skirt of the canvas. My mind would wander to the fate of my friends. Images of Varrick wrung and Rummer crumpled flashed across the back of my eyelids. Remembrance of Laughing Dog's lifeless body being dragged desperately by his sister into the cave, his blood following after him plagued me. Ember's face refused to take shape. The harder I reached, the further the image blurred. *Wendy... swinging.*

I felt sick and uneasy. My box began to strangle in around me. Tap, tap. The hum of the night was interrupted and hushed. I struggled against my bonds, but there was nothing to see.

Tap. Tap. I looked above me, but there was only the silhouette of the seal over head. Another tap against the dry canvas. It was behind me, just outside my cage and cover. I twisted my body as far as I could to be greeted by a looming figure that was gently dancing in the breeze, feet dangling free. A red spot began to spread across the canvas with each toe tap. She began to jerk wildly, gagging and choking. Her arms reached up and clawed at her noose.

The canvas began to crawl forward, slipping down the front and up the back. Slipping, *tap, tap.*

Blood pooled, and body fluids drained into the dirt. Slipping, *tap, tap.* Gargled screams. *Wendy?*

The cover hit the ground with a puffed exhale of dust. A lonely tree stood with the guard sleeping at its roots. I could finally see the world around me. Four cages were covered, only the moonlight giving form to the night. Hekate's Crossing streaked brilliantly against the sky. The silhouette of iron beams peeked over the tree line. *The bridge. We're here.*

The canvases fell with a whisper, exposing their captives. Cerbina looked just the same but burdened in heavy chain. Belle was company to a withered Telal. Bill was in the raw, curled in a dirty corner.

Ember was in the furthest cage, more sealed and warded than any other. Her big green eyes penetrated into me. She and I were alone amongst those who sought escape in their dreams.

Her strawberry hair was clogged in knots. Her skin rejected the moonlight. Something vile squatted inside her and set its will on me. I had no way to protect myself and was thankful for the wards they had put around her.

As if she read my thoughts, she glanced to the ward written in salt and ash around her cage, and diseased joy infected her. She held her hands up like a stage magician so I could see as she popped the binds apart with no visible effort. Slowly, with blackened fingers, she carefully pulled off her gag, our mated gaze never broken.

Her blue cracked lips held a quiet Mona Lisa grin as she reached a small hand between the bars and swept the seal away. The wind went stale, and the light faltered. She began to rock with madness. Ember had a plan.

My heart counted its beats, my breath forgot itself. I was naked without my skills. I desperately hoped for one of the

Hounds of Heaven to show up but was greeted only with a wet snore. I tried to create a bubble of protection but was met with great pain as the faerie stone did as it does.

She let out a banshee howl, her mouth gaping, her features distorted. It revealed true visage, the white face demon from the cabin. The pale green of Ember's eyes were drowning in a sea of black. I started to tear at my wrists, nearly breaking my thumbs. *Oh Goddess! Help me!*

She blinked out of her cage, and her body moved between this world and the next. Her young frail frame shifted out of time and place. My little girl struck absolute terror in me. She was damnation, and she was coming for me.

The cold of the void, the sweet smell of dead flowers and the stench of sour rot invaded my cage. She slowly made her way to me as ice crystals formed under her steps.

Bill awoke in a panic and began to scream against his gag. He knew this evil; it had kept him company all this long while. She stepped to him and raised a little finger to her mouth. "Shhhhh." He instantly held himself still.

She approved and took her time building the moment for herself. She avoided a glance at Cerbina, but the servant's beady stare watched Ember's every step. Belle let nothing escape her attention as she tried to control her dread. Telal kept his head down, his red eyes peeking through his dirty mane.

Ember squatted next to my cage, and her foul energy wormed under my skin. "Mommy, I've missed you." Ember's soft voice escaped from the corrupted body.

Below the surface lurked the creature who had nearly swallowed me whole. The feelings of pitch and pain grew like a cancer. I began to tremble with chill and desolate panic.

She flickered, her face only inches from mine. The foul stench made my stomach threaten revolt, a bad idea with a leather gag over my mouth.

"Mommy, you miss me?" Crusted blood hung like macabre chandeliers from her lashes and dangled from her nose.

Ember? I wanted to cry, to scream, to fight and burn the world for her safe return to me. I raged against the faerie stone, the pain it inflicted giving me focus in the chaos of emotion. The indifferent stone cracked.

"Like my face? I chose it just for you," said the familiar growl of the devil I knew. Its presence pulled disease from the ground itself. "Getting this body was so easy." Ember's tongue was black and chewed. "You know, since gingers don't have souls."

She reached up and threaded my hair through dirty fingers. I jerked and pulled to get as far from her as possible. "I've been patiently waiting, since before time had a name. Your daughter was taken from you, and you did nothing. You're pathetic. What kind of witch are you?" Her eyebrow arched, a genetic trait from mother to daughter. "I was worried you weren't going to make it here, but you did... with my help, of course. You owe me a thank you." She grabbed my hair, and crawling things were set free into my matted curls. She tapped my gag with a finger, and it fell to the ground.

"Say it."

I pushed out the stone. "Leave my daughter."

"Not yet. Say it."

"No."

"*Say it!* Or will bite your daughter's fingers off one by one." She placed her index finger in her mouth and gnarled.

"Thank you," I snarled.

"Good Mommy." Its voice was back to Ember's, and she let go and squatted before me with cracks and pops.

"Why be Hopkins' bitch if you have all this power? Just leave my daughter and find someone else."

"You would curse another innocent to save your own? I like her. I chose her, she chose me... it is our shared destiny." Ember was amused.

"Who the fuck are you?"

"You can call me Alex. Alexander the Great! Ember's still here, of course. The things I have done to and in this body.

This little bitch will never be the same. Maybe it would be best to kill her." Alex bit down hard on borrowed lips, fresh blood began to fall.

"You were the one in my house? At the cleansing? Belle's? The cabin?" I swallowed hard.

"Yes, I was worried you wouldn't make it, so I made sure to keep an eye on you and to invite your delectable daughter." The demon began to rub between its stolen legs.

"And you serve Hopkins." I turned my head and pushed to change the subject.

She let out a piercing cackle. "He serves his destiny, as do we all."

"Yours is to be his bitch, in service to the Church."

"Church! Fuck those pustule cunts. Without me, those fucks are nothing. *I* took your fucking daughter, not *him!* You know well there are many gods, but none as vain and prideful as the Christian God. They call me 'enemy' to give them purpose. I am the corruption they swallow. I am the filth in which they bathe. In their fear, I was born. In their hate, I was swaddled. In their ignorance, I was educated."

"What do you want from me?"

"Nothing short of your blood and soul."

I tried to keep centered, but it was impossible locked into her shark's gaze. I started to pray like I had never prayed before. "Hekate, hear my prayers..."

"Shut the fuck up, you're wasting your time. She's not here. What does she care for a witch with no faith, and a fear of power?"

"Lady Hekate, hear me..."

"You should have taken the emerald. You could've wiped the world clean of these sanctimonious shits and freed your daughter. You could've plucked their eyes with the very crosses they wear, hung them by their intestines at their own altars, ate their flesh and blood like they do their own savior, gave them the death they worship and deserve. You could've made them pay for what they have done to you and your girl."

Hekate, I pray to you, please protect me.

"It was the Christians that allowed me to steal your daughter. Her father and new Catholic whore lied to you. Ember was sick. She was empty, and her broken heart fed me, piece by piece. I made a festering nest within her. Oh, your daughter didn't fall too far from the broom. She is like you, a natural. I dug my way in. Allen and Jennifer are such great fucking parents, they ignored her, told her it was all in her head, told her to pray, and everything would be okay." Alexander laughed. "It was their God who allowed this to happen to her. They called their church, and their priest saw me, the real me." A voice of Hell burned through and its true face flashed. She paused and watched me closely. "The priest told them that poor little Ember could only be helped on sanctified ground. Daddy and new Mommy were expecting a new bundle of joy, and they thought I was too much trouble. They would have been right... So they sent me off to live in a fucking convent, to be healed. But the church locked Ember in a room, abandoned with only me to keep her company... for months."

Rage tore through me, hot tears blistered.

"They let me grow and feed." It knew it had me. "They gave me to Hopkins. You could've punished us all, but you took the coward's way out."

Breathe in, breathe out. Breathe in, breathe out. No. I found my silence, my beautiful stillness. "I would see the worst of them as their best, and treat them as they had treated us. The few do not define the many. I know good Christians, with the lesson of love in their hearts." I thought of the smiling and welcoming faces of my neighbors Rick and Camille. "You're the fucking coward hiding behind a little girl. I'll destroy you and banish your soul to oblivion. I swear it," I answered it with cold loathing.

Ember was unmoved as I saw my Dark Lady take form from the frosted mist.

Ember quickly turned in surprise as she felt the presence

of the Crone. Ember let out a great hiss, her true form showed where Hekate's cloak of fog brushed against her. Hekate stepped forward as the fearless, dangerous goddess she was.

Her hauntingly beautiful face morphed with subtle shifts between a maiden, mother and crone. Her dark eyes fell upon the squatter. "Be gone." A blended emotionless voice, that rolled like thundering waves, commanded.

"For now, old woman. We know her fate." Ember spit.

Hekate raised her claw-like hands with purpose, and Ember flickered and appeared beside Telal's and Belle's cage.

"She may be yours, hag! But they aren't." Ember stood straight and forced her arms wide. Belle was afraid, baled her body tightly, but Telal was beyond terror.

"Hekate, please!" I called out but she was gone.

Telal and Belle were twisted and stripped by invisible hands. Their gags tossed. I was the only one who could hear their screams and their bodies crashing against the iron bars. The guard lay still and quiet, deep in his dreams. Bill covered his ears and squeezed his eyes shut like a toddler hiding, his tears flowing freely.

They both had their flesh ripped and peeled, legs brutally spread. Each wound was forgotten long enough to heal, only to be redone. Belle's tears fell and my heart broke. I wanted to look away but I couldn't. Ember just smiled as her will proceeded to rape and defile them beyond the line of death for any human. Alex knew exactly how to exploit the vampires' healing gifts and made it their curse.

"Stop! Please, *stop!*" I choked on my shame and sorrow.

Chapter 50

Sunday
Solstice

"Sir, one of the vampires is dead," the guard yelled after waking from his blissful, ignorant sleep. I found no sleep having borne witness to nightmares, a demon's delights. After Alexander had grown bored with Belle's and Telal's tears and screams, it simply went back to its cage and replaced its constraints, the guard none the wiser.

"Why are these cages uncovered?" Blackburne's heavy boots made quick strides. "He's alive, but he is no use to us." Telal, the High Vizier of the house of Lilitu, was broken and unresponsive. "We will use the woman." Belle's bright bloody tears tracked down her face as she shook violently, her flesh wounds healing slowly.

"Your pet demon is playing you for idiots," I seethed.

He turned around towards me. "I don't know how you got your gag off, but it makes no difference." Blackburne started rallying the troops and organizing their efforts. Alexander sweetly smiled at me from behind Ember's green eyes.

"Welcome to Hell's Gate Bridge, Miss Keening." Hopkins was in full robes. "If I were you, I would take this time to prepare yourself and make peace with God." My canvas was thrown over my cell with a quick flourish.

Muffled, frantic planning and preparation for the ritual was nonstop as the shadow of the painted seal moved across my cage like a sundial. The tarps were torn off when sun had began to set.

Hekate's Crossing. A bright streak in the sky, focused on its destination without care about this little planet and its looming fate.

"Get everyone into place carefully. We're losing the light fast." Blackburne took the lead on every detail. Hopkins was nowhere to be seen. He was taking his own advice and preparing himself for what was to come.

We were taken from our cages one by one and walked onto the bridge, its steel bracers crisscrossing over us like rusted spider legs. Its wooden planks cracked under the new weight. An intricate pentacle, a specific design used for necromancy, the darkest of magicks, had been carefully burned and carved into the wooden beams.

We were carefully marched into the seals that marked the points of the dark star. Cerbina, a small old woman, had been the hardest to move. It had taken ten large men to simply lift her from her silent protest. Ember's excitement was barely contained as she skipped into place.

Bill was barely able to find his feet and collapsed on top of his marker. He held a profound sadness. I wanted to tell him his son and wife are okay, and that they loved him very much.

Belle had no fight left. Both tired and beaten, we met each other's gaze across the bridge. Even in that moment of shared despair she had a beautiful, noble strength. She smiled as I did. We touched our necklaces in a shared habit, and we understood.

Torches that lined the bridge were lit by red-cloaked men, marking their sacred space to birth the apocalypse. The Hounds of Heaven brought a standing altar into place. My heart and mind stuttered as bleak anticipation grew. *How the hell are we going to get out of this? Hekate, where are you? How could you let this happen?*

The bridge straddled a large, deep creek. It was shielded from civilization by a small pocket of forest in winter hibernation. Curious clouds began to gather, as they do when magick is afoot. They were swirling with power, but retained a pocket of clear night sky framing the five tailed comet and ringed moon overhead. The air began to grow very cold, and snow began to fall.

I'm sorry. I am so sorry. Hekate, forgive me. Ember, forgive me. I am so sorry. Hot, salty dewdrops slipped down my cheeks.

Hopkins walked to the edge of the bridge, flaunting his pride and elaborately embroidered black robes. He went to the center of the pentacle and placed a wrapped mirror on top of the black altar. I could see a familiar energy vibration. My inner ear began to tickle. "Help me." *Walker?*

"Lydia, thank you for this." Hopkins held up the bone-handled Athame. "We wouldn't have been able to have done this without you.

"Secure the old woman." The robed men held and cranked chains down tightening them to the bridge girders to which Cerbina was attached.

Hopkins approached Cerbina carefully. "Hold her steady." He held the Athame with great care.

Cerbina was utterly unafraid. Hopkins was dead calm. "Her head." One of the men wrapped a harness around her head and cranked the connecting chain till it was tilted back, exposing her throat. He held the dagger up to her face and slipped the knife between her lips, cutting golden strings. "These were sewn in by King Solomon himself." He was in awe of the moment to which his fate had led him. My hairs stood on end as dangerous, powerful magick was released. "A secret he wished to keep."

Instantly, a nest of herbs shot from her mouth, and a loud clank of a ring onto the bridge followed as her body began to turn inside out. Her insides vomited up into a new form. Hopkins quickly grabbed the ring and left the circle seal. Cerbina's growing bulk broke through the enchanted chains. Raw, unformed claws caught a slow guard as she continued to bubble over in thick pinkish gray flesh. A solid form began to take shape, and the old woman's shell emptied completely.

Sulfur permeated my senses. All of us who were held in the seals could only stand and watch with awe and trepidation, even Alexander.

Cerbina reformed with three large dog like heads mounted on a massive canine body. She had fur like porcupine quills, paws as big as truck tires and six eyes that glowed hot white blue. Cerbina chomped down on the man she had snared and chewed him whole. Hopkins' mask of self control cracked with uncertainty.

He put on the large golden ring of Solomon's. He grabbed the mirror that held Walker inside, slamming it in the center seal, shattering it into pieces. I saw the spirit energy of Walker flow out and empower the Cthonic seals.

Cerbina howled furiously, launching herself at Hopkins but hitting the invisible wall of the seal. Her monstrous bark vibrated my bones. He raised the Athame and commanded "Be still." Cerbina let out a whimper and was silenced.

"What kind of Christian are you!?" I questioned him as I watched Cerbina's hot breath escape her new form.

"Dedicated. I'm willing to make the ultimate sacrifice to God and his Church."

"To open a portal to Hell."

"I thought you pagans didn't believe in Hell?" he smirked. "I'm going to open Solomon's Gate, and then the world will fear evil, knowing God once again."

Chapter 51

11:03PM Sunday
Solstice

The clouds continued to gather like an angry mob, encircling the lone comet and the inquisitive moon. Flashes of lightning danced through cover under the weight of heaven watching.

"It's time." Hopkins pointed Solomon's Athame to the angry skies. The Hounds of Heaven raised their faithful hands to the darkening firmament. Thunder crashed, and the winds began to sweep across the trees and down onto us with fevered excitement.

"I call to the dark gods forgotten, those who lie in wait behind the veil. I call the dark gods of pain, fear and death. I call to you to set this world free of love, hope and will. I open what Solomon closed. I undo what Solomon created." Solomon's Athame sparked from indigo to a black crackling energy. He spun around counterclockwise, casting the sacred boundary. Blackburne patiently waited with a small crew by his side just outside the glowing lines.

"I call to the night watchtowers. The blood," With the madness of obsession, he pointed to Belle. She began to transform to her dark self against her will. Her teeth unsheathed, her eyes turned and her skin grew pale, all softness fading into an uncompromised killer. A faint auric red-black glow like heated iron, hugged her flesh. She was the purest form of the darkness inside, something that rode the jagged edge of serpentine and feline. I was awestruck, yet terrified.

"The blood," the Hounds of Heaven repeated. The carved seal began to pulse under her feet.

"The bone." He motioned to Bill. Bill began howl violently, and his skin began to glow and pop with a smell of burning flesh. It wasn't the smooth transformation I had seen before, but a violation and desecration of flesh and bone. His skin broke apart, giving birth to the silver backed lycan. He towered over all but Cerbina, and his aura burned my eyes and skin. His own reflective eyes held no humanity only brutality and gruesome death.

"The bone." The next seal hummed.

"The flesh." He resolutely turned to Cerbina. Cerbina's heavy body was slowly etched with ancient symbols by invisible hands as she raged against the night. The tips of her quills began to glow with the same luminescence of the caves as a third eye emerged on each of the large snarling heads. Her own sweat began to sizzle and steam off her skin.

"The flesh." Some of his men were beginning to show doubt in their determination.

"The will." He turned toward Ember, who greeted him. Ember's solid black eyes were pierced with blood-red pupils. Her skin split as bony spikes broke through, and her mouth ripped ear to ear, freeing gnarled teeth from bleeding gums. Ember's flesh crawled from underneath. Alexander was freed.

"The will."

"And the spirit." He looked at me; our eyes locked. My very soul began to vibrate with power. My mind began to run a race with my heartbeat. I was overtaken, as I had been at the club, but it felt like home. Auras were no longer nebulous mist but thunderclouds. My being held the elements, my heart the universal secrets. My hands blazed with starlight. Terrifyingly cold silence was within me. I was one with the universe but was just as removed from the world I lived in.

"The spirit." A shock of electricity hit me hard as my seal was charged and locked.

"The channel." He pointed to the cracked mirror from

which Walker had been released. A young man took spirit form beside Hopkins in the center seal. He was being torn and stretched into the corners of the necromantic pentacle. Walker's ghostly visage was cycling from his living human form, through the states of decay of death, and back again. His face showed perpetual screams and torment.

"The channel."

"And the vessel." He pointed to himself. His handsome face tightened, and power came through his sunken features. He collapsed to the ground writhing in pain. He began to jerk and foam at the mouth, like he was having a terrible seizure, his body empting itself of food and bile. Hopkins' eyes glazed over milky white. His flesh turned clammy and gray-blue. His aura dissolved into nothingness.

The men began to panic, but Blackburne told them to hold their places. After a minute Hopkins straightened himself and wiped his mouth with his ornate sleeve. "*Say it!*" He demanded as he choked up the last of his body's contents.

"The vessel." Their voices were cracked and out of sync. Some were looking over the sides of the bridge, maybe to judge if they could survive the fall to freedom.

Hopkins was unsteady, but he clumsily opened a box on the altar and removed a golden goblet, roughly formed, ancient. He slowly made his way back to Belle. He cut off her tattered shirt, exposing her chest. She snapped at him with fanged teeth and a low growl, but the seal held her still.

"The eternal!" He began to carve the eternal symbol into her chest and gathered her fresh bright red blood into to the cup. It overflowed to the floor and began to follow the pattern on the wood beams of the bridge. He followed the river of blood as it rushed toward Bill.

"To the ever-changing." The dagger dug into Bill's barrel chest, carving another symbol through tufts of coarse fur and black flesh. Bill's large jaws snarled wide, but he was held in check by the seal's magick. Hopkins did as he had with Belle and let garnet fluid lead him to Alexander.

He cut off her nightshirt and let Alexander stand there in soiled Barbie panties. "Hurt me, Daddy." Evil dripped from her every pore. *My baby*.

"To Corruption." He carved the rune into her small body as it cried out moaning orgasmic sounds as he gathered her black blood into the chalice.

He continued to follow the blood to Cerbina to my right. "To the Beast." He was growing weaker, but he refused to fail. Cerbina's violet, glowing blood was gathered and guided as with the ones before.

"The seer." I was stunned into submission, not even a scream could escape my lips as the Athame's blade carved my symbol. I watched as our five bloods mixed together in a whirlpool. The blood spilled connected under our feet, bringing the sacred space fully alive.

Hopkins walked back to the center of the pentacle under the portal. "The path," he stood beside Walker, and with the enchanted dagger he was able to carve into ectoplasmic flesh. Plasma dripped into the cup,

landing with a bright flash.

"I am the host." He carved his own symbol into his chest and mixed his blood with ours. "*Ati me peta babka*. I am your master." Hopkins drank down our blood and held the bearing with Solomon's Ring high.

Our lifeblood was pulled into the center of the marked floorboards by the plasmatic vortex that was created by the cuts in Walker. Walker let out a yell, and our blood was pulled up through him, skyward shooting through his mouth and creating the opening of a portal above our heads.

The black rainbow of energy that surrounded us was growing like a typhoon. Blackburne held steady against a broken tree at the edge of the creek ravine. The others had to brace themselves any way they could against the gale forces. The portal roared like a hurricane as all six of us were lifted into the air and held in place. Screeches and howls flew past, trees broke and twisted, and the water rushed and hungrily climbed the gorge walls. The fast, wet snow stung, and my hair was being ripped out of my head.

"*Ati me peta babka.* I am your master." Hopkins' feet hit the ground, then he collapsed and began to wail in pain.

"Stand strong," Blackburne yelled at the top of his lungs to the men, but he was barely audible.

Hopkins' voice changed into a twisted groan. "*No!* I *command* you to open and serve me. I am a servant of *Almighty God*! I have the ring! *I have the Athame!*"

Alexander began laughing uncontrollably. "You have *nothing!*" An army of chaos was breaching the rim of the portal. The demons were to be birthed soon into this world. "You are no Solomon!" Alexander hissed.

Hopkins' voice choked as his body began to transform. His teeth began to fall out of his head, and new needle like fangs pushed through his gums. His limbs stretched and became gnarled. His skull could be heard to crack from the inside, and long finger-like horns crested. His flesh became stone as splintered bone was shoved from his fingertips to become jagged talons.

Everything went quiet for me. I looked down at my hand and saw drops of blood melting. The white, frigid snow was now the color of crimson. In the stillness of the eye of the storm. I saw the comet split in two.

Blackburne's men began to panic, even he looked unsure. This had not been a part of the Hounds' plan. "Don't break the circle!" It was no longer Hopkins' voice coming from his disrupted body.

A great thing, a horror beyond words, began to reach out from the vortex. Hordes of demons' shadows ripped through the air. Creatures squeezed in between the crevices of the Horror to newfound freedom. "No!" Hopkins threatened as his men began to break form. His demonic voice only frightened them more.

Great crackling and lighting started bouncing off the glamour ward around the Hounds of Heaven's camp. *Is someone trying to get in?*

Panic finally overtook the men as the Horror howled with frustration from the mouth of the portal. Several jumped off the bridge. One by one they broke the circle, setting the winds of damnation free. The seals broke, and we all dropped hard to the ground, freed from our bondage.

Alexander was the first to attack one of the frantic men. It jumped onto the red-robed man and began tearing him apart with unbridled enthusiasm.

Cerbina crashed through the crowd sending more over the edge. Men hit rocks and girders on their way down. She made a joyous crunch as she gulped one down. She reached up and grabbed a demon in mid-flight and swallowed it whole. Her bristles vibrated and purred with delight.

I watched as Alex's victim floated in the river below past the ward, making it explode, pushing everyone off their feet but freeing more vile things from the portal.

"Kill Hopkins!" Belle was no longer in her pure dark form but as the vampire she was.

Bill, turned beserker, charged towards Hopkins but was thrown towards me by Alex's will.

I raised my hands without thought and pushed Bill with my will over my head. He landed safely outside the bridge.

There was only one way to kill Hopkins. "The Athame!" I knew Alex wasn't going to let us take Hopkins out. The Horror was about to pull its way out of the mouth of the portal and free the legions that waited behind it. *I'll have to kill Ember. I can't, but I have to.* I was sick, but I had no time to think. *I have to act now.*

"Take your places!" I heard a familiar voice call out over the unholy torrent. Chains of men and women encircled us, lining both sides of the bridge. Their auras shined as only witches' auras could. I saw a face I never thought I'd see again, Wendy. She stood there as bold as the sun, holding hands with friends and strangers.

"Do it!" She locked hands with her followers and began

to chant. People from all paths with a single will and goal. The chant began to build, and the demons were herded back to center. A charge grew within me as they gifted me their gathered energy, my hands glowed with power. *Breathe in, breathe out.*

Bill was going one-on-one with Blackburne. Blackburne let loose a shotgun blast of faerie dust, but the enraged and empowered Bill didn't care as it burned into him. He was a train on a collision course, and Blackburne was on his tracks.

Cerbina had her focus on the crunchy delights of the demons, finding joys in the musical screams and curses. Alex took great care to keep its distance from her while protecting Hopkins.

Belle nodded at me, and I knew to prepare myself. She flew on top of the thing that once was Hopkins and knocked the Athame from his gnarled grasp towards me. Alex knew what I was about to do. We both dove for the indigo dagger.

Cerbina blocked Alexander's intentions as she chased another morsel. I willed the Athame to my hands, my heart beginning to crumble. *I have to do this.*

"Goddess Hekate, I invoke you! I call upon you as your daughter! Please! Please help me!"

"Shut up, witch." Alexander sneered as it began to gather its strength. A black crackle and shadow grew around my daughter's small frame.

"Goddess Hekate, hear me!"

"Quiet! Your goddess is not here!" Alexander laughed.

"Then I will do it myself!" I knew the eclectic coven's chant kept Alex from gathering its full power, but not for much longer.

"You're going to kill your own daughter?"

"Mercy is not a part of this world." Heavy tears ran down my face. Alex and I crashed into each other, raw primal magick pulsing and creating a cocoon around us. Ember's clawed hand smashed into my chest.

"You are of no more use." Alex used its foul will to choke

my heart and still my lungs.

"I love you, Ember." I thrust my blade into my daughter's side. I could feel the heartbeat of the demon pulse into the blade. I watched my daughter's eyes return, and her big beautiful green eyes grew dim by my hand.

"I will drag her soul to Hell." Alexander choked.

"Mommy, I'm scared." Ember's true voice was weak and fading.

"I love you always."

I regained my inner silence, and a desperate inspiration hit. I began to focus my will. I pulled the demon that squatted inside Ember through Solomon's Athame and into me.

"Come into me." I used every ounce of my will and strength and tore the thing from my daughter's body. Alex dug deep into her like the parasite it was. I watched its black aura curl like a viper inside her dying body. "Come into me." I pushed my aura into her body and wrapped the darkness in my light, dragging it kicking and screaming as I swallowed it whole.

I collapsed, catching myself hard on my knuckles and knees. The *wrong* squirmed inside me. Rage and perversion infected me. I convulsed as crawling bugs rocketed out of my mouth. Alexander would not go easily.

Ember's limp body bled freely, "Belle, get Ember away from here!" Roaches and maggots dripped from my lips.

"My witch!" Belle danced between the Horror and Cerbina who were in all out combat. Belle swooped with speed and precision of a nighthawk. She grabbed my daughter into her arms and began to break free of the bridge, when Hopkins caught her by the throat. "Bill!" Belle threw Ember.

Bill caught her in his monstrous arms and broke off his battle with Blackburne, making his way to the witches' line.

The possessed Hopkins lifted Belle into the air. She screamed and fought, but he was too strong. His dead face sprouted quivering things as he pulled her close. He tore out her throat with one gruesome bite. Her flesh and blood dangled from his putrid mouth. He threw her aside like trash.

Her body wrapped around a girder, and her head separated from her body with a sickening snap of flesh.

Silence gave way to numb rage. My will crushed the parasite inside me into a box. I willed myself to move with grace and speed. I felt as though I was flying.

Hopkins caught me by the throat like Belle, just like I'd hoped. I sliced through his wrist and severed his hand from his arm with the Athame. He roared. I caught myself on the wooden planks and snatched up his still moving hand.

Alex scratched and burned at the box inside me, trying to break free. For a split second in stilled time, I thought I saw Lady Hekate standing at the edge of the bridge, watching, giving me a vision of joining the ring with the Athame. *Breathe in, breathe out.*

I willed myself to once again fly into Hopkins. His bursting chest with jagged rib bones acted as armor as I plunged the dagger deep into his corrupted heart. I pushed all the black energy within me into the vessel that was the leader of The Hounds of Heaven.

"Get out! You are not welcome anymore!" I yelled. Alex scratched and clawed ferociously to keep inside me. "Get out, foul thing!" Alex crashed into Hopkins' already cracked soul.

The black energies began to battle within him. The power tore him apart from the inside out destroying what was left of his soul, his body and his mind. My third eye revealed a monstrous battle that would give me nightmares to my dying day, but that day was not today!

"Cerbina! Hopkins!" I called her away from the Horror above.

Two of Cerbina's heads turned towards me. She lowered her ears and showed her powerful diamond-like teeth. Her hackles raised higher, and she jumped at Hopkins. The demons inside were too busy fighting among themselves to notice a hellhound on a mission. All three heads snapped down with extreme prejudice.

I grabbed the ring off Hopkins' dead hand and placed it

on the hilt of the Athame. The Horror's raw, fleshy, brutally grotesque mouth snapped at me, pulling its unimaginable body through the portal. Cerbina took point in front of me and snapped at the beast that was ten times bigger than her gigantic self.

I joined the chant of the witches gathered. I pulled their energy into myself and found the silence within. With a soul breath, I said "Be gone. You are not welcome here. *Be gone I say!* Go go back to whence you came! In the name of the Crone Mother Hekate!"

The ring and dagger focused the gathered will and energy, and the vortex began to devour itself. The horrid thing lost its grip in this world, its claws scrabbled for the iron legs of the bridge. The demons raged against the hungry portal. The Horror lashed out at me, catching me across the face. The bridge began to buckle, and soon gave up its fight and started to collapse. I ran for solid ground and fell to my knees on the edge of the chaos.

"Be gone, and tresspass no more." I repeated my demand till my voice abandoned me.

"So mote it be!" The chorus of witches commanded. Our combined energies drove it back and the portal sealed with a massive blast of our focused will and power.

Chapter 52

Saturday

Morti and Grace kneaded my blanket as they tucked Ember into my bed. I shut the lights off, grabbed my hot cup of cocoa, and went out on my front porch. I looked to the stars and the waning moon and enjoyed the peace of the moment.

Hekate's Crossing had passed, but it had left its mark. It had not been yet a week, but the reports of magick and the strange were taking up the news. We had stopped the Horror, but we didn't catch every escapee. The veil between this world and the next was thin and barely more than memory. A new age had begun, doubt and compliance being replaced by fear and revolution.

Laughing Dog's funeral was yesterday but open only to the Dark Spiral People. Belle's funeral rite was to be held on the dark moon. Wendy and I were making plans for Joy's service without telling the others. I lit a candle for her and Belle nightly till I would be able to show my proper respects.

I took a deep sip of chocolate, and I thought of Belle's laugh and the soft touch of her lips. *I will always miss you, my sweet devil.*

Everyone had gone to their corners of the world to tend their wounds and regain their centers. Bill was mourning with his family, and Telal was chauffeured back to New York. I don't think either of them would ever be the same; hell, none of us would be. We all had new and heavy scars to carry, within and without.

Clack. My brooms fell. I spread my energy across my land, and I knew my visitors. Varrick drove his sports car carefully down my dirt road with Wendy in the passenger seat.

They both stepped into the night and greeted me with broad smiles. Varrick had healed his wounds but would every now and then flinch in discomfort. Wendy's neck was still bruised and scabs peeked from under her whimsical scarf.

"It's been a long, strange journey, my sister." Wicked Wendy limped up the steps with her ankle in its fresh cast and gave me a big hug.

"Understatement." Varrick smirked.

"It's good to see you two." I had found myself immersed in the mundane and feeling so removed and alone. Only those who shared in the past month could ever understand the surrealness of shopping for milk and eggs.

"How's Ember?" Wendy sat down next to me on the porch swing as Varrick leaned on the cracked wood railing.

"She seems to be doing better. She'll have scars, but her body is healing itself thanks to Sky's and your concoction. Her nightmares have stopped thanks to that makeshift coven. Mine, not so much." I smirked.

"We're thinking of making the coven a permanent arrangement. What do you think of the name 'Tribe of All Paths'? Kind of a Southeastern witches' congress, and first responders in a crisis."

"Y'all worked a miracle on both of us." I liked the idea but was wary.

"When is she going back to her father?"

"Two days. They're feeling very guilty, and they're moving into town to have Ember close to me. I don't think they'll ever be able to understand, but I think they know that."

"Good." Varrick said it with such an inflection as to add "they had better or else."

"Have you seen the news?" Wendy asked.

"They have the same story as the cops do. 'Cult leader kidnaps local author and child.'"

Varrick pulled a black velvet pouch out of his leather jacket. "I wanted to give you this. I think she would have liked for you to have it."

I took it with some playful hesitation, inside was Belle's stone necklace. I could see the faintest residue of energy from her many years of wearing it. There was also the softest whisper of jasmine.

"Thank you." Tears began to well up, but I quickly choked them down. He just smiled and nodded.

"The Codex is back at Belle's mansion under August's watch." Varrick added as he rubbed the back of his neck.

"How is he doing?"

"August has lost people before. He will need time, but that is something he has plenty of. He says if you change your mind, he would gladly give you the book." Varrick answered.

"Well, we've got to get moving, we have to make it to Birmingham before too long. The House of Markus and the Red Mountain Black Paws are in talks after the park thing. Luckily, they both had connections to cover our asses. We'll see you at the Belle's rite?" Wendy looked much older and more tired than she had just a month ago.

"Yes," I answered.

"Your students are eager to have you back." Wendy adjusted her scarf.

"I'll have to think about that." I sipped my cocoa and I remembered the question that had nagged at me. "Wendy, how did you find us at the bridge?"

She laughed to herself. "The clouds and a whisper." I was not satisfied. "We knew what town. We just had to watch the sky for the opening. Plus, we had a little extra help, but I'll fill you in the next time I see you." She began to very carefully turn to head down the porch stairs, "Till then take care, my friend, blessed be."

"Blessed be."

"*Ena te noct prak üt, ish üt prak te noct.*" Varrick took my hand and kissed it gently, his silver eyes finding mine.

"And you, my friend." He might have been an asshole, but I was glad to have him at my back.

I watched them drive away as I pulled my computer into my lap and began to type.

"In this unseen war, mercy and humanity are not an option. The devils we fear are those who protect us, and the angels we worship are those who condemn us. We walk in shadow because you can't. I'm not a devil and I am not an angel. I am a witch."

Lydia will return in

Wyndigo Rising

The Second Novel of the Keening Chronicles

Made in the USA
Charleston, SC
08 November 2015